ANDREI TKACHEV

THE DARK SUMMONER

Enjoy the adventure!

BOOK ONE

MAGIC DOME BOOKS

The Dark Summoner
Book # 1
Copyright © Andrei Tkachev 2025
Cover Art © Linni 2025
Cover designer: Vladimir Manyukhin
English translation copyright © JJ Shaw 2025
Published by Magic Dome Books, 2025
ISBN: 978-80-7702-158-6

TABLE OF CONTENTS:

CHAPTER 1

THE QUIET TINKLING OF THE BELL notified me of a new arrival, but I wasn't about to just drop what I was doing. The days when I eagerly awaited every single visitor were long gone — replaced by a faith in myself and the services I provide.

"Excuse me," a man addressed me politely, and, putting down the next glass to be wiped, I took a look at him. "I believe you're expecting me."

"Booth number five?" I asked. I gave the stranger's clothes the once-over, although I didn't really need to as he'd been described to me beforehand.

"I think so," he replied hesitantly.

"Through there on the right," I said, pointing the way. "You want the seventh door on the right. The number's on the door, you can't miss it."

"Thank you." The man nodded modestly and, straightening his shirt collar, he headed off in determined fashion.

Once I'd made sure he'd got the right door, I went back to what I was doing. There was no better way of fostering a sense of peace and well-being. In an hour, I'd have to go and remind some guests that their paid time was up. This had started to slip people's minds more and more. Sometimes force had to be used as a way of explaining to the especially dumb that this really wouldn't do.

I mean, you do your best to build your reputation, and then along come certain individuals who don't get anything and see themselves as better than everyone else... Okay, okay, let's try and stay tuned into that sense of well-being. And the number of dishes I've broken in the last month... Hmm...

The big hand of the clock told me it was only just past noon, and there I was with three booths full already — top-of-the-range ones, too. And almost none of the usual customers. The regulars would only start turning up after work, so the busiest time was yet to come. You weren't likely to meet many decent folks at the bar during the daytime, and the drunks had got my message a long time ago.

Away from prying eyes, a ghostly light flickered on the counter in front of the number five, which meant some guests wanted to see me. I sighed, put a glass to one side and headed off to the booth in question.

"Was there something you wanted?" I asked, smiling politely at a gray-haired man as I closed the door behind me.

"Yes, Mr. Vetrov," he answered me in no less courteous a manner. "I ask you to bear witness that the transaction concluded by us is made with the full consent of both parties and without coercion."

"You're aware of the fee for such a service," I said with a slight shrug of the shoulders.

"Yes, but this young man isn't convinced" He looked disparagingly at his companion, who clearly felt out of place and couldn't hide it.

For a second, I imagined what we must have looked like to an outside observer. There was Christopher Lazarev — patriarch of the appropriately named family, famous for its healers who could pull someone back from the other side, even if their heart had been ripped out. And the young man, in all likelihood, was one of the service nobility. He bore all the signs of someone who'd entered that narrow circle of the aristocracy, yet he had the manner of a commoner who didn't know how to conduct himself in the presence of distinguished gentlemen. And there was I, a nobody, really, by comparison, who the patriarch of a well-known family spoke so politely to, like I was his equal.

No wonder the young man was looking at me in such astonishment — he couldn't understand what I'd done to deserve such an honor.

"As you wish," I said, shrugging again.

A slight click of the fingers and an intricate sigil appeared above the heads of the two men. It began to spin slowly in the air, becoming darker and darker by the second. Bright purple sparks appeared now and then on its surface, and I nodded to myself with satisfaction.

One simple act from me would've been enough, but experience shows people prefer the spectacular. For some reason, they're much readier to believe impressive gestures.

"Speak the words of the oath," I said, prompting them to proceed.

Lazarev's expression didn't change. He merely gave the magic seal a barely noticeable sideways glance. This wasn't the first transaction he'd made like this.

"I testify that this contract is concluded by me with my consent and without coercion," he enunciated majestically, gracing his companion with a slightly ironical look.

The young man was still somewhat taken aback after my performance, and I had to clear my throat to bring him out of his momentary trance.

"I...I...I," he stuttered, but he then pulled himself together and continued more resolutely. "I testify that this contract is concluded by me with my consent and without coercion."

"The contract is concluded." That said, I rolled up the seal, which made a blast of icy wind blow through the little room.

The document lying on the table rolled itself up into a scroll, and the seals of the Lazarev family and that of the service nobleman appeared on it. His coat of arms wasn't one I was familiar with.

"Maybe I can bring you something?" I said, addressing the patriarch of the Lazarev clan.

"Thank you, Gregor. We still need to discuss a couple of points, and then we'll vacate the room."

"There's no hurry," I said, with as warm a smile as I could muster. "Your paid time hasn't run out yet."

Christopher Lazarev raised a quizzical eyebrow but said nothing in reply.

Back behind the bar, I took an order for a couple of steaks and beer from some people sitting in the far corner — a favorite spot among the customers. I watched the table out of the corner of my eye to make sure they behaved themselves with Natasha, who worked as my waitress. They turned out to be smart. I was glad I wouldn't have to lay out any money on their treatment, what with her being very scrupulous where her modesty was concerned.

Natasha was prickly, striking, and full of surprises. She had blonde hair, which she often wore down, her locks cascading down her back in a long soft wave. She had a figure any model would envy. But Natasha, as the aristocrats like to say, was a commoner, which, along with her appearance, often led to boozy customers showing a lack of respect. And given that she was touchy and knew more than one martial art, anyone who misbehaved was risking serious injury.

No sooner had I finished wiping the remaining glasses, than the nobleman I'd recently encountered shot out of booth number five, nervously fiddling with the end of his tie. As soon as he'd gone through the exit, the light on the counter lit up again, requesting my presence.

What did the patriarch want from me now?

This time I didn't ask anything. I sat straight down in front of him and folded my arms without saying a word.

"Gregor," said Mr. Lazarev somewhat pensively. "Thank you for helping me conclude that agreement. It was important to me."

"Always happy to be of service to you," I said with a smile, to which the patriarch began to rub his neck wearily.

"And where did you get that from?" He shook his head sorrowfully. "Such an appetite for money... Wealth rarely brings happiness, you know..."

"Says a man whose services only princely families can afford," I interjected. This wasn't our first conversation on the subject, and I knew he wouldn't take it the wrong way.

"Unfortunately, if it were otherwise, I wouldn't have any free time at all," Lazarev shrugged his shoulders contritely, although we both knew that he didn't feel guilty about it in the least. The patriarch of a large family isn't really one for sentiment. "I would like to make you that offer again..."

"Mr. Lazarev," I interrupted him straight away, waving my hand. "We've talked about this. I'm not looking to go back to that serpentarium they call 'high society'."

"But your family mustn't die out!"

"I'm Vetrov now," I objected. "There aren't any Vorontsovs left. They're all dead! And the senior branch of the family — abandoned me."

"Your blood says otherwise," Christopher said with a sigh.

"So much for blood!" I even raised my voice in anger, but quickly took myself in hand and continued in a calmer manner. "Our family was destroyed because it set too much store by power and influence. I don't hanker after what ruined my relatives. As you can see, I need much in my life."

"Why do you need so much money, then?"

"Are you trying to say my services could be cheaper?" I raised an eyebrow. "Don't get your hopes up. I won't be dropping the price or offering discounts just because it's me you're talking to in here, and not one of your business partners."

"Just who is it you take after?" Lazarev sighed once more.

"Huh, my relatives, obviously. Why don't you stop beating about the bush? We've had this conversation, in all its variations, more than once now. Tell me: what does the patriarch of the Lazarev family need from a humble bar owner."

"Humble," Lazarev repeated, unable to suppress a smile. "I want to pay for the use of your talents for a single matter."

"Money or service?" I asked, trying to appear not only indifferent, but even completely uninterested.

My mind, in fact, was frantically going over any recent events which, in one way or another, might've affected the Lazarevs' interests, while at the same time wondering what exactly they needed a dark magician for. That they'd have the money to pay for my services — I didn't doubt for a second.

"Perhaps, this time — a service." Lazarev smiled at me, and there was a flash of cunning in his eyes as he looked to see how I'd react.

"Strange. And what is it you want to pay me with a service for?"

"I like what you did with this office." He carefully ran his hand across the table. "I want the office at my estate outside Moscow to enjoy the same properties."

"Ah, all those conversations... now I get it..." I drawled, already calculating in my mind how much time it would take. "That, I'm afraid, is going to cost more than one service."

"I agree," Lazarev replied without hesitation, stopping me in my tracks.

"And how much do you need this?" I looked at him with surprise.

"You've no idea how tired I am of having to travel here to Petrograd to this protected room every time I need to discuss issues best kept private."

"You want something exclusive for yourself," I scoffed.

"That, too." Lazarev didn't bother denying it. "Your establishment is one of the few in the empire that can boast such a level of protection."

"Flattery won't get your price down. Two services and fifty thousand. Take it or leave it," I said firmly, wondering whether he would agree to such conditions or not.

"Done," he replied with a faint smile, slamming his hand on the table.

"Okay." I scratched the back of my head, perplexed. "I wasn't expecting that. Okay, I'll need a couple of weeks to sort things out at the bar, and then I'll come over to you."

"Fine, Gregor." Lazarev rose from the table and stretched out his hand towards me. "A pleasure doing business with you."

"Let's see if you're still saying that when I come round." The joke was just asking to be made. I shook his outstretched hand. On it, without him noticing, a seal appeared, manifesting itself in full as soon as he touched it. I'm no fool, and I don't make just verbal agreements, even with someone I think I can trust. "I have to warn you straight off that it'll take some time to make your office — it's not a quick job, you know."

"In that case, I'll have the guest quarters made ready for you, so you don't have to spend money on a hotel room," Lazarev said, nodding to himself. "Prices in the capital are extortionate."

"Most obliged." I bowed my head slightly and, refraining from irony, continued: "That'll reduce my living expenses for you while I'm at work. I'll provide you with a list of materials I need before I get started in the next few days."

With that, the scraping and bowing was concluded, and I escorted Mr. Lazarev to the door, once I'd let his driver know, so he wouldn't have to hang around on the street. A small detail, but the kind of detail my whole small business is based on.

"Misha, look after the bar for me, will you," I asked another of my employees once Lazarev had finally gone.

"No problem." Misha's response was positive as always.

This dark, muscly guy worked as a bartender and had already filled in for me more than once receiving guests (he was particularly popular with the ladies). I didn't need to worry about leaving the bar in his hands. Meanwhile, I went up to the first floor and, removing the security seals, went into my office. Everything had to be thought through in detail.

Flopping onto a large leather sofa, which I'd received as payment for a cushy job I'd done, I put my hands behind my head and began to reflect on what had just happened.

Until then, I'd never agreed to do that kind of work, especially if it meant being away from Petrograd for so long, but the Lazarev family patriarch was one of those who'd helped me promote my business before I'd built up a reputation. It's true, I approached people like him myself and offered them my services if they visited the bar. Their being there was the best possible advert for it, and had an effect I wouldn't have got from the more traditional ways you go about making a name for yourself.

So, I was sitting there wondering why this old intriguer (there's no way the patriarch of a rich family can be anything else) really wanted to winkle me out of my familiar surroundings. Two healing services from the Archon are extremely expensive, but something tells me that I still sold myself short.

I don't like it when I can't put the right figure on my work. Really don't like it.

And why this conversation about my relatives which would have them spinning in their graves? Lazarev knew perfectly well I had no warm feelings towards them, and he'd taken the news that I'd been deprived of my noble status gladly, yet he still liked to remind me that I couldn't quite consider myself a commoner.

Betwixt and between is no-man's land. Ordinary people with magic, by and large, can't just do what they want. They're either taken into public service, or, more often, they become servants to one of the noble families. Either way, they're valuable resources that can increase the power of the clan and are never allowed to just go to waste.

For several years after what'd happened, I was no use to anyone, and before my relatives from the senior branch knew it, I'd already managed to find my feet enough to have no problem in telling them where to go. Oh, the rage on the face of my dearest auntie when, without mincing my words, I sent her on her way and told her never to darken my door again. No, it was so worth it.

I got distracted. Back to my job order.

Modifications to Lazarev's office. Everything needed to be thought through so I could do it as quickly as possible. The important thing was that my seals didn't conflict with the protection he already had. The ideal would be to use another, empty room, but I didn't think Lazarev would agree to holding his meetings in a specially prepared place. Familiar surroundings would be much more comfortable, and those who didn't need to know about the room's features just wouldn't, which could even be to his advantage. Narrowed it down to the only room that's an option. That was easy.

Maybe I'd make him a room not VIP level, but one where conversations can't be monitored, and it's difficult for an intruder to get inside. Spirits — they don't like it when their patrimony is invaded without the owner's permission. They're the best defense, in my opinion.

Except "spirits" isn't quite the right word. I can call them that as I'm the only one who can give them orders and put them to work. I could call them hedgehogs, if you like. One professor I knew, when I was demonstrating one of my seals, wanted to give the creature I summoned a classification, but the name was a combination of so many mind-bending terms in different ancient languages — some of them dead — there was no way I was ever going to remember it.

Distracted again... I needed to drop Lazarev a list of standard materials with a few expensive ones thrown in, more for the sake of appearances.

Seals can, in principle, be affixed to ordinary paper, but then, I wouldn't be able to vouch for their durability, and the spirits themselves could exploit this for their own ends. I had a not very pleasant experience of this kind once and have no desire to repeat it. There are the scars on my right side as a souvenir, which even a healer of Lazarev's level wouldn't be able to remove.

Yeah, maybe that's what I'd do. Conclude all current business and set off for the capital as soon as I'd given my staff some instructions. Have a break at the same time. What with the bar and private jobs, I'd not had the chance to go anywhere for over a year.

I spent the next five days running around buying in stock for the next month, then hastily concluding jobs I'd normally have gotten round to over the next four weeks. I had to tweak my plans. In the end, I did everything, or almost everything, I needed to. And if I forgot anything, then it wasn't so important, and I could deal with it when I got back.

I set aside another three days for myself to rest and for the paperchase involved in applying for a bankcard, which would make paying for things in the capital a lot easier. Before then, I'd managed almost completely without cash — there didn't seem any point in walking around with a wheelbarrow full of paper, but this was a different case entirely, and besides, I wanted to buy something for my employees. As for me, I was hoping to treat myself to a visit to the capital's auction houses.

Maybe I'd strike lucky and be able to add to my collection of ancient artifacts.

Like others, I, a dark magician, also had my own little weaknesses. But while the whims of some inhabited the realms of fantasy, mine I can afford, being self-sufficient like I am.

Before I knew it, it was the day before I was due to set off. It was only then I realized how attached I'd become to my bar and my employees, which took me by surprise — something I'd never have expected. This probably stemmed from my childhood when I'd had to do without a lot, so now I just wasn't ready not only to hand over what was mine, but to leave it behind. What was "mine" to me wasn't only material things, but also the people working for me. I paid them a decent salary and had turned a blind eye to their less than exemplary pasts. They could always ask for my help if they needed to, like Natasha and Misha had when they became my first employees and the mainstays of my establishment.

As I paced up and down in my office, trying to think if there was anything else I could leave off doing, I was being closely watched by Serby who was clearly annoyed that I was disturbing his sleep.

It was funny seeing from the outside the alert way a miniature German spitz, who didn't even reach my knee, was following me with his eyes. Unfortunately for him, the moment I created his physical shell, I didn't really know much about dogs, so I embodied his essence in what happened to be in my mind at the time. It turned out to be an interesting combination — a cute-looking pet on the outside with a demon descended from Cerberus on the inside. But it didn't take much effort for him to maintain this shell, and after causing a couple of fires, Serby calmed right down and only misbehaved now and then. A demon is a demon, after all, and can't get by without some mischief.

"Enough hustle and bustle, already," he grumbled, fed up with watching me.

"So, your instincts are coming out on top?" I asked, looking at this canine specimen with amusement.

"I'll scorch you," Serby growled menacingly, and laser-like red coals flashed in his eyes just for a moment.

"Alright, alright." I raised my hands apologetically. Today I was picking on him out of habit. I didn't really want to tease this little demon. "It's just I'm not used to leaving this place, so I keep thinking I've forgotten something."

"So, don't go, then," the spitz snorted. He didn't get why I was dithering.

"I can't. The contract's already been concluded."

"You could've *not* concluded it," Serby muttered, making himself more comfortable on his litter.

"True, but I'm curious about the need for me to be uprooted from the comfort of my home."

"He's curious," my four-legged friend snorted once more.

"Says the demon who foisted himself on a young dark magician when his spell didn't quite work out?"

"Didn't quite," the demon said, aping me. "Yes, if it hadn't been me, you would've been gobbled up by something a bit more powerful."

"I appreciate that, and that's why I let you live in this world in peace." I smiled at Serby, which made him shudder, like he'd seen something terrible, and then he tried to appear unruffled. "As long as you don't forget that, you can keep on living in peace and gathering your energy."

As I knew from my research, for any summoned entity, our world is a virtual paradise. There's a lot of energy available, and nothing trying to steal it from you. You can quietly draw on it from the world around you without worrying about anything coming along and eating you.

In their worlds, everything is a lot harsher. While there's possibly also quite a lot of energy, there are many more entities feeding on it. As a result, there is constant fighting over scraps. The more energy you — if you can put it like that — digest, the higher you rise in the hierarchy. Judging by what the spirits told me, their worlds are worlds of endless battles, with only the occasional lull, and that tends to come after a large-scale massacre. Which is why spirits respond so eagerly when they're summoned — they don't want to miss the chance to increase their power without anything going after what they manage to store up. And that such a chance comes at a price doesn't put any of them off — the spirit still ends up being the winner.

Take Serby, for example. He moans all the time that I didn't make him a shell worthy of him, and then he melts when Natasha strokes him, like a regular dog, and nobody would suspect his other-worldly nature. He manages to find plus points even here. He gets to chill out. So, how can you take his griping seriously?

"You know what?" I'd just had an excellent idea, which I had to share with him. "I was going to leave you here to look after things, but maybe I'll take you with me. You never know, you might prove useful."

"Why do that?" Serby looked at me warily, his left ear twitching. "Better if you take the sword, then I can stay home."

"The sword is a great idea, by the way," I beamed at him. "But you're coming anyway."

"I don't want to," the demon muttered under his breath. But he knew full well he couldn't defy a direct order anyway.

"Sometimes you have to do what you don't want to," I said philosophically as I turned away from him.

I thought I'd give him time to get used to the idea of running after me on his short little legs, something he really didn't like. Maybe it would bring him down a peg or two and even be of some benefit to him. Otherwise, God forbid, he'd get fat, assuming that applies to the material shells of spiritual entities.

I couldn't help smiling as I imagined what Serby would look like on a treadmill. Wondering what would happen first — him getting tired or going nuts — did amuse me, but I thought it best not to say it out loud or put it to the test either.

Hanging on the wall of my office was a sword made by a Russian blacksmith from a fragment of a katana, which looked like an ordinary hand-and-a-half sword. But whether the smith wanted to fashion something new, or something went wrong, the sword ended up as a combination of the remains of a Japanese sword and a classic Russian magic sword, sawn right down so it was a lot shorter than it could've been. But the best thing about it for me was that it became a wonderful vessel for a spirit that hadn't yet departed for the other worlds — that of Miyamoto Musashi — one of Japan's foremost swordsmen, who carried on honing his art even after his demise.

It wasn't easy for him in his new incarnation, but a master is a master. Miyamoto adapted to the new sword very quickly and set himself a goal — to nurture in me a worthy successor to the school he'd developed during his earthly existence. At that time, I had a thing about Japanese culture and didn't find anything wrong with the idea, by which time it was too late to refuse. And to disembody a spirit, who could still prove useful — that would've been a waste.

So, that's how my ghostly teacher came to me. I was glad he was silent most of the time — it eliminated the likelihood of gaining a reputation as a crazy who spoke to a sword. Speaking to a dog wouldn't surprise anyone — many dog breeders do it, sometimes treating them as if they can talk back. While the sword was in its scabbard, Miyamoto slept without being aware of the passage of time. There was no need to wake him up yet.

At that time, these two were the only recruits I had a contract with. And while they were more like my familiars, they were enough to give any potential adversary an unpleasant surprise should the need arise.

"I'm not getting in that!" Serby looked in horror at the carrier I was holding, which I'd hidden away in the office some time earlier.

"It's up to you — you can either run after me the whole way or travel in comfort. Or, well, I can tie you to the gas tank, so you don't fall off." I grinned as I gave him his options.

"The last one, the last one," the demon replied, looking at me aghast.

"Shame, that" I said, shrugging my shoulders, and I threw the carrier aside. "I'll stick you in it another time, then."

Serby growled helplessly, but I just brushed it off. He can't cause me harm of any description, and nor, in fact, can I to him, and these little jokes always help to brighten up our life together.

"Well, then, come on, let's go." I waved my arm, and the dog had no choice but to jump up from his warm, comfortable spot and trot along on his short legs after me.

After checking again that my employees remembered everything so there wouldn't be any mix-ups or incidents of any kind while their boss was away, I went out through the back of the building to the garage, where my pride and joy and, there's no point hiding it, my childhood dream, was waiting for me.

I remember that when I first saw this beauty, I knew straightaway I had to have it. A Harley-Davidson V-Rod, black body with dark red accents. I spent my first paycheck on it as soon as the bar started to turn a profit. And with the greatest of pleasure, I firmly transplanted myself from a seat on public transport to the one on my chopper.

I only had to approach the motorcycle and run my hand along its bodywork before it immediately started revving its engine impatiently.

"I know, I know." I patted it soothingly on the gas tank. "We've not had a ride together for a while. Believe me, today I'll make it up for all the time you've had to stay in the garage."

"Don't tell me you're about to go to Moscow on that?" said Serby, frozen in disbelief.

"What did you think I meant when I said I'd tie you to the tank?" I asked quite seriously and not getting any response, I continued: "I'm not about to get on any stuffy trains or planes. I don't trust them, as you know. My iron horse, however, is a different matter." And I patted the bike until it revved up again.

Yes, I couldn't just buy a motorcycle and not make it the vessel for a fire horse.

"And, well, this is practically a compatriot of

yours, so there's no need to panic," I said.

I put my travel bag on the seat and fastened it securely with the specially made straps. I had to fix my sword to the side using the clasps there — not ideal, but there was no way I'd lose it. Serby desperately refused to budge, but I'd prudently prepared for such an eventuality by buying a seat specially designed for dogs so he could travel with me in style.

"Right, let's go," I said with a contented smile.

The motorcycle reared up on its back wheel and, revving the engine several times, took off like a real-life, restive horse from its stall.

And the advantages of animate technology? Well, it can act without being directly controlled by a human. So, the journey, which should've taken me the whole day, was completed in just four and a half hours with us only stopping a couple of times at a roadside diner so I could stretch my legs and have a bite to eat.

When we were just outside Yaroslavl, Serby insisted he was hungry, and I had to take him with me into the diner, as I had no success in getting him to wait outside for me. You should've seen the waitress' face when I ordered ten medium-rare steaks. Being just above average height and thin with it, it was hard to imagine me putting away so much food, but the girl got over her surprise and brought me my order.

But when I put all this on the table and released my slavering hound, well, now, that was funny. The customers at the diner just looked at me confused at first, but when Serby ate one steak after another, their eyes just grew wider and wider.

Because of his physical shell, he's got a small mouth, but, reverting to his actual size, he could've gobbled up all ten of them in one go.

Once he'd dispatched all the steaks, he jumped off the table onto the seat beside me, a great deal happier. By this time, they'd brought my order, and so now it was over to me to abandon myself to the pleasures of stuffing my face.

Out of the corner of my eye, I saw a group of teenagers who were bursting to ask me about my unusual dog, but they couldn't bring themselves to, which was fine by me. The demon disliked being disturbed after a meal and had used his powers to exercise some gentle pressure on them to arouse an irrational fear of him. It was hardly surprising people were asking themselves how he'd managed to stick all that away. But I wasn't about to explain to anyone, let alone openly declare, that this creature is not of our world, and, that he isn't in fact, despite his familiar-looking appearance, an animal at all. With Serby, all his food turns into energy. And he doesn't experience the physical needs associated with digestion, which is very convenient — there's no need to worry about him leaving any vile-smelling piles anywhere.

We made another stop in one of the Moscow suburbs. To be honest, it would've been better if we'd just kept going. No sooner had we started to walk away from the bike than some jerks tried to jump on it, and they paid the price with some serious burns. And I had to explain to the law enforcement officers why there were such dangerous security spells on my vehicle. We argued for half an hour, they failed to find a reason to detain me or issue me with a fine, so they let me go with just a warning.

Those jerks should've been grateful they didn't turn into dead jerks — that'll teach them to lay their hands on the property of a dark magician. My, shall we say, fellows in the trade aren't known for being particularly laissez-faire where their property is concerned.

Nothing else interesting happened on the way, except that at one point I was admiring a sports magicar racing near me, and almost missed my turning.

Cars with engines that run on magic energy are nothing new in themselves. But what grabbed my attention were the capabilities of the sports versions. Even a Master-level spell couldn't leave a scratch on the one I was staring at, let alone something less energy-intensive. I'd need to save long and hard if I set my sights on a set of wheels like that.

I rode up to Pushkino outside Moscow, where the Lazarev estate was located. For some reason, the princes and boyars weren't keen on living in the capital itself, and only kept their official residences there as it was more convenient for conducting business and organizing receptions. Most of them settled in the outlying areas, which led to the emergence of entire towns inhabited by aristocrats and those who served them. And if you consider that many of these clans have households of over a hundred people, the number of them who must be servants is rather large. Gradually, these towns became diluted by commoners, but the tradition endured, and no one showed their face in the nobles' neighborhood unless they had good reason to.

I had a travel permit from Christopher Lazarev. And although they allowed themselves several remarks regarding my appearance, the nobles' security had to let me through. I expected to be stopped like that more than once on my way up to the estate. No problem. Just one of the minor drawbacks of owning a vehicle like mine, and I'm more than prepared to put up with it.

CHAPTER 2

"NOT A BAD SET-UP the Lazarevs have here. Understated," I couldn't help but comment.

I stopped as you should at the set of wrought iron gates, lavishly embellished with ornate decorations of shoots and flowers of some kind, and waited patiently for someone to notice I'd arrived. I hadn't received any instructions from the patriarch and considered making my own way into the grounds to be overstepping the mark. I put Serby down and took a good look at the estate.

The three-story mansion stood in the middle of a large area of land, and a lot of effort had been put into fencing it all off from the outside world. As well as the main house, there were several other buildings, slightly smaller, but just as charming, although I couldn't work out from there what they were for, nor did I care.

Once on the ground, Serby busily played the

dog, sniffing around every nook and cranny. He was actually looking for where the power lines feeding the estate's protection were laid. They had to be powerful enough for security to be able to deploy the shield in a fraction of a second in case of emergency. If you connect yourself to the power line carefully, no one will notice the losses as they'd hardly be registered.

I wasn't about to stop him, but I closely followed what he was doing in case I had to restrain him. He has been known to overdo it on occasion.

Two hours passed. I had the definite feeling someone had been watching me for a while, and yet no one came out to meet me. Anyone else would've lost their temper a while back, but I kept standing there quietly, leaning against my motorcycle, and looking around.

I very much doubted Lazarev's people hadn't been told I was coming. Maybe I was early, and the patriarch was now hastily rearranging his schedule. And me? Nothing to worry about. I can wait. In any case, I could construct models for a new seal here without any difficulties because I wasn't planning on feeding it with any power.

Just another half an hour later, I'd nearly worked out why my seal wasn't working properly, when a black Cadillac drove up to the estate. The iron gates opened. I decided to take full advantage of the opportunity and rode into the grounds while the way was clear.

Before I'd even had time to congratulate myself on such cunning, two guards jumped out and, judging by their expressions, they weren't about to give me a warm welcome.

"I'm here to see Christopher Lazarev," I told them before they had the chance to do anything.

"Stay there. We'll check," snapped one of them who looked like he was in charge.

He went off to a small lodge that served as a checkpoint and started to talk to someone through his communication bracelet.

Usually, you see guards with walkie-talkies or, in extreme cases, cell phones, but for an underling to have one of those on his wrist, even on a rich family's estate...

Communication bracelets appeared on the market about a year ago, whipping up a frenzy with their technical capabilities. Despite the huge growth in their popularity, it was still pretty difficult to get hold of one. They were made in limited batches, so there was a waiting list of several months. True, there were always people ready to sell a place in the queue, but that cost more than the device itself. And that wasn't cheap. About a thousand imperial rubles — for the economy version. At this point in time, owning one is merely a dream.

You'd have thought the competition would've come up with their own version by now and released it, but the rumor was if you tried to open the bracelet or scan it at all, you were left with just melted rubber and plastic. So, there was no way of anyone else cloning the technology.

No one knows who the inventor is, and you can

only buy them online. And some clever so-and-sos set it up so that even who sends them out is a mystery. And that, basically, is all I know, as I haven't gone any more deeply into it than that.

"Apologies for the delay," the guard said politely after his inquiries were complete. "You'll be escorted to the guest quarters."

"Is there a garage there?"

"What do you mean?" The guard didn't understand.

"I'd like somewhere to park my bike," I said, patting the side of my iron horse.

I'd used my time standing at the gate to activate extra seals so that it didn't cause all hell to break loose.

"Yes, the guest cottage has its own garage. You can leave your motorcycle there," he replied after a short pause.

The conversation ended there when we were interrupted by a cute girl wearing a pantsuit. She greeted me with a meek smile:

"Mr. Vetrov?"

"Yes, that's me," I said with a nod, my gaze briefly settling on her green eyes.

I've always loved girls with green eyes. You can't tell me Lazarev didn't know that. Or am I being paranoid? We'll see.

"I'll accompany you to the apartments that have been allocated to you," she said, looking me up and down.

"Could you just wait a second?" I asked, remembering I'd forgotten someone.

I went back to the open gates, where I found Serby, who at the time was about to eat one of the power lines feeding the magic charms there. He'd got so carried away by what he was doing he hadn't even noticed I'd gone inside.

"There you are," I said, scooping him up into my arms.

"Let me go," he protested.

"Remember what we said?" I thought it was time to remind him what we'd agreed upon. "As long as you don't attract attention at the wrong time, you can do whatever you like."

"Yes, I remember," Serby replied, and he proved it by staying quiet and playing the sulky pooch.

"I'm sorry, my dog ran off." I smiled at Lazarev's servants as I showed them Serby.

"Er..." Seeing the dog, the maid seemed lost for words, but she soon snapped out of it. "This way."

She walked ahead, and I followed her, wheeling my bike. After a while, the path veered off to the right, to one of the buildings I'd seen from behind the fence. Then I was given the tour of the garage and the rooms I'd be staying in while I did my work.

"So, these are guest quarters, eh?" I whistled in surprise.

The designers were obviously very accomplished — their touches weren't ostentatious, and they merged seamlessly into the background but, even so, everything still had that faint whiff of wealth and luxury.

"Is there something not to your liking?" the maid asked anxiously.

"No, not at all," I said to reassure her. "It's just I'm used to more... humble surroundings, shall we say." The girl clearly didn't know how to respond to that, so she didn't.

"We might have one problem, though." I felt I should break the awkward silence.

"What's that?" She looked at me blankly.

"You didn't tell me your name." I shot her as charming a smile as I could.

"Anna Gromova," she said shyly and give a quick bob.

Hmm, Gromova, eh?

"That's more like it, Anna." I gave her another smile. "It's just I didn't know how I'm to address you."

"Well, if that'll be all?" Anna looked at me inquiringly, to which I just spread my hands. "Then I'll take my leave. I'll let you make yourself at home and relax after your journey. Mr. Lazarev didn't expect you to arrive so early, and he's currently busy, but he'll be sure to see you in the evening."

"Thanks. I'll do that."

Settling in didn't take long. I had one bag, so unpacking wasn't difficult. There was a time when I used to get by with a lot less, but, hey, I'd made it to twenty-four.

"Nice house," Serby declared after a thorough inspection of all the rooms. "Why don't we live somewhere like this?"

"Huh! Because of the cost."

"As far as I understand what you humans call accounting, you should have enough money for more than one such house," the dog answered, looking and sounding completely serious.

"Right." I had to laugh. He looked ridiculous. The seriousness, or rather, the attempt to appear serious, looked sweet on his little face, but it was best not to tell him that. "I could, you're right, but I don't want to. I much prefer my pad."

"When is feeding time around here?" he asked shortly after.

"All the things to talk about, and you're just about food," I scoffed. "I'm not sure they'll be inviting us both to dinner, but I'll think of something. You won't starve."

"Very funny," he muttered, and he trotted off to attend to his business.

Serby didn't need human food to stay alive, he just fell in love with it during his time in this world and wasn't one to miss the chance to enjoy something other than pure energy.

Making sure Serby was far enough away, and checking again that my sword was fixed securely, I embarked upon the main business any self-respecting dark magician starts with — ensuring my own safety.

Arranging myself comfortably on the kitchen sofa, I closed my eyes so I could open them again and explore the world through different eyes. With a wave of the hand, my standard draft seal appeared in front of me. Unfortunately, or fortunately, this is the only way I can use magic.

As a rule, sorcerers use a certain amount of willpower to affect the world around them. Most of them favor the element which comes most easily to them, and that's the one they develop. For them, this element is their main tool for working with the world's energy, and their main weapon. And a magician's rank depends on the amount of magic energy they can use in one go.

In my case, everything is somewhat more complicated. I had the fortune to be the last of the Vorontsovs who specialized in dark magic, which gives you a certain perspective on things. It's very hard to be peace-loving when your gift belongs to the realm of curses and black magic, a realm that also happens to be closely monitored by an ever-vigilant state.

My family couldn't say its influence was that great, being a junior branch, and when I was born, the situation deteriorated. Especially when it turned out I didn't have any kind of magic ability at all. My father was unable to produce another heir due to injuries he received, and my grandfather, a very lively and agile old man, didn't get the opportunity because of his age, although he definitely wouldn't have minded giving it a shot.

Circumstances and pressure from their relatives forced them both to resort to a dangerous ritual in the hope of instilling magic in me. They came up with the ritual themselves based on one or two theories and set out to create in me a magician even more powerful than themselves.

I was all of fourteen at the time, and I still

didn't really know what was going on, but the freezing cold altar I lay on, the heavy chains that shackled my body, and the pain of the cuts inflicted by the ritual dagger are not things I'm ever likely to forget.

My memory has wiped most of what they did. Drowned out by the pain and horror. It was only when I came to in the middle of a half-ruined estate that I realized what'd happened. Everything was in flames, and all around lay the dead bodies of my family. Yes, I was still a minor, but I understood perfectly that my still being alive was a piece of luck that could come back to haunt me. I grabbed whatever there was left of value and ran.

You can imagine my surprise when I accidentally performed magic for the first time while absent-mindedly doodling on a piece of paper. For ages, my father didn't believe I was completely ungifted (he consoled himself with the hope that I was a late developer, which can happen) and he diligently set about preparing me for the future by initiating me into the basic theories.

And it's thanks to what I learned, unsupported as it was by practice, and to the skewed gift that eventually came out, that I managed to survive and achieve what I achieved. Not the nicest of memories, but that experience made me. Made me who I am.

I must be getting old. Starting to philosophize.

Looking closely at my draft again, I mentally added new lines and symbols to it. If another magician saw me, they'd just laugh watching me doing this by hand (but I just find it quicker and easier). The fashion now is to cast spells with just one flourish of willpower, especially when starting from an intuitive level. Anything else was the stuff of antiquity and subject to ridicule, since most see it as like using a "crutch", and not proper channeling of the power.

Gradually, the sigil became more and more convoluted, but that's what I was aiming for. Unrolling it in front of me, I double-checked the key elements and immediately energized the design with a fifth of my available reserve.

This release of energy made the seal manifest itself in material form and become visible even to anyonewithout the gift, although thankfully there was no one else there except me. The seal's elements and circuits began to act according to their in-built guidelines, and then, with a flash, a dozen small semi-material creatures appeared. So far, so good.

Perhaps you can't call me a sorcerer in the classic sense, but I do have the power to summon creatures from other worlds, and they'll do whatever I tell them to. The creatures now hanging in the air, although small, were very dangerous, and they could get out of control and cause a lot of trouble even before the bonds keeping them here started to get weaker.

They only needed to keep me secure for a week while I was at the Lazarevs', so it didn't make sense to bind the seal to a material bearer — the energy I gave them would be enough for just that length of time. And, as a bonus, these creatures would provide me with the level of comfort I'd become accustomed to.

I didn't need to give those I'd summoned any orders, as all their conditions had already been written into the seal. When these entities appeared in this world, their instructions were affixed to the seals, which, after hanging in the air for a moment, disappeared. And then everyone went about their business.

A light flashed a couple of times, and you could no longer see what the creatures were doing.

All well and good. They'd also sweep the house for monitoring spells — I'm used to being on my own when I'm alone, and I don't like being spied on.

All this meant I could have a little snooze. I managed to sleep a bit on my bike — the good thing was it took me where I was going all by itself — but it's still nothing compared with a proper sleep on a nice soft bed.

I was woken by persistent signals from my security web. Among the summoned, there was an entity that could weave a special web of energy across the area it was ordered to. Its threads were so fine that a magician who wanted to enter the protected area wouldn't be able to see them straight away against the waves of background energy. This entity could do much more than that. The security net was just a small part of it.

Tutting at the spider hanging down from the ceiling in the corner, I got up from the sofa and went to the front door, which was where the persistent signals were coming from.

"Hello again, Gregor." It was the girl I met earlier. She smiled politely.

"Nice to see you again, Anna." I smiled back.

It didn't escape my notice just how closely she was looking at the door, which only confirmed my suspicions. She was one of the gifted, otherwise she wouldn't have been taking so much interest in the details of a house she'd have seen many times before.

"Mr. Lazarev is ready to see you. I'll escort you."

I closed the door of the guest cottage and followed my charming companion.

"How long have you been in service to Mr. Lazarev?" I asked, making conversation as we walked.

"My family's been serving the Lazarevs for generations, so, it's safe to say — from birth," she replied, and, for some reason, she took me not to the front door, but to one of the servants' entrances around the side.

"And how do you like it being under the healers' wing?" The question was somewhat impertinent. In high society it might even be considered insulting.

"My family doesn't have much power or influence — we'd only be someone's junior branch anyway," she replied, not offended in the least. "The Lazarevs are very warm towards us. I don't think whether or not I like it here is applicable. I can't imagine my life being any different, really." Anna paused for a moment. "Here we are." She pointed to the door made of dark wood decorated with a floral motif of creeping vines.

"Thanks for the company."

"Will you find your way back or shall I wait for you?"

"Ah, don't worry about that," I replied as gently as I could. "Our conversation is likely to drag on, so..." I waved my hand vaguely.

Anna gave a slight smile and walked back down the corridor.

"Gregor, don't be a stranger. Come in," the patriarch of the Lazarev family called out as soon as I entered his office.

Closing the door behind me, I occupied an armchair opposite him.

Not bad at all. Tastefully done out. The hearth with its real fire and crackling logs made the room uniquely cozy. And the furnishings made with different expensive types of wood spoke volumes to those in the know. Like myself.

"Hah, you look tired," I said, taking one look at him. "And there was I thinking always being on the go was no problem for a healer of your level."

"I don't like using magic unless there's a call for it," he replied, wincing. "And maintaining the body with magic isn't the best option. I don't deny it's difficult to do without it sometimes. Well, that's all by the bye," he said dismissively. "I'm sorry I couldn't meet you right away."

Yeah, sure. Though I didn't say it out loud.

"Come, now." I tried to look slightly embarrassed. Just slightly, insofar as a dark magician can. "You're the head of an entire household. You've a lot to keep on top of."

"You got here earlier than I expected." Lazarev rose from his chair and walked over to the bar. He fished out a bottle of wine, uncorked it theatrically, and fetched two glasses. "I take it you won't say no to us getting through this? As it's evening, a little wine won't do the body any harm. Trust me, I'm an expert."

"Personally, I prefer cognac, but I won't say no." I was all for it and accepted the glass gratefully. And that wine, by the way, I found out, costs a lot more per bottle than the average, and that's an understatement. I heard somewhere there are only about a thousand bottles of it in existence, and there was one just sitting there in his office. Boyars know how to live, there's no denying it. This was a very generous gesture, all the same, and it didn't go unappreciated. "And about my arriving early... I just don't like being late," I said, with a shrug of the shoulders. "I managed to finish up all my business quicker than I thought, so I decided to leave there and then. I expect you wouldn't mind your office being ready ahead of schedule?"

"Of course, I'm not against it being completed as soon as possible, but you also need telling," he chided me.

"Anyway, I doubt my being here will cause any problems." I let that go, too.

We'd long hit upon this way of communicating.

It suited us both, and my rather insolent behavior didn't bother Lazarev in the least. So, I took full advantage.

"Oh, and you're not the only unexpected guest to descend upon me." Lazarev wearily rubbed the bridge of his nose and set his glass aside.

"One who arrived in a Cadillac without your coats of arms, either."

"I asked my assistant not to let anyone in. He was somewhat overzealous in carrying out my orders," Lazarev said, passing the buck to his subordinates. "And about the car..." he heaved a huge sigh. "That was my niece who decided to drop by unexpectedly. Hence no coat of arms — she didn't want me to know she was coming."

The girl described clearly didn't know the meaning of discretion and secrecy, arriving in such a provocative vehicle.

"Family strife," I said with a grin. "I know all about that."

"No, no, nothing like that," Lazarev tried to explain. "It's just she's supposed to be in college now, but she decided to take off without permission."

"What about the bodyguards?" I wanted to know as I savored another gulp of the quite marvelous wine.

"They told me what she was up to, only they didn't know the ultimate purpose of her visit themselves. Take no notice." Lazarev gave a faint smile. "It's just the carping of an old man. Her coming here threw out my schedule a little, that's all."

"So, when can I get started?" I thought it was

time to cut to the chase.

"Some of the materials you requested have already been delivered, so you can start tomorrow. Are there any other tools you need?"

"Don't worry. I have all the tools I need."

And with that, we finished the bottle in silence, and I took my leave of the office owner, who, it seemed, had decided to sit there a bit longer. Perhaps the open bar and the pensive mood that had overtaken him had something to do with it.

It didn't feel like we'd been talking for that long but, outside, it was already dark. Everything would've been plunged into complete darkness had it not been for all the lights. My head felt nice and fuzzy, and I didn't want to think about anything serious now. I decided not to go straight back to my temporary lodgings but to take a stroll around the estate, instead.

I picked one of the paths leading off to the side and started following it at a leisurely pace. Everything I saw spoke of an estate that was scrupulously maintained. Yes, even over there, the contents of the flowerbeds had been so neatly pruned, it was as if someone measured them every morning and removed anything sticking out. I couldn't understand the point in going to so much trouble just to make them look slightly better than they did before.

Behind the main house, as well as the outbuildings, some generously lit greenhouses and a small lake revealed themselves.

I wasn't about to go poking around in the

greenhouses, as there could have been plants in there that were incredibly whimsical and expensive. Well, what else would a family of healers be growing if not medicinal herbs? Better to give the place a wide berth and tell Serby not to stick his snout in there, otherwise I'd have to spend the services I'd been promised (but hadn't received yet) on writing off any screwups.

My path took me alongside a lake. As I approached it, I could make out a small gazebo among the vegetation, commanding a wonderful view of the water. This was confirmed when I sat down on a bench there, upholstered with a stain-proof cloth.

Part of me could've looked out over the lake for hours, but I wouldn't be me if I hadn't thought of a way of taking the edge off such a soothing scene. A small seal appeared above my left hand. After a couple of seconds of contemplation, I added symbols to the seal to determine the parameters of the desired creature, and then I energized it.

Now I just had to wait for the spell to find a demon capable of meeting my requirements. It was probably no more than ten seconds before an initially formless cloud appeared above my palm. Soon, however, it began to take shape. A minute later, and a small fairy that looked like a drawing from a children's cartoon was already standing there on my hand. Despite its appearance, it was a very bad creature — something vaguely reminiscent of a demon, although it wasn't quite that. But the important thing to me was whether it performed the task I'd assigned to it or not.

I nudged the fairy towards the lake, and, gliding on the surface of the water, it began to dance to inaudible music. With each of its movements, a sheet of ice was formed, which was in no hurry to melt, despite the warm weather.

I followed each graceful movement of the tiny figure, curious to see what would happen next. The performance ended with the creation of an ice-castle, right on the surface of the water. It was so detailed it looked like an exact copy of an existing castle.

Unfortunately, the ice-castle heralded the end of the summoning, and, with a wave of its hand, the summoned spirit melted into the air. For a couple of seconds, the ice structure fought for its survival, but then it collapsed before finally "drowning". All this splendor had been sustained by the magic of the summoned creature, so it departed at the same time.

"That was beautiful," rang out a melodious female voice to my right.

It was only down to my peaceful mood that I let a stranger get so close and didn't order one of my summoned critters to attack.

"Oh, just a little trick." I said, looking closely at the stranger.

She turned out to be a tall brunette with gold-colored eyes — a shade you don't see in common folks. She was wearing a flimsy light-colored dress that reached down just above the knee and offered an intriguing view of her slender legs. And the view from above revealed some fairly large... In all, I was transfixed. The unknown woman was young and beautiful in a way that made it hard to take your eyes off her, but in that there was something witch-like, which was actually quite sobering.

"I've never seen anything like it," the girl said in admiration. "That wasn't an illusion," she asserted, before adding: "I sensed it was a living creature."

"Not really — it was just a semi-material shell," I blurted out before I realized what I'd said.

Giving details about your abilities to strangers is not the best idea in the world.

"How's that?" the girl asked with surprise, moving closer.

"It's... done with a spell," I said, finding a way out of the situation. "As for how to do it — that's my secret," I said, putting an end to any more questions on the subject.

"But I just love unraveling secrets," the stranger confided in a quiet whisper.

"Hah, good luck with that."

"I haven't seen you here before," the girl said, leaning against the handrail of the gazebo. "Are you a new employee?"

"You could say that. And you are?"

"Arina Lazareva, the niece of the owner of this estate," she replied proudly, standing in semi-profile. She appeared to be aware that the moonlight falling on the gazebo was showing off her figure to great effect.

"I was lucky enough to meet the young mistress on my very first day." I clicked my tongue, enjoying the view, not caring that my interest was self-evident.

"Don't." Although it was clear Arina was pleased with the reaction she got, she frowned slightly. "That may be the way at the English court, but here everything is much simpler. And I'm not fond of such behavior."

"You've studied in England?" I raised an eyebrow.

"I did practical training on an exchange at the Royal School of Arts," she answered. Just what you'd expect from a niece of Christopher Lazarev.

Only someone from a very influential family could drop one of the best educational establishments for magicians so casually into a conversation. Or a very spoiled child, anyway.

The Royal School of Arts, or RSA, as it's often abbreviated, was founded, according to its official history, by Merlin, one of the most powerful sorcerers of his time, to help druids, witches and magicians hide from the flames of the Inquisition and progress their art. Along with magic itself, the RSA was opened up to the whole world, and it announced that it was officially recruiting to its hallowed cloisters.

The only school that could better it was our Academy of Magic under the patronage of the emperor. It was one of the strongholds of modern magic and contributed in every way to its development as well as to humankind's technological advancement. As if in opposition to the Academy, the

RSA advocated that the human and the magical shouldn't be mixed, for which they had their own reasons. I guess it's hard to trust people when your ancestors were persecuted like mad dogs and exterminated in various imaginative ways.

Unfortunately, I'm not destined to see the inside of either of these places.

"It must've been an amazing experience," I said, eager to squeeze some more details out of her.

"The teachers there really are wonderful." Arina gave a faint smile. "And everything is so different from what they teach us here. Before visiting the RSA, I had no idea that magicians still used magic helpers."

"You mean their staffs?"

"Yes. They say the senior students germinate the seed of the nascent staff inside themselves, so it becomes an extension of their energy. They even have a practical course on obtaining suitable materials so you can make your own," she related enthusiastically, glad that I was interested. But suddenly her mood changed drastically. "Only there are more than enough conceited idiots, too hung up on their family trees and the fact they had home schooling, which is often much better than at the RSA."

"Yes, I also heard they still have home schooling and often develop spells within the clan that remain a family secret and aren't in any registry," I said, showing off my knowledge.

"Only they don't have families, but houses,"

Arina corrected me, frowning in a comical way for a second. "They have a slightly different way of classifying the composition of magic families," she said, as if quoting a textbook.

"You were clearly asked to leave so as not to embarrass the other students with your intellect," I said, teasing her slightly.

"Exactly." Instead of being offended, Arina raised her head a little and adopted a proud pose. "They just couldn't take it."

And with this, she broke into peals of laughter. It was so contagious I didn't realize at first that I was laughing as well.

"You should be more careful, with a personality like that..." I shook my head.

"Don't." Arina waved her hand. "My uncle has already bored me half to death with his lectures on the subject. Why have I been so open with you, I wonder?" Her question wasn't directed at anyone in particular.

"Probably because I'm an outsider who doesn't care about you or your feelings?" I suggested, with a crafty look.

"Perhaps." Arina shrugged indifferently. She paused for a couple of seconds, and then turned around abruptly and, pointing accusingly, said: "By the way, you didn't introduce yourself."

"Gregor Vetrov."

"Vetrov, Vetrov," Arina repeated, as if tasting the name. "I'm sorry, but I don't remember that family."

"That's not surprising," I said, watching her

fumbling around. "I don't belong to any."

"But you're a magician!" she exclaimed accusingly again, as if I were deliberately deceiving her.

"Well," I said, "that's just how it turned out."

"Another mystery," Arina uttered under her breath.

But I heard her perfectly well and really didn't like that she was still anticipating getting to the bottom of my secrets.

"And you owe me a repeat performance," she said in a peremptory tone just as I thought our conversation was over.

"And why's that?" I asked calmly.

"Gregor, your employer is my uncle, and I, as his niece, can give servants and employees orders," she explained patiently, as if to a child.

"You're right and wrong at the same time," I said with a revealing sigh. "Yes, my employer is Christopher Lazarev, but at the same time it was he who hired me, and it was with him that I signed a contract. So, I'm sorry, but your claims are addressed to the wrong quarter."

"Is that so? Arina narrowed her eyes slyly. "We'll see about that."

With these words, she turned around, flicking her hair in the air, and headed off back towards the house. I couldn't shake the feeling that the patriarch's niece, as they say, had the "bit between her teeth"... Well, that would make my stay here more interesting, anyway.

CHAPTER 3

THERE'S NOTHING LIKE a warm sunny morning to foster a feeling of bliss and relaxation. Especially when the hands on the clock are slowly creeping towards noon, and there's nowhere you need to hurry off to. I felt completely rested and was listening as some little birds were singing outside my window. I would've lolled around in bed all day, but, sadly, I'm not here just to lie on a soft featherbed.

In a dark corner of the corridor, a spirit summoned in the form of a spider was patiently waiting for me. As soon as I came closer, a web appeared next to me with the number four in the middle of it. It was the number of times uninvited guests had tried to get into my quarters. It was also good that I'd removed the visitor notification beforehand, otherwise I wouldn't have got enough sleep. And not getting enough sleep puts me in a foul mood and makes me do bad things.

I remember that it took two painful weeks to try to explain to this spirit how it was to communicate with me. I could've not cared and been content with the fact that I'd been protected at least, but at that particular moment I wanted to see the results of this protection. And this was all I ended up with...

Serby was already in the kitchen, pretending to be asleep and unaware of what was going on around him. In fact, it was the way his ears cocked in reaction to the sound of my footsteps that gave him away completely. What could I do? The demonic pooch couldn't quite get used to his material form, and sometimes his canine behavior betrayed his emotions.

Without paying attention to the spitz (let him nurse his self-esteem), I went to the refrigerator, which I'd completely forgotten to inspect the day before. After resting by the lake, I took the opportunity to sneak into the kitchen and lift some supplies from there. Why hide it? — I wanted to know what the inside of the Lazarevs' kitchen looked like.

The precious appliance met all my expectations. It was filled to the brim with a variety of food that you just needed to heat up. So, making breakfast was a breeze.

The aroma of meat being warmed up in a skillet reached Serby, who'd already cast off the role of a sleeping dog to set about his favorite sport — speed eating. I went for a light salad and a couple of sandwiches along with some strong coffee — the latter gave off a barely detectable magic energy, which revealed that an earth magician had had something to do with it at some point.

"So, how was your walk?" I asked when the demon had eaten everything and was lying on his side, looking over at me from time to time, contentedly.

"It's a large area with some serious protection," he replied. "Although they didn't sense my interference at all. It was funny to watch them when I deliberately brushed against one of the security threads, and the guards who ran up saw only a harmless mutt."

"You're lucky they know you're my pet. Otherwise, they'd consider you a trespasser and destroy you accordingly," I scolded him. "So, try not to draw too much attention to yourself. The less distracted I am, the sooner I'll finish the job, and we can go home."

"I know what to do and how to do it," the spitz said proudly. But he wasn't about to protest, which was already a good sign.

In general, although Serby liked to demonstrate his bellicose temperament and assert himself as a real demon, he was sometimes terribly curious and peace-loving. How is it he managed to survive among his compatriots with a character like his? It was only because I intervened in his fate that he was still alive today.

After cleaning up after me and the dog, and stretching contentedly, I went out onto the porch where I was confronted by a frankly angry-looking Anna.

"So, you've finally deigned to surface," she said, laying into me straight away.

"Were you waiting for me?" I looked at her with surprise.

So that's who was trying to get into the house!

"I've been charged with accompanying you while you're here," she said sternly. "And you decided to apply additional protection to the house, because of which I've had to stand here waiting."

"Sorry, my bad," I said, trying to smooth things over. I didn't want to start such a nice day with an argument. "I didn't think I'd be assigned an escort. I mean, the owner of the estate must've forgotten to mention that."

"Mr. Lazarev is a busy man," Anna said, sighing. "It seems I was the most available of the servants at the time, so I was entrusted with looking after you."

"Got it." I looked thoughtfully at the girl who was flushed with indignation. "Then, please," I motioned towards the main house. "You're free to go."

"What do you mean, go?"

"I don't need an escort." And Anna had made such a good impression on me. "Order that the materials I need for my work be delivered to Mr. Lazarev's office."

"But... how... I..." Anna began to gasp for air.

"Anna, come on. I'm relieving you of your duties. And to be honest, I don't need an escort. Unless, of course, you've got something else in mind?"

I gestured in a way that left her in no doubt what "something else" meant.

"Why, you!" The Lazarevs' blushing servant was incandescent. She turned around and left. She was almost running.

"Yeah, it'd be a blast, I'm sure."

Humming a cheerful tune from some song I'd heard, I went up to the main house. Intending to go through the front door, I stopped for a moment, and then turned onto the same path Anna had led me down. Why? She'd taken me that way for a reason, and now, after yesterday evening, I thought I'd worked out what it was.

On the way, I still couldn't help myself, so I dropped into the kitchen, making off with a couple of delicious smelling buns while the cook was distracted by his underlings. Say what you like, but at the Lazarev estate they cook as well as the best restaurants in the capital. That's what money gets you.

Fueling myself en route, I eventually arrived at Lazarev's office. It was locked. I could, of course, have gone and looked for one of the servants and have them find the keys, but... I couldn't be bothered. A small seal flashed over my left hand, and before it activated itself, I directed it towards the door. A slight click, and the handle turned easily. Access was granted.

I felt like a master burglar. Straight up.

Once inside, I switched over to magic vision and thoroughly examined every corner of the room. As I'd noticed yesterday, almost everything that would've been of interest to a magician had been removed. There were none of the valuable artifacts or trophies that the status of an estate owner demands be there. What can I say, even the safe I found behind the bookcase was empty as if it had been scrubbed clean. Christopher Lazarev clearly knew I was coming.

Despite the lack of any interesting knick-knacks, there was something on the desk that caught my attention. On the tabletop made of a rare type of oak, there were several little pouches which I untied one after the other, to check that the components I needed for my work were inside. Not only that, whoever had assembled this order turned out to be sufficiently well-versed not to put together any herbs or minerals that were incompatible.

The way I intended to protect the Lazarev patriarch's office was all about the creatures I was going to summon. But, for them to limit their activities to just this room and keep carrying out the duties assigned to them properly, I needed material bearers.

There were plenty of stationary anchors in my bar the summoned could feed on. And they could draw on more energy than normal in an emergency. Here, I was going to use a combination of herbs and minerals, the properties of which made them good accumulators of natural energy in themselves. I didn't use this method at home due to the cost and difficulty obtaining some of the things on the list, and because I didn't have the right connections... yet.

Okay, enough sitting around! Time to get to work.

First off, I pulled out a few sheets of paper from the desk drawer and, using a pen, quickly began to sketch out a schematic diagram that would let me achieve the result I wanted using the minimum of power. While I managed all this quickly and easily, no-one saw how many drafts I had to destroy before I arrived at the right level of artistry.

Just an hour of careful and painstaking work, and the whole desk was a carpet of sheets of paper covered with drawings of sigils and pentagrams. Sitting with my eyes closed for a few minutes, I eased the trembling in my still tense hands and proceeded to the second stage of the work I'd mapped out for the day.

From the outside, it might've looked like I was rushing between the pouches of materials and the complicated diagram I'd drawn without any discernible system, but there was something correct and logical to all of this. I'm not quite all there at such times. I know perfectly well why I'm doing this or that and where there are errors to be corrected, but, when I'm at work, I'm seized by something like inspiration and just go with the flow. It was a while before I realized all the pouches were empty, and small mounds of herbs and minerals were already laid out on the table at the nodal points of the scheme.

My father and grandfather's damned experiment! If I understood just a little bit more of what it was they did to me... then maybe I'd be more aware of what I'm doing.

To hell with them!

I cleared my mind of all unnecessary thoughts and, stretching my arms out parallel to the table, I garnered energy equal to about eight hundred units, and powered the entire circuit with it. A soft blue light emanating from the seals filled the office. At the nodal points, the piled-up mounds of materials rose into the air and began to squeeze themselves into tiny spheres. A few seconds later, they started to solidify, and symbols appeared on them. After hanging in the air for a little while longer, seven spheres dropped down onto the table.

Carefully putting the hot spheres into the pouches, I collected up the sheets of paper and, with the help of another seal, first burned them, and then removed all the ashes. With this, you could say, the most difficult stage was completed. I had to wait until the spheres cooled down and started to fill with natural energy, and then I'd be able to move on to the final part.

I double-checked the pouches and heaved a sigh of relief. Now I could safely say I'd managed to create some fairly good concentrations of magic from natural sources, which could easily feed all the creatures I was about to summon.

It would've been great, of course, to make those anchor rods I used in my bar, but it had taken me three months of meticulous work to create them in preparation for a ritual, after which I couldn't get out of bed for about two weeks — my body was completely exhausted. It was good I'd allowed for that eventuality and made sure everything I needed to help me recover was close by.

I had no desire to go through that again, which is why I chose a way that was more expensive, if we're talking about money, and yet cheaper at the same time when it came to my strength. There is, of course, a chance someone might take an interest in spheres capable of accumulating magic energy, but in such a case, the summoned creatures would attack them, destroying the sphere at the same time. I don't like it when someone tries to uncover my secrets.

Closing the office door behind me, I decided to go down the central staircase where I almost banged heads with Anna Gromova who was hurrying off somewhere. The surprise made her rock on her heels, and she was about to fall backwards. Thankfully, my reaction saved her from counting how many steps there were on the not-so-small staircase with her ribs.

"You should be more careful," I said, holding the servant in a state of limbo.

She instinctively wrapped her arms around my neck and looked at me bewildered. Her eyes registered what was going on, and then I'm sure I could see anger welling up in them.

"Let me go," came Anna's muffled voice.

"Sure about that?" I expressed my doubt, looking down the stairs emphatically. "I know the Lazarevs are healers, but it's still going to hurt."

"Let me go," she repeated hopelessly, the light

in her eyes ebbing away.

I no longer felt like poking fun at this servant of the Lazarevs, so I helped her down onto the stairs.

"Were you looking for someone?" I asked, examining the somewhat disheveled girl.

"I've found them, now," Anna said with a heavy sigh. "I've been looking for you everywhere!"

"We kind of talked this morning... I mean, this afternoon."

"I should have handed you the key to the office."

"There was no need," I said with a wave of the hand. "I got in anyway."

"But how?" She looked baffled. "Only I had the key."

"Don't know," I said, hands open. "Now, if you'll excuse me, I'd like to have something to eat."

"How the..." Anna looked around her in confusion.

I wasn't about to hang around any longer because my stomach was already telling me in no uncertain terms that while work is work, I also needed to eat. Steadily making my way down the stairs, surprisingly without passing anyone, I sniffed the air andfollowed my nose in search of the dining room. I could, of course, have gone outside and come back in again through the same side entrance as before, but I wanted to check out the mansion's interior decor.

So, I took my time admiring the antique paintings and vases which, I noticed, had fresh flowers in them, and still managed to find the dining room, where I was plunged straight into the bustle of dinner being prepared.

The chef I'd seen before was shouting at his subordinates, calling them bungling oafs. Their reaction was phlegmatic, but they did start to speed up, especially when one of their bosses was walking past.

I think I'd have done the same to escape the attention of such a meathead. It was really quite strange that such a pumped-up man-mountain, who looked like a special ops soldier, was the chef at the Lazarev estate.

"Who let him into my kitchen?" He'd spotted me.

"I come to eat." I put my hands up straight away.

Anyone else would've done the same. The guy was pointing a rather large cleaver at me, which, by the looks of it, could be used as a projectile should it prove necessary.

"When you come, eat and stay out of here," he said menacingly, shaking his huge knife at me.

"Okay, so, where is it I'm supposed to go?" I threw out my arms, trying to look apologetic.

"You," the chef prodded the guy nearest to him. "Take the new guy to the dining room."

The chosen assistant silently wiped his hands on a towel and gestured to me to follow him.

"Zhenya," he said, stretching his hand out as I scampered after him.

"Gregor," I answered with a handshake. "In

there, is it always so…" I waved my arm vaguely, not knowing how best to describe what I'd witnessed.

"Ivan Semenovich is a man of the world," Zhenya, who turned out, on closer inspection, to be covered in freckles, said, with a faint smile. "But he has a really heavy hand."

"Yeah, and voice," I replied, rubbing my ear which was still ringing.

"But the experience we're getting under his guidance is massive," he said proudly. "Some of the guys got jobs in the capital. One as assistant chef, another, with Ivan Semenovich's recommendations, has even become a highly respected chef himself."

"Then you really are lucky. But you still need to watch your ears."

"That's true," Zhenya said, laughing as he took me to a door at the end of a labyrinthine journey. "This is the staff dining room."

The room contained a long table to seat about twenty people, and, opposite it, a self-service area complete with dishes catering to every taste.

"You've got everything here, and some," I said, taking it all in.

"There are quite a lot of employees on the estate and not all of them can eat at the same time," Zhenya said. "So, Ivan Semenovich decided to arrange somewhere everyone can eat when they're not working. There's food here even at night, which is the main thing for those on the night shift. So, help yourself," he said with a good-natured smile.

"But I have to go."

"Thanks."

Having gathered up a selection of tasty treats, I picked a corner far from the entrance and began to sample one after another. Faces I didn't recognize came into the dining room, which confirmed what I'd been told about the servants eating here during their time off. They also took some food, and ate slowly, chatting quietly among themselves, paying me almost no attention. Everyone confined themselves to curious glances, but no one dared come any closer.

So it was until the guard I recognized from my first day here walked in. Taking only a mug of coffee, he made a beeline for me.

"Hello," he said politely. I indicated that the seat next to me was free, and he took me up on the offer. "Sergey."

"Gregor," I replied, without looking up from a tender slice of cutlet, doused in some awesome sauce.

"Why did you offend Anna?" the guard asked suddenly.

I almost choked in surprise, but managed to get it down me, all the same.

"I really don't know what you're talking about."

"Just be gentle with her." He sighed heavily and looked to one side. "She hasn't been at the estate for long... she just finished her studies... and..." he said, a little disjointedly. "I mean, Anna's still finding her feet, and she's been entrusted with accompanying a guest and helping him, and the guest doesn't appreciate her help at all."

"But I really don't need her," I said, shrugging.

"You heard what I said," Sergey replied in a more menacing tone, then left the dining room.

What do they all want from me?

After finishing my early dinner or late lunch, whatever you want to call it, I decided that was enough chat for one day and tried to get back to my lodgings, discreetly.

How wrong to think that I'd be able to slip away unnoticed.

* * *

"Why am I here, again?" I asked with a heavy sigh.

"Greg, you agreed to come with me yourself," Arina said with a look of surprise.

"Arina Lazareva, when did we start addressing each other so informally?" I looked at her just as surprised.

"If we're too formal, it'll attract attention," she said with an expressive frown. "Everyone here is about the same age, anyway."

With this, Arina grabbed my elbow and dragged me towards a fairly large group made up entirely of young folks.

Ask me how I got here. Well, Christopher Lazarev's niece intercepted me right outside the guest quarters and somehow managed to persuade me to take her to some local gathering.

I couldn't help but notice how the guards were

strangely placid and reacted quite calmly to the sight of Arina on my motorcycle. I wouldn't be wrong in thinking there'd be quite a few of her bodyguards at this party, melting into the background. It's hard to think otherwise when the children of wealthy families are all in one place.

I was, clearly, taken for Lazareva's chaperon, since no one asked why there was a commoner there. And to be honest, I was curious as to what makes the up-and-coming generation of the empire's aristocrats tick.

Arina began to attract looks almost immediately, which she openly exploited, smiling radiantly at everyone she knew. I got the feeling she liked all the attention. I, however, had to maintain a detached expression so as not to end up in hot water.

To think I could've been in similar company, had things turned out differently...

"Arina, I'd given up all hope of seeing you today," a blond guy standing in the middle of the group greeted her.

"Yura, dear, how could I miss such an event?" Arina smiled ironically. "Just as well that I did!"

"You're right," he said with a laugh and drew closer. "Won't you introduce us?" He looked me up and down.

"Greg Vetrov," Arina introduced me. "He kindly agreed to accompany me to tonight. And this is Yura Volkonsky — the ringleader around here and my friend since childhood."

Volkonsky, hey? It was my turn to size him up,

and I couldn't help but notice he was in excellent shape. From the way he moved, it was clear the guy had carried on the tradition of his military commander ancestors and put in a good few hours a day of martial arts training. At the very least, he was being taught combat training. As far as I'd heard, his family was very strict about that.

"I'm always glad to see new faces in our little group," he said, holding his hand out to me and smiling affably.

"I was just at a loose end," I said with a chuckle. His was a firm handshake. A little too firm, I'd say.

"And what have you got lined up for us today?" Arina asked, interrupting our exchange of pleasantries.

"I managed to get a section of the road closed off for our race," Yuri answered, undisguised triumph in his eyes.

"I see..." Arina drawled pensively. "We've not had a race before. Who's in it?"

"Anyone willing to risk their wheels. A couple of people I know said they wanted to take part, so it should be interesting. Come on, I'll show you." He gestured to us to follow him.

Yes, Yura wasn't lying — it really should be interesting. And how could it not be, when most of the cars in question were magicars, and so stuffed full of magic, that even I could feel the power emanating from them. Didn't I see one of these cars on the way here?

"Wow," Arina said, taking the five cars in.

"Who's agreed to risk these?"

"I invited my friends from the academy, and they said why the hell not. Unfortunately, racing is banned in the capital. Here, it's a bit easier," Yura replied.

"Aren't you worried about this being in the papers tomorrow?" I asked Yura.

"We keep these meetings kind of private, so we can let off steam out of the spotlight. Our families' servants see to that," he replied politely.

"I see you've thought everything through."

"And who's that?" Arina pointed at someone wearing motorcycle gear who was standing apart from everyone.

"That's our 'dark horse'. We'd pretty much settled on the number taking part, when he turned up and said he wanted to make it six."

"Six?" I asked. "But I only see five cars."

"That's the thing," Yura said with a self-satisfied smile. "He's going to race on his bike."

"Is that fair?" Arina asked, somewhat doubtfully.

"The others agreed," he said. "Frankly, everyone thought it was funny, this fella wanting to race, that and the fact that no one knows who he is. Absolutely no one gives him a chance against top-of-the-range magicars."

"You don't know who he is?" Arina was intrigued.

"No. He refused to give his name or show us his face. As you can see," Yuri pointed to the guy standing on his own, "he won't even speak to anyone, and the girls are annoyed they couldn't get a word out of him."

"Very interesting," I said.

"That's why we decided to have him in the race," Yura said to me. "He'll make it a bit different, at least, even if he's behind from the off."

The conversation between Arina and Yuri moved on to their mutual acquaintances, and I stepped back a little to give them some space.

It was interesting to examine the nascent flower of the empire so close up. I thought it'd be something unique, but so far it mainly resembled any typical party for bored rich kids on the look-out for new sensations and entertainment. All the fact that the competitors were driving magicars said was they all came from the kind of families that could afford them.

Well, what did I expect? Pushkino wasn't that far from Moscow. World-famous names had their estates there. And the children of noble families are bound to know each other, after all, a lot of them go to the same colleges, and who said they weren't allowed to make contacts in such an informal setting?

I looked on as small groups of these members of high society sauntered around the starting line, bowing politely to other such groups, often stopping to exchange a few words. The servants guarding them rushed in and out of the crowd, their behavior and demeanor markedly different from that of their masters.

I, of course, wanted to take a closer look at the

magicars to be awarded to the winner, but no one was allowed near them. No doubt they were afraid some crafty character would try to influence them and give one of the racers an advantage. The mysterious stranger really stuck out. He was just standing there next to his bike, waiting for the race to start.

What was that all about? I suspected there was more to the guy than met the eye, and that Yura was making a big mistake being so quick to dismiss this "dark horse".

"Hey," I called out to a group of guys passing by. They were having a loud discussion about the relative merits of one racer versus another. "Anyone taking bets here?"

"This your first time at one of these?" said a guy with brown hair and eyes standing closest to me, who got where I was coming from.

"Yeah. Looks like I was too late to enter." I said, hands open.

"Speak to him." He pointed to a tall guy who was smoking a cigarette, standing next to a store or something that was now closed. "He takes care of the bets around here."

I thanked him and headed towards the guy in question.

The bookmaker at today's get-together didn't look any different from most of the others there. The same expensive clothes and friendly nods to acquaintances. It was only his gaze that betrayed the poorly concealed ennui of a man who had already been to so many of these things that they now bored him half to death.

"I'm told you're taking bets?" I asked him.

"Got any dough?" He took another puff, looking at me somewhat skeptically.

"You take bank cards?" I asked, and after an affirmative nod in response: "Then yeah."

"Who are you betting on?" The bookmaker started to display more interest.

"On the motorcyclist there." I chuckled.

"You sure about that? It's not, of course, any of my business, but his chances are way too low."

"What are the odds?"

"Fifty to one."

"Great." I smiled. "Three thousand on him, then."

"I'd say 'good luck', but you'd clean me out if you won," he said once the card payment was complete.

"That's what I like to hear."

What I spent wasn't going to hit me too hard if I lost, and, if I won, I'd get my hands on a hundred and fifty thousand... I just hoped my instincts hadn't deceived me, and that the guy rose to the occasion.

While I was doing this, Yura was hanging out with Arina, and they were enjoying themselves chatting with other children of the aristocracy. I felt like a spare part at this gathering and, had I not been able to put a bet on, I'd have been bored stiff. My lifestyle really was very different, and there was no getting around it.

Only aristocrats could come up with a race between magicars, let alone put up as a prize a car few people could afford. It seemed to suggest a certain disregard for what their parents had achieved. They weren't in the least embarrassed that they'd had everything handed to them on a plate. I'm not saying they aren't trained to be aristocrats from childhood and that eventually some of them will turn out to be worthy successors, but at that age...

To be honest, I was a little jealous they could be so carefree before they were saddled with family responsibilities. Maybe that's why I was in such a gloomy mood.

"Gregor, please don't tell me you're bored?" Arina appeared to my right from nowhere. "They've gone to all this trouble."

"I'm not used to this kind of thing," I said with a sigh, not even trying to explain to her. At best, she wouldn't understand; at worst, she'd even get offended. "When's the race?"

"That I can help you with," Arina said with a smile. "It starts in half an hour. They've nearly finished setting up the cameras so we can all watch it."

"All that effort?" I raised an eyebrow in surprise.

"Yes. I mean, this isn't just a way of enjoying yourself, but also showing off your organizational skills. That's why Yura's making sure everything's top class."

"I thought the Volkonskys were of military stock."

"Yura has two older brothers, so he won't become heir," Arina explained. "And, anyway, he's not cut out for war games. He prefers arranging evenings like this for the elite. And if he proves to his relatives he can cope with such 'trifles', they'll start trusting him with something a bit 'bigger'," she said, hinting at something.

I got it. While historically the Volkonskys served in the military, theirs was quite a big family, and they all had to find something to do, didn't they? I'd not really gone into it, but I would've assumed they had more than one business with a military contract at their disposal. Who knows what kind of business this guy would be given to run. So, this wasn't a bad way of showing his family what he could do.

"Look, it's starting," Arina said, pulling me away from my thoughts.

And indeed it was — the competitors were already sitting in their cars, getting ready for the off. The magicar engines were making as much noise as they could and distorting the air, but that was due to the magic particles they were emitting rather than the heat. The motorcyclist, however, stayed detached from this spectacle, and was just sitting there on his iron horse.

Maybe it was worth joining in? I did wonder how my chopper would fare in this race. But no. A stupid idea. If I bet on myself, though... The thought was soon nipped in the bud by a fiery flash announcing that the race had started.

The magicars immediately pulled away, leaving the motorcyclist in their wake, raising hoots of derision from the crowd. They'd already given up any hope of seeing him doing anything of note, and so switched their attention to the cameras showing the leading pack. Luckily for them, they were all wearing communication bracelets, so they had no problem picking up the images from the cameras.

I was getting jealous — I still didn't have one. Maybe I should request one in return for one of my services?

Thankfully, Yura had also provided a way of watching the race for those who hadn't managed to get hold of such a luxury gadget. I grabbed a tablet from one of the servants and began to scroll through the cameras until I found the one showing the outsider. The screen showed the dashboard of the unknown rider's motorcycle. What looked like symbols on it lit up, and suddenly the bike shot forward at such a speed that it only took him a few seconds to catch up with the last car.

Either he couldn't keep such a speed up for long, or he was afraid he wouldn't be able to handle the maneuver, but the motorcyclist then slowed down and tried to get around the car in front of him from the right, moving the body of the motorcycle in the same direction, which forced the driver to slow down so he didn't hit him with his wheel. He made a few more attempts to get in front, but they were no more successful than the first.

But then the motorcyclist did something I didn't expect — he pulled a wheelie, and when the car began to brake, he didn't go around the side, but somehow got up onto the roof and simply rolled over it. Taken by surprise, the driver didn't see the turning in time and flew straight into a wall. It was only the car's safety system crammed full of magic that saved him, otherwise the consequences would've been tragic. And so, the only damage was a slight crack in the wall of some store and a shocked driver, whose race now was probably run.

It was still looking like I'd been wrong in my choice of winner, but even if I had, the motorcyclist had at least surprised and entertained me.

Selecting another camera, which was now expertly following every move of this "dark horse", I was able to see how effortlessly the rider overtook two more cars, literally slipping between them. It seems they decided to try to sandwich this all too nimble stranger and ended up paying the price by colliding with each other. But the motorcyclist accelerated sharply and was able to squeeze through the narrowing gap before it closed.

Unfortunately, the impact of the two magicars caused a burst of magic particles, affecting the camera, temporarily disabling it. While I was looking for one that worked, the guy I'd bet on took the lead, his rivals left far behind.

Impressively skidding to a sideways stop, the mystery rider dismounted, removed his helmet and left it on the seat of his bike. He turned out to be a dark-haired young man of average height, good-looking enough, I imagine, for quite a few girls to find him attractive. It was obvious straight away that his aristocratic lineage went back more than just one generation.

"Why, it's Alexey Belsky!" The gasp of surprise came from Arina, who'd been standing next to me all this time. "I thought he was living as a hermit."

"I didn't know the patriarch of the Belsky family had such a grown-up son," I said in reply.

Indeed, the guy looked about twenty, and as far as I knew, Vasily Belsky, the current head of the Belsky family, had several adult daughters, but his two sons were still too young to be taking part in events like this. It was believed that Patriarch Belsky had had other sons, but that they'd died and so couldn't become heirs.

Meanwhile, the bookmaker was already bustling around the race winner, handing him a card of some sort that he put away safely in his jacket. The bookie then pointed at me, and Alexey headed over towards us.

"Alexey Mstislavsky," he said, introducing himself.

"But," Arina interrupted the hero of the evening, wanting to protest politely.

"No, it's Mstislavsky," he repeated, looking at Arina, strain and fatigue audible in his voice. She was taken aback and decided to leave it there. "They say you're the only one who bet on me?"

"Gregor Vetrov." I said with a nod. "Yes, I thought you had the best chance."

"Really?" Alexey looked at me in surprise. "Well, thanks for believing in me. I didn't until the end." He gave a somewhat crooked smile.

I could see the guy was getting rid of his nervous tension now it'd sunk in that he'd done what no one expected and won the race.

"Hah, that's the way to do it," I said. "Surprise your opponent, and he won't stand a chance."

"I'll remember that," Mstislavsky replied in a serious voice after a brief pause. "Now, if you'll excuse me, I still have to figure out how to collect my winnings."

"Of course. Congratulations on your victory."

I grinned, and why not? This guy, Belsky, had brought me a hundred and fifty thousand from out of the blue. I started to think maybe I should take up gambling.

"I assume this is finished, then?" I said, turning to Arina.

"Hey?" She was deep in thought and didn't hear me right away. "Oh, yeah, sure. We can go, now."

CHAPTER 4

THE MORNING STARTED with my spider-spirit reporting that I had visitors. Silently swearing, I looked at my watch and gave a muffled groan. It showed it was only ten in the morning, and given that I went to bed at three, that was early...

Hurriedly putting on my jeans and throwing on a shirt, I tried to smooth my hair down and went downstairs, as the unexpected guest, in no mood to leave, was pounding on the door, causing me no end of aggravation.

"Who is it now?!" I practically roared, wrenching the door open.

The visitor turned out to be Anna, who squealed with surprise and suddenly blushed. Following her gaze, I shot her a cheeky smile.

"Come in." I waved, inviting the Lazarev family servant inside.

At this point, I was more interested in eating

than finding out what it was she wanted from me. I had to at least do myself up, though, otherwise I'd just be embarrassing a girl who hadn't actually done me any harm for no reason. Her reaction did tickle me, though.

And where had Serby got to, incidentally?

While I was busy making a light breakfast, Anna went and sat down on the nearest chair. She clasped her hands together, then checked herself and unclasped them again.

"I've not had breakfast yet. Join me if you want," I said a little more abruptly than I could've done, putting some bacon and eggs and a mug of strong coffee down in front of her.

Contrary to my expectations, Anna didn't protest. She picked up the fork somewhat reluctantly, taking a cautious bite. From her look of surprise, she obviously liked it. After which, she set about her morning meal with greater gusto.

Well, so? I've been living on my own for a while, now, and I like to eat well. So, I had to learn to cook to my taste, and not buy takeaways all the time. You'll never save up any money doing that.

"So, then, tell me," I said, feeling much better disposed already.

"What, exactly?"

"Why you're knocking on my door again first thing in the morning?" I explained patiently. "I've already told you there's no need to accompany me around the estate, and Mr. Lazarev is well aware of my working hours. If he needed something, he'd have sent for me after lunch."

"I am charged with the responsibility of escorting you," she said stubbornly. "And I intend to fulfill it, whether you like it or not."

Such headstrong servants the Lazarevs have! Things would be so much easier for me without all this tiresome shadowing.

"Okay." I let out a sigh. "Just don't get in the way."

After all, I'd be here for just under a week, and there's no point making enemies for the sake of it.

"Maybe you need something for your work, then?" she asked, wanting to help.

"Yes, in actual fact, we have to wait another day," I said. "Oh, and warn people not to come to Mr. Lazarev's office for the time being."

"Okay." Anna said and then fell silent.

"Are you waiting for more instructions from me?" I asked when the silence had been going on for too long. Anna just nodded. She was somewhat reserved that day. Had she been reprimanded over that incident on the stairs, perhaps? "I want to take off into town and buy some clothes."

"I can help you find the right stores," Anna immediately piped up. "Just give me your preferences, tell me what you want to buy, and I'll draw up an itinerary."

"There's no need," I batted away her offer and eyed her closely, which made her start fidgeting, not knowing what to expect. "Only you'll have to change. A pantsuit is not the best for traveling in."

"Why not?" Anna looked at me in surprise.

"Are you going to get on a bike in that?" I

asked, with a raised eyebrow and a slight tilt of the head. And seeing the look of incomprehension on the girl's face, I explained. "I don't like other people's transport. I'm going on my bike. If you want, you can follow me by car, but I won't wait for you."

"Okay." Anna seemed resigned to the situation, but she didn't want to let me go that easily. "I need half an hour to get changed."

"I'll wait."

In fact, to get to the place that provided the local aristocrats with their amenities, you didn't even need to leave the surrounding area. There was already a small town there before the wealthy clans picked this place for their mansions. Now it had grown, thanks to its powerful residents.

Anna was surprisingly punctual, and ready by the time I was wheeling my bike out of the garage. She'd decked herself out in a light-colored chiffon blouse, tied just above the navel, revealing her belly. Instead of trousers, she'd put on blue jeans, which emphasized the feminine shapeliness of her legs. And her hair was tied back in a high ponytail.

An amazing transformation from office girl to young woman, intent on going shopping. Interesting. Should I take it she dressed like that for me, or was that her everyday look? Nothing is ever straightforward with them.

"More like it." I gave her an approving nod, once I'd finished looking the slightly abashed girl up and down.

Anna raised her head a little and tried to show that for her there was nothing unusual about this, but she still couldn't hide her blushing, her neat little ears turning treacherously red. You'd think I'd been looking at her for an hour.

"What do you need a sword for?" She pointed to the sheathed blade attached to the side of the bike.

"There's a special cord on the scabbard that prevents anyone from pulling the sword out," I explained. "So, don't worry."

"But it's a weapon!" Anna exclaimed. "We'll get stopped by the first police patrol carrying that."

"You don't need to worry," I said with a smirk. "I have a permit for it." I sat on the bike and started the engine. "Take a seat."

Without any further ado, Anna positioned herself behind me and grabbed me firmly around the waist, and we took off. Despite the abrupt takeoff, she didn't even squeal, which I found both surprising and pleasing. Maybe this wouldn't be so boring after all.

There were no problems leaving the estate, unless you disregarded the disapproving look from Sergey — the guard who'd had a word with me in the dining room. Well, he himself asked me not to push the girl away, and look, I'm not doing. He only has himself to blame for that.

"I'd like to change my wardrobe. Where is the best tailor around here?" I asked Anna. We were going slowly enough that we didn't need to raise our voices.

"What grade of establishment is required?" she asked.

"Hmm." I started to think, as I hadn't really given it any thought. "Whatever befits an aristocrat."

"Then you need Bogolyubskaya Street, and I'll show you the right place from there," Anna replied after a short time thinking.

"Just tell me when to turn. I don't know my way around here at all," I replied and opened the throttle.

You've no idea how I had to restrain myself from giving free rein to my metal horse, but scaring the girl behind me was the last thing I wanted. For now, anyway.

So, with Anna acting as navigator, we got to a small eighteenth-century-style cottage. It made for a bizarre sight, hard up against the backdrop of modern buildings and glitzy complexes.

"And why hasn't this house been demolished yet?" I asked quietly.

"This is a branch of the Lamanovs. No one would dare touch a building belonging to the tailors to the Imperial family," Anna replied with a barely concealed tone of superiority, jumping down onto the ground. "Its prices are slightly higher than other places, but it fully matches your request."

So, she's starting to bite back. We'll see about that.

"I hope it's not a disappointment," I said disparagingly, putting my bike on its stand.

Despite Anna's high opinion of the place, it didn't make much of an impression on me. What can I say? It didn't even have a fancy sign outside, just the inscription: "Atelier". No wonder I had serious doubts.

Leaving my bike by the entrance, I pushed open the door and went inside. The interior of the shop was in keeping with its exterior. I had the distinct feeling I'd gone a hundred or a hundred and fifty years back in time. The whole of the inside was made of old wood, which, I sensed, was old, but not aged. To my left there was a huge mirror mounted on the wall, which made the room look much larger than it was. To the right there were bales of fabrics and closed cabinets, adjacent to niches filled with all kinds of junk, of some use to the tailor, no doubt.

It was the walls that grabbed my attention more than anything else. As well as the elaborate walls, there was a visitors' area in the form of a three comfortable leather chairs around a small tea table, on which, at the time, were some pastries. In the middle, there was a large table, which, by the looks of it, was where the tailors did their work. In the far corner was the fitting area, concealed by a dark brown screen.

As soon as I thought I couldn't see the proprietors, out from behind the screen stepped a well-groomed woman of about fifty. She was wearing a long dark blue dress with wide sleeves, which almost completely covered her hands.

"Welcome to our atelier," she greeted us with a melodious voice. "Would you like to order a suit for your lady?" she addressed me, walking up to the table and putting down some sheets of paper.

"I'm not his lady!" Anna flared up, but then stopped short, adding in a more measured tone: "I'm escorting him."

"Very good," the woman bowed her head slightly. "What can I do for you, young man?"

"I'd like a suit I can wear at a dinner party and on my motorcycle."

"A most unusual choice," said the proprietor, bowing her head and looking somewhat puzzled. "Pray, come this way."

The woman pushed back the wooden screen. Behind it, I saw a small circular platform which she directed me to stand on.

"Please hold your arms out to the sides," she asked. "Very good. Now, don't move."

"What exactly...?"

"And no talking."

The shop owner pulled up her left sleeve to reveal a communication bracelet, and, activating it, brought a holographic screen up in front of her.

Maybe Anna wasn't so mistaken in her appraisal? And I was getting jealous already — almost everyone I met had one of those things. Also, from the confident way the woman was using it, it was clear she'd had the device for some time and was quite conversant with it.

Meanwhile, with another motion from the tailor, three small spheres appeared from the ceiling, which, judging by the tingling in my fingertips, had started scanning me.

I don't know about other people, but I can often feel it in my body when magic is directed at me like that. It's even saved my life a couple of times.

By the way, a magic scanning system, and in a tailor's, too. That really is something.

"Very good." The woman looked pleased with herself, and she finally let me lower my arms and come down from my "pedestal". "I have several options for you that wouldn't even need taking in."

"I can take a look," I said. After everything I'd seen, a somewhat crazy idea struck me, which I decided to voice anyway. "Do you make suits to order?"

"Of course, we're a tailor's," she said, a little irritated.

Before proceeding, I quietly created a small seal for Anna and sent the summoned creature over to her. She was looking at some fabric at the time. She shook her head as if something had flown past her face, and sat down in an armchair, feeling suddenly dizzy.

All well and good. I really don't need Christopher Lazarev finding out about such an unusual purchase.

"I'd like you to make me a suit that protects against magic, as well as being blade-and-bullet-proof," I whispered in a conspiratorial tone.

"Most interesting." The lady shot an inquiring look at Anna, and then me. "I don't get many coming to me with such orders."

"But, as I can see, you are more than capable of indulging me in such a whim?" I'd decided to employ a little flattery.

"Normally, for such unusual orders, I'm obliged to obtain client recommendations, but since you're accompanied by a servant of the Lazarevs..."

I'd never have thought Anna's presence could influence someone's opinion about me so much.

"I don't belong to the Lazarev family." I objected to the clear suggestion that I was associated with them. "I'm just doing some work for them."

"Why do you assume I'd accept such an order?" the woman asked, giving me a suspicious look.

"Surely it isn't beyond your talents?" I winked at her. "And if it's a question of money..."

"Twenty-four thousand. Imperial rubles, naturally," she replied immediately without answering the question.

"Then again." I scratched the back of my head, a little taken aback. I wasn't expecting it to be that much.

"Fabrics which are even only a little protective against magic have always been expensive. And you've also requested protection against physical weapons," she explained. "That also includes money set aside for my silence regarding the features of such a suit, should anyone develop an interest in it. As I said, I usually only carry out such unusual requests with recommendations. But you..." The woman's eyes darted towards Anna.

"I hope it will meet my requirements at least a little," I responded tetchily.

"That's easy to verify," the woman scoffed and

gave me a strange look in which I detected a hint of defiance. "I prefer to schedule special orders on the spot. Your spell, as I understand it, distracts attention?" she asked, pointing to Anna, who was looking in the opposite direction.

"Something like that." What she'd said had piqued my interest.

"In that case, let's go to another room." She beckoned to me to come over to the closet containing the fabrics. She pressed one of the decorative protrusions, which I had previously taken to be ordinary stucco molding. After that, something inside made an audible click, and the cabinet moved back and to the side. "I've loved stories about secret passages since I was a child," she explained. "So, at my request, we had this unusual way to the inner rooms made instead of a door."

"Hmm. And does everyone have such an honor conferred upon them?" I asked.

"Only those I find interesting." The lady then turned around abruptly. "You don't meet a summoner very often these days."

"Is that so?" I was on my guard, and I put my hands behind my back so she couldn't see what I was doing.

"Don't bother," she said, shaking her head. "I'm not about to tell anyone. I'm just curious about what you, young man, are capable of... No, not like that," she said with a dismissive gesture. "Rather, I'm curious to see what you'll do next."

"I'm not about to involve myself in anything," I countered, and I carried on creating a complex seal without looking.

"Summoners always get involved in unpleasantness. Whether they want to or not, such is the nature of your magic." The woman shrugged her shoulders and turned her back to me, leaving herself open to a blow from behind. I really had to restrain myself. "So, then, let's go through, otherwise we'll have been away for too long."

I pulled myself together, deciding not to act hastily, and followed her. That's not to say I was particularly surprised by her perceptiveness. Summoners weren't common among sorcerers, but they weren't so rare as to be considered fantastical. I was alarmed by her reticence, as if something had been left unsaid. It's difficult to convey, but I got the distinct impression this woman knew much more than she was saying. For some reason, she'd decided to let me know she'd worked out what I was, while maintaining an intriguing silence about the rest.

Okay, let's see what happens next.

"Welcome to my humble workshop." The woman waved her hand and the lamps in the room lit up.

You can't say it wasn't impressive, but it could easily have been down to motion sensors. If the atelier used magic instruments to take clients' measurements, then they were simply obliged to have such hi-tech.

Overall, the emergence of magic, or rather, its disclosure to the world, didn't have an adverse effect on technological progress. On the contrary, it fueled it. What can I say? Some families spent their time solely on new developments at the point where magic and technology met. The magicars came about from such a fusing of the two.

As soon as the lights came on, I saw a room that looked more like a tailor's premises than where we'd just been. There you also had several tables on which were laid out offcuts of cloth and sewing tools, and several quite large machines, that looked like they were designed for more detailed work. And, of course, a bunch of needles and threads that seemed to be on all the tables. Everything gave the impression of being a creative mess with, at the same time, instruments carefully arranged according to their purpose. In the middle of the room there was an area kept clear where there stood a mannequin.

"Could you help me and put that to one side?" the woman asked me.

I found no reason to refuse this small request and carried the silent dummy over to the wall.

"Now undress and stand in that circle," she instructed.

"Do I have to undress?" I frowned.

"If you want your suit, then, please, do as I ask," she said sternly.

Still not particularly happy about this, I undressed slowly, hoping this would annoy her, but she was busy with her preparations and seemed not to notice me at all. Eventually, left in just my shorts, I went and stood where she asked.

"What interesting scars," the woman said pensively while holding a roll of dark cloth against me.

And that's why I don't like getting undressed. Girls are usually impatient to hear the story behind these scars, most of which are bound up with unpleasant memories. Especially those around the area of the heart. The perfect pentagram carved there raised too many questions. With the help of a certain expert, I'd managed to disguise it as a tattoo, which immediately made my life easier.

"I can tell you about them if you drop the price by half," I said cheekily, not really expecting her to agree.

"Perhaps..." the woman said, putting her hand to her lips. "I'll decline all the same. It's not only women who are enhanced by mysteries."

She said it in such a strange way, but any thoughts forming on the matter were knocked out of my head by what she did next — needles rose into the air, a lot of needles, probably all the needles in the room.

"I wasn't somehow planning on becoming a hedgehog, and I don't go in for acupuncture, either," I said, making a summoning seal in my mind. I just hoped the tailor didn't notice and did something before I ran out of time.

"How stupid," she said with a faint smile. "Our family may not be able to boast any great lineage, but we do have some abilities. To the extent that my family became personal tailors to the emperor." She frowned slightly and gave me a severe look. "And stop doing your magic, it can interfere with my control, and you don't want me to stick needles in you, do you?" she asked slyly. "Believe me, there are much easier ways of killing you."

"You persuaded me." I grinned, and reluctantly stopped making my seal.

The atelier owner's arguments backed up with metal scissors by my neck were too compelling.

"You men always see conspiracies everywhere." The woman sighed heavily and shook her hands, as if she had an orchestra in front of her which she was about to conduct.

Needles slid obediently around me. Some of them picked up scraps of cloth and began to place them against my body while cutting the material to size and fixing it in place with short stitches.

I just stood there, afraid to move. Too often, needles, pins, scissors and knives flew before my eyes. Who knew if the hand of the tailor would shake and suddenly something vital of mine would be cut off.

A few minutes later, I was wearing the outline of my suit-to-be, but I really wasn't happy after such an exhausting process. The tailor snapped her fingers and, with the help of some needles, delivered me from my new outfit.

"There we are," she said with a satisfied nod of the head, and, being given the go-ahead, I changed back into my familiar, comfortable clothes. "I'll be able to run up your suit much quicker with these."

"Shouldn't you have asked about my preferences?" I asked nervously, doing up the last button on my shirt.

I made too sharp a movement, and the button

flew off, bringing a patronizing look from the tailor. She shook her head and waved her hand, picking the button up with the end of a needle. A moment later, and it was back in place.

"Believe me, you'll love it," she said with a smile.

When we returned to the main room, I saw Anna had fallen asleep in the armchair, and I quickly recalled the overly effective spirit. Apparently, she'd started to resist, and the usual fog was no longer helping, so it'd had to turn the girl into a sleeping beauty.

"Duty bound to escort me, and she fell asleep," I gently scolded Anna who woke up with a start when I touched her.

"Forgive me, I only closed my eyes for a second." She was ashamed and, jumping to her feet, she bowed to me. "It won't happen again."

"Not to worry."

I had thought about being a lot harsher towards her, then maybe she'd have finally left me alone, but Anna looked so sweet when she was asleep that I stopped myself.

"Your purchase will be ready in two days," the proprietor of the atelier said, digging out a tablet from somewhere. "Twenty-four thousand nine hundred and fifty rubles in total. Will you be paying by cash or card?" she asked.

"Card."

It was a good thing I'd arranged with a broker to have all my winnings transferred to my account the night before — otherwise I wouldn't have had enough funds to pay for something so expensive. Yes, with that kind of money you could splash out on a second-hand armored jeep or maybe even something a bit bigger.

"As I understand it, the parcel can be sent to the Lazarev estate?" the tailor asked me once the payment went through.

"Yes, I'll be staying with them this week," I confirmed.

"Thank you for using the services of our atelier," she said with a smile.

As soon as we left the shop, I was greeted by a scene, which wasn't to my liking at all. Two teenagers circling my motorbike, while a third was sitting on the ground, desperately blowing on his hand.

"Yes, the engine was probably just hot," one of them sounded sure, turning to the one sitting on the ground. "You didn't have to stick your hands in it."

"So, according to you, I'm dumb enough to stick my hands in the engine?" the guy said, jumping to his feet. "I grabbed hold of the handlebars, and they were like red-hot!"

"Come on, that's bullshit," the third teenager scoffed. "Look!" With these words, he boldly jumped onto my motorcycle and looked at his friends triumphantly. "Nothing happened."

"There's something I don't like about this," said the guy with the burnt hand. It seemed that once bitten, he was twice shy and was moving slowly away from it already. "Get off before something happens."

"Huh, don't be such a wuss," his friend said. "Just take some pictures with it. Everyone'll be jealous of us later."

"Can you smell frying?" the first guy asked unexpectedly, sniffing the air.

And as if they were just waiting for these words, the clothes of the teenager still bravely sitting on my chopper set on fire. He jumped off with a scream and began to roll around on the ground, trying to put the flames out.

"Casting security spells of such severity is forbidden," Anna said, frowning at me.

"No one asked them to touch my bike," I said, shrugging my shoulders. "If you'd taken a few snaps with it in the background, there wouldn't have been a problem," I said, pushing aside the one guy not harmed by my magic, who was in shock. I sat down on my chopper and started the engine. "Come on, let's go," I told Anna.

"But they need help," said Anna, a little distraught.

"Okay," I said. "You, call an ambulance for your friends," I said to one of the teenagers, who kept nodding. "Quit nodding and call them!" I said angrily, and the kid snapped out of it and pulled out his smartphone. "Happy now? Let's go, then. I was hoping to have time to drop by a couple more places today."

Making sure the guy had called an ambulance, Anna obediently took her place behind me. I expected her to start reproaching me, but she just let out a deep sigh.

Our subsequent purchases weren't as spectacular as the first one, so we arrived back at the Lazarev estate by dinnertime. This time I wasn't kept waiting at the gates for several hours — they opened as soon as I approached.

"Thanks for your help," I said to Anna, once my bike was back in the garage.

"I'm glad you didn't run away from me this time," she said defiantly.

"And this is by way of an apology for my rudeness." From my back pocket I took a small gold pendant on a chain and handed it to her before she had time to react.

"I can't accept this," she said in a shy, barely audible voice.

"It's a gift." I took the pendant from Anna's hands and, while she was still dumbstruck, deftly fastened it around her neck. "Yes, I knew it would look great on you."

"Thank you," Anna said quietly, putting her hand over the pendant, and she almost immediately started walking towards the main house.

That's it. Now, thanks to the small spirit confined in her pendant, she'll "forget" to come and find me, which means no one will be knocking on my door early tomorrow morning, and I can sleep in peace and get my work finished.

"You can smell the pheromones from this female directed towards you," a voice familiar to me rang out unexpectedly.

"Ah, the missing person has finally turned up."

I threw open my hands, looking at Serby. "And where have you been?"

"I don't suppress my needs, unlike some," the spitz scoffed, going into the house.

"Why, did you manage to make the rounds of all the local bitches?" I asked in a good-hearted way.

"And what's wrong with that?" came the disdainful response. "Physiologically, I'm almost the same as your dogs, so the process is complicated only by the fact that my partner can't speak. But I wouldn't necessarily say that's such a problem."

"Ugh, how about keeping those kinds of details to yourself? I'm more than capable of imagining what goes on without your elaborating."

"How much longer are we going to be here?"

"Have you not enjoyed courting the local 'ladies'?" I asked by way of a reply, and I collapsed onto the sofa opposite him. "Three days, no more. I'll finish the job tomorrow and we can get ready to go home."

"Where did you get three days from?"

"I ordered a couple of things that'll be arriving from the city. We just have to manage until then," I explained.

"Okay, it's just I'm kind of used to your bar, now," Serby replied grouchily.

"Out with it — you're missing Natasha," I chortled.

Serby said nothing, which only goes to show I was right.

The next day I woke up closer to lunchtime

and, judging by the spider's silence, this time no one had disturbed him, which meant Anna had safely "forgotten" about me. Which was good. The summoned spirit would exist just while I was here. At least I could sleep to my heart's content.

I stole into Christopher Lazarev's office no problem, like the last time. It was surprising, though, that with so many servants around, none of them asked me where I was going. In fact, there were no people in this wing of the house at all. Did they do the cleaning at night, or something?

Well, none of it mattered.

As soon as I entered the office of Patriarch Lazarev, I noticed a slightly heightened atmosphere in the room. I always felt it when I used my magic. Such an atmosphere only confirmed that the day before yesterday I'd done everything right and all that remained was to summon entities from other planes and bind them with the rules of a contract.

I'd arrived at such a system myself by trial and error, familiarizing myself with my grandfather's notes. He didn't use a single definition, calling these entities either spirits, demons, or something else. What marked them out was that they were only theoretical studies which he was unable to verify in practice. I had the "privilege" of finding out whether his theories worked — the hard way.

I remember that in my first poorly controlled emissions of power, I was terrified of anything I managed to summon into our world. I was lucky these were only short-lived flashes, and the summoned creatures lived only a couple of seconds before the energy that kept them here ran out. To eliminate such danger, I had to bury myself in my grandfather's surviving records and develop my own method of controlling the power available to me.

It was more complicated for me because my family had been destroyed, and the senior branch wanted to use their knowledge for their own interests. To some extent, I became a voluntary exile, and so I couldn't use their library or any of their connections.

But despite this, after several years of diligent research, I found out that although my abilities were different from the usual element-based ones of the empire's magicians, they still weren't truly unique.

As the owner of that tailor's shop said, people like me are called "summoners". We can't use the usual methods to develop our gift. Instead, we summon beings from other planes to serve us. As long as there's enough energy to make a tear in space and secure the summoned creature with the chains of a contract.

Generally, they try not to flaunt children who can do this, as the creatures they can summon are far from good and have the potential to cause a lot of trouble. These creatures are proof of life beyond our world and others.

Which is why they're studied in secret laboratories.

A couple of years ago, I found out about one such summoner, and even got to talk to him. He turned out to be an old man, no longer able to use his powers and therefore considered useless. He was just thrown out onto the street, and no one believed his tall tales. He'd earned the reputation, most likely not without some outside help, of being a heavy drinker who saw even more outlandish things when in a drunken haze.

It was he who pointed out the difference between my summonings and those he could perform. According to him, the following happens — summoners pull entities from other worlds and, using their magic, force them to stay in our plane of existence. Usually, without constant nourishment, such a period of time is finite, and a weak summoner can't use the creatures for long. The ones I summon, unless there are limitations imposed on them, can exist independently in our world, absorbing energy as if it were second nature to them.

This frightened the hell out of the old man, and he started to shout something about a dark summoner. His fear led him to believe that I was a threat to his life, and he rushed towards the freeway, where he was knocked down by a truck and killed.

Of course, it was a pity to lose a source of information, but if you think about it, he couldn't tell me anything new. But it was thanks to him I realized that those creatures only I can summon are rightly called demons, and at every summoning you must limit their free will and not let them escape.

As a result, Serby and Miyamoto were the only summoned entities of mine that weren't constrained by stringent parameters and had relative freedom, as far as that's possible.

Hmm, I got distracted for some reason.

I created an intricate seal in the air and placed the first of the spheres I'd prepared in the center of it. A wait of a few seconds — needed to find the right spirit — and there in front of me materialized a fairy very similar to the one I'd created on the lake a couple of nights ago.

"Contract for five years. Afterward, you'll forget everything, but you'll be able to keep the energy you save as a reward for your service," I said firmly, looking the demon in the eyes.

"I will obey," it said in the slightly hoarse voice of a woman and meekly bowed its head.

You wouldn't know it now, but it'd taken me almost a year to find the right combination of seals to ensure such obedience.

With a wave of my hand, the spirit disappeared along with its sphere, hiding among the things in the cabinet. The sphere is the only thing that keeps the summoned creature in our world, and it's well aware of this, which means it'll take good care of it.

After this, I took out the remaining spheres and summoned the remaining demons in turn.

"So, there we are," I said an hour later, giving my hands a shake. Although I'd prepared the energy containers in advance, I still had to use up quite a lot on calling up such "specialized" spirits in a short space of time. And, with that, it seemed, my work there was done. Perhaps I'd keep that to myself for now and, in the meantime, help myself to more of the Lazarevs' generous hospitality.

CHAPTER 5

"YOUR ABILITIES HAVE ALWAYS surprised me," Christopher Lazarev said as he inspected his updated office.

"I know a thing or two," I said with a modest shrug of the shoulders.

"By the way, about that," Lazarev said, sitting in his armchair and gesturing me to take the seat across from him. "As far as I remember from our conversations, you're self-taught, aren't you?"

"Yes." I wasn't going to deny the obvious. "You know that perfectly well yourself. I was deprived of the opportunity to undergo, shall we say, 'home tutoring'."

"Haven't you considered attending the Academy of Magic?" he asked.

"But who needs me there?" I looked at him with surprise. "I'm officially a commoner and don't have the right to study at such an institution."

"Well, about being a commoner, I'd dispute that" Lazarev said, chuckling. "But looking at it from that angle, there is for commoners the possibility of paid training or a grant."

"No way." I folded my arms. "I've no intention of paying for training, and as for sharing my practices... The state wouldn't be able to afford it."

"Is that so?" The patriarch raised an eyebrow. "Gregor, how much, for example, does the secret of creating protection for this room cost?"

"That, I'm afraid, would be beyond your means, Mr. Lazarev." I threw out my hands and smiled apologetically.

"Even in exchange for your favorite services?" His eyes narrowed slyly.

Downright serpent of temptation. Well, well.

"In that case, it wouldn't be only you who owed me a service, but your family, too. Anything else would be small fry," I scoffed.

"So be it. But I'll convince you to enroll in that college someday."

"You start up this conversation year after year. And my answer is around about the same every time," I said with a sigh. "I've no interest in studying with the children of aristocrats. I'm completely happy with my business, and nothing would give me greater pleasure than to spend time at the counter of my bar rather than behind a desk."

"You are capable of much more, but another time, maybe," Lazarev said with a faint smile. "The money you requested for your work has already been transferred to the account you specified.

And, of course, I know I owe you two services.”

“Four, if you count the others.” I gave him a friendly grin, well, as far as that was possible.

“Are you putting a collection together?” Lazarev’s irritation was too telling.

“Money tends to depreciate,” I shuddered involuntarily at the memory associated with that phrase. “A service, and one requested by an aristocrat, costs a lot more.”

“Let’s assume someone like me would fulfil all the terms of the deal,” Lazarev said after a brief pause. “But what would you do with those who don’t keep their word?”

“Nothing. But they’d definitely regret such an ill-considered act.”

“What happened to you to make you like this? Lazarev asked, sighing bitterly.

“Perhaps I’ll leave that question unanswered.” I tried to say it as gently as possible and began to get up from my chair. “My work is done, so if you’ll excuse me, I’ll be going home.”

“Very well.” Lazarev nodded. “But we’ll come back to this.”

“We always do.” I laughed, waving as I closed the office door behind me.

Our conversation took place in the evening after all my affairs had been wrapped up and my orders had arrived. My employer was the patriarch of a large family, after all, and couldn’t spare me his time at the first request. And to be honest, that was to my advantage.

Breathing in the cool air, I stretched happily

and moved off towards the guest quarters which had been my temporary shelter for these past few days. Serby had already been warned not to get held up anywhere and was waiting patiently for me on the porch.

"Finally finished gassing," was his grouchy greeting. "You humans can't get enough of your pointless conversations, can you?"

"You don't understand a thing about human society or the rules of decency," I said, sighing, laughing inwardly at his serious little face. It still looked funny then... oh, yes.

"If I even began to tell you what's been going on here, you wouldn't be able to sleep," the spitz snorted as he got up.

"I believe you. I believe you."

Serby threw me another glance and headed off to the garage, where the chopper and some of the bags were ready to go.

"I didn't put you down as someone who talks to animals, Greg." On the path leading to the guest house appeared Arina Lazareva.

Today, the aristocrat was sporting a dark medium-length dress, open at the shoulders. Her hair was loose and cascaded gently over her shoulders, drawing the eye to them.

"Hah, sometimes he seems to be being smarter than he looks." Fortunately, only I knew just how true that was. "I didn't realize we'd agreed to start addressing each other informally, Miss Arina," I said with a slight bow.

"Well, of course." She looked at me in surprise.

"We agreed to dispense with formalities. So, don't argue," she said abruptly in a menacing tone. I said nothing. The estate owner's niece didn't stand on ceremony and opened the door to the guest rooms. It was a good thing I'd already removed all the spirits, otherwise I would've had to explain why she couldn't get in. Having little other choice, I followed her. She went into the living room and sat down on the sofa. "As I understand it, you've finished your work and are going home?" Arina asked it in a tone that would make it clear to anyone what she was driving at.

"Yes, back to Petrograd," I replied, smiling faintly as I leant against the doorpost. "I've left my bar unattended for far too long."

"Do you like places like that?" she asked with little interest. She obviously didn't like my answer very much.

"Miss..." The look Arina gave made me raise my hands in placatory fashion. "Okay, okay. You didn't quite understand me. I own a bar in Petrograd. And I dare to hope I've managed to turn it into an interesting place. At least, Mr. Lazarev likes to be there when he comes to the city." I couldn't resist boasting a little.

"Is that so?" Arina was suddenly interested again. "I didn't know my uncle frequented such places."

"Each to their own." I'd said enough. "Have you come to say goodbye, or was there something else?"

"How else can we talk?" The girl smiled coquettishly, and rising from the sofa with a graceful movement, she came towards to me. "Maybe I want to uncover your secret," she said, stopping one step away from me.

Arina was shorter than me. The bottom-up look from her golden eyes combined with her low-cut summer dress... The girl had clearly decided to play the experienced seductress.

"Aren't you afraid those secrets could swallow you up?" I took a step forward, holding her gently by the chin so that our lips were literally a few millimeters apart, and she had to stand on tiptoe.

Although she started this game herself, Arina was practically trembling in my arms. From her eyes it was clear she realized how stupidly she had let herself fall into a trap. Although it only got her even more worked up.

"And what if they do?" she whispered defiantly.

"No," I said firmly, roughly releasing her from my embrace. "It might all be just a game for you, but for me this is real life. Find someone else to practice your moves on."

"Oh, you!" she shouted angrily.

It was understandable. The young aristocrat had probably got all kinds of ideas into her head, and there I was not following the script at all.

"I don't want to spoil my relationship with your uncle... or you," I added as she stared at me. "So, don't test my patience, otherwise I'll forget which family you belong to."

"I wouldn't do that!" Arina replied emphatically, but it seemed the intensity of her emotions had already begun to subside.

The storm had passed... perhaps.

"Okay, okay." I put my hands up and laughed. "Let's not fight."

To this, she just sneered and left the house, slamming the door.

"I hope she doesn't get it into her head to exact some kind of family vengeance?" I scratched the back of my head meditatively. "Okay. Christopher Lazarev is a smart man, he'll figure it out himself, and I should probably go before Arina thinks anything else up."

With these words, I picked up my last bag of things and headed for the bike. Serby was there already waiting. Well, I say waiting — the mini version of a dog was just shamelessly napping on the seat of the motorcycle. Without waking the grumpy demon, I secured him carefully with the straps.

I only had to touch the gas tank, and the bike started up, the engine growling quietly from time to time.

"Clever girl." I gently ran my hand along the side of my iron horse, which somehow realized that it wasn't worth making any noise now — there was plenty of time for that. "Right, let's go."

Moving off gently, I pointed the bike towards the gates, where I was stopped by the guard I knew.

"You're leaving us at this time of night?" Sergey inquired dutifully.

"Yeah, I decided not to overstay my welcome,"

I said, looking at the man's not-so-happy face.

"Have a safe journey." He gave me an unexpectedly kind smile and opened the gates for me.

That really was a surprise. Although maybe he was happy to get rid of me at last?

I wasn't about to test his patience and taxied onto the road home.

* * *

I decided to make my way back at a leisurely pace. However you slice it, traveling is traveling, and it's tiring. So, at the first opportunity, for the sake of variety and to at least relax a little, I turned off the main highway and headed for the city I now called home by a quieter route.

Soon, I was almost the only vehicle on the road, only coming across the occasional car, blinding me with its headlights. It must've been the first time ever it didn't truly bug me. No doubt all down to the calming effect of the night.

Some don't like the night, but that's precisely the time, when the sun hides behind the horizon, that I feel truly relaxed. I like how the streets gradually empty, and no one infringes on your enjoyment of a stroll through the quietening city. And if they do... well, they asked for it, and I can't be held responsible.

After a couple of hours, I started passing small towns, which only a few decades ago were simple villages. Before, habitations were built near large rivers, now they are built near highways. Also, to some extent, rivers of a sort. Time passes and everything changes. People's way of life, too.

Philosophizing again.

Riding past one such town, I felt an unpleasant, all-too-familiar shooting pain in my heart, and it was only by sheer willpower that I managed not to hit the brakes. Slowing down gradually, I stopped at the roadside and tried to work out what was wrong with me.

"Why've we stopped?" Serby asked in a sleepy voice a minute later.

"Can't you feel it?" I snapped, getting more and more annoyed that I still couldn't put my finger on what was causing it.

"Well, think about it, someone's dabbling in magic," the dog replied with a grunt, failing to understand my concern. "Not many people have the gift."

"Not many summon demons, either" I replied in a hushed tone.

"You mean..." Serby immediately drew himself up.

"Yes, some dimwit's decided to call up forces he doesn't understand."

"Well, maybe we should leave things be?" the spitz suggested, unsure of himself. "Whoever it is will get what's coming to him."

"Pacifist." I grinned.

"Idiot," Serby replied in a similar tone. "You're always looking for trouble."

I said nothing in reply to this and smoothly led the bike into a residential area, obeying my instincts.

Unfortunately, at the point when sorcerers stopped hiding from society, problems arose from the general availability of the Knowledge. Since then, not a year has gone by without there being some kind of incident involving the inept and, generally, unsuccessful use of magic.

It's commonly believed that only aristocrats can be magicians, and that is why they are a privileged class in every country, but in fact this is not quite the case. Naturals capable of operating with magical energy also occur among commoners. The clans immediately attempt to take them in as servants in order to increase their own power. And many simply don't know about their own abilities and never will. Of course, it's also impossible to discount the various illegitimate children the aristocrats managed to sire over that time. It's partly because of this that the relatively small magic community doesn't dwindle.

Except that, as the century of technology and the internet developed, manuals on how to awaken your power began to appear on the net. Most of them were complete nonsense, but many was the time when one of the aristocrats' children, out of stupidity and with the connivance of their bodyguards, spread genuine information, and that's when problems started for all of us. Worst still is when "especially gifted" idiots circulate something about ritual magic, now considered too backward to be worth studying.

Needless to say, most popular on the web was

summoning demons who can fulfil any of your desires, and no matter how hard they fought against it, something always slipped through the government's net. And there were also many who thought up rituals themselves, basing them only on gut feeling. The chances of an unlucky experimenter dying himself were high, but worse still was such a fool could bring much more terrible consequences than just his own death in his wake.

"It's here," I said, more for my own benefit than for Serby's, as I stopped near one of the town's typical three-story buildings.

"It's not too late to turn around," Serby reminded me.

"Huh, I wish I could, but the demon might sense you or me and come hunting for something tasty," I said.

"You have a high opinion of yourself," the dog muttered, trotting alongside me.

"So, you've no issue with becoming a tasty snack, then?" I retorted.

"But who will be food for whom?" Serby said, grinning ominously.

Well, he thought it was ominous. I mean, when a small dog grins, all the more so one of his breed, you're more likely to find it cute than frightening. I've seen him milking this misconception on more than one occasion.

"You first," I chuckled, and I nudged Serby gently with my foot.

He muttered something incomprehensible but set off all the same.

The building was small, with only three apartments to each flight of stairs, but we had to climb to the very top to get to where I could just about sense traces of magic being performed.

Through not the most pleasant trial and error, I'd already established that the magic of a summoning is felt only by me and others like me. Ordinary magicians can feel something only when the creature that appears as a result of the ritual begins to use its powers to the fullest. Although, among the entities there are those who can exert their influence while successfully concealing themselves, lost in the big city until they encounter a magician with greater powers.

I wasn't about to knock on the door — with a quiet click, I opened all the locks using a small seal. It wasn't the time for etiquette. In such situations, it's better not to warn anyone you're coming but to drop in unexpectedly.

Gently pushing the door, I sneaked inside and saw a very ordinary corridor that connected three rooms, a very small kitchen and what looked like a combined bath and shower room. Your typical small apartment. There were only three jackets on the hanger nailed to the wall, which indicated either that most people living here were out or that not many people actually lived there. It wasn't hugely important — I just really didn't want to be surprised by any random witnesses.

Sniffing the air again, Serby led me to the last room, which turned out to have very good sound-proofing, as I couldn't hear any noise at all until I

went close up to the door. I'd know that character-
istic smell of burning wax anywhere — that's how
much I hate it. They're completely useless, but
that doesn't stop people using candles in their rituals and that isn't likely to change any time soon.

Opening the door a little, I began to inspect
everything carefully. It looked as if there used to
be furniture in the room, but someone had decided
to remove it and draw a pentagram there — something which is by no means widespread on the internet, but much-touted by films of various kinds
— and a hexagram, which, at a glance, was also
geometrically precise.

Such accuracy was rare in someone contemplating a summoning ritual. Usually, they execute
them carelessly and hastily, don't fully understand
the process, and are completely unclear about
what exactly it is they want to achieve.

Okay. On the floor in the middle of the room
was a neatly drawn hexagram, at its points candles forming a circle. What I really didn't like was
that along the outside of it, and filling the inside of
it, were extra elements which I was only vaguely
familiar with. It all spoke — no, it didn't even
speak, it all screamed that a commoner I didn't
know had found some bona fide, not bogus,
knowledge from somewhere.

It wasn't impossible that lots of mistakes had
been made there, but the very fact that someone
had got their hands on the kind of knowledge that
should be kept behind seven seals in the private
library of a boyar clan... Just like me to turn off

the beaten track and end up in a real mess like this.

But where was the guarantee that I'd just have been able to ride past? The summoned demon could sense me because, as Serby had said himself, to them I have a unique odor. Or it could even sniff out Serby. And it wouldn't make any difference whether it was led by curiosity, hunger or aggression — it would attack me on the highway, and I'd have to defend myself on the fly, and that's not one of my strengths. It was better to meet the creature then, while it was still weak after its transition and hadn't had time to adapt to our world's energy.

By the looks of it, I came just in the nick of time — just as the ritual had started, but the summoned entity hadn't yet appeared.

The initiator of the summoning was a young guy of about eighteen. He wasn't exactly what you'd call "presentable". He was overweight and, while having acne doesn't do anyone any favors, frankly, he'd let himself go. But that wasn't the main thing. This kid was reading out quite confidently the words of a spell I didn't know, all while checking some printed sheets of paper in his hands. Some of these printouts were scattered around the room, and on them I saw a diagram of the summoning sigil, and on most of them were clearly shown the symbols to be used.

The strangest thing was that it didn't feel like he was having any kind of magical effect on the seal, yet the hexagram was reacting to his hand gestures — the symbols were shining, and the flames of the candles flared up. Everything became clearer when he stepped to one side, and I could see that in the center of the hexagram there lay an unconscious girl about the same age as him. There was no evidence of an argument or any violence, but she was lying completely naked, shackled for effect by chains he'd managed to get hold of from somewhere.

Christ, it would've been easier to tie the limbs with duct tape or zip-ties — just about anything was easier to find than chains. Hmm, slightly off-topic.

The potential victim of the ritual was damn attractive, and all this would've looked just like some kind of role-playing game, if it weren't for the seal draining the energy from her. I don't know how, but this guy had been able to find someone with the gift to use for his own purposes. Judging by the intensity with which the energy was leaving the girl, one can only wonder how such a strong magician as her hadn't come to the attention of one of the families or their servants.

I hoped he wasn't a total numbskull and hadn't kidnapped a member of a clan — the town would be laid waste to for the insult, and no one would've been able to figure out who was right and who was wrong.

Meanwhile, I was calmly observing the ritual, waiting for the right moment to intervene.

Charging in all guns blazing and interrupting the proceedings... well, there are better ways to die. That's what makes all these summonings dangerous — if you do something wrong, you get no end of trouble. And if the flow of intersecting energies goes to pieces, then there'll be such an explosion that not every Adept can handle, and a slight movement of the hand from one of those monsters would raze a town like this to the ground. An exaggeration, of course, but things wouldn't be looking too rosy, either way.

The guy finished reading the last lines and the air above over the girl became hazy. She cried out in pain, but didn't wake up. The demon that appeared instantly transformed itself into an elegantly dressed man, the only difference from a human being the small horns poking out from his hair and the all-too perfect appearance.

Then began the crude bargaining. The guy offered the demon the girl along with all her energy in exchange for his being attractive and irresistible to women. And, of course, that they'd do anything he wanted.

What else did I expect? If someone doesn't want revenge, power or money, then this is the kind of thing they come up with. Unfortunately, despite his accurately executed seal, the kid had proved himself to be feebleminded and, it seemed, was already imagining himself as some great Casanova.

But who in their right mind summons an incubus? A simpler entity could've coped with such a request, believe me. I understand, of course, that there isn't much readily available information on dark entities, but you have to know that incubi specialize in working with women, not men. There's the very real risk of a mishap, where the guy becomes attractive to members of his own sex — the demon would be very happy to take advantage of anything ambiguous about the wish. And the guy was clearly struggling with this — his speech was so garbled, you could've done anything you wanted and still been right.

Finally, the moment came when the demon completed its transition, and I calmly entered the room.

"Hi, everyone." I gave them all my best smile.

"Who are you?" The kid looked at me, astonished. He had no imagination at all.

But if he couldn't gather his thoughts and didn't get who I was and how I came to be there, then the incubus looked at me with a hint of curiosity and a smug smile.

"The spatial transition control service." I'd decided to play the fool a bit (nervous, I guess), hands behind my back. He won't remember me later, anyway.

"Summoner." How the demon managed to hiss as it pronounced this word, I'll never know, but it was what it was. "And... Guardian?" The incubus was bemused to see a miniature spitz by my side.

"Do they still call you that?" It was the first time I'd heard Serby addressed in such a way, but he ignored my question. Okay, once you start putting on an act, you have to keep it up. "You violated the ban on summoning dark entities," I said menacingly to the guy who was now really quite confused.

"What ban?" he stammered and then, suddenly getting all worked up: "I've never heard of it!"

"Do you know this phrase?" I said, and then narrowing my eyes, continued: "'Ignorance of the law is no defense'? This here, is exactly that. In relation to which, I order you to cancel the summoning, and we'll deal with you later."

"Kill him first, then grant my wish!" the guy flared up, pointing his finger at me in a way I found quite rude.

It was also slightly insulting that no one was paying any attention to Serby. And there I was hoping it would give me some extra time, but it was looking like I'd have to speed things up a bit.

"Not very polite," I said, shaking my head as I completed my final preparations.

If I hadn't needed the time to create the necessary seals, I wouldn't have had to indulge in such small talk. It was lucky the boy turned out to be so naive, and that the demon didn't sense anything until it was too late. But to create more than one seal, let alone keep them in an inactive state when I couldn't see them — that was something of a challenge.

I quickly raised my hands towards them both and, while an energy spirit flew at the guy and instantly knocked him out, three seals were dispatched to the demon. The first chained up the incubus so it had no chance of escape. The second cut off the energy coming from the girl. The third one finally closed the breach made for the transition, cutting off the dark creature's last chance of ever slipping away.

"Can we make a deal?" the demon asked desperately, after it'd tried to destroy my seals.

"Nope." I shook my head and threw a stone towards the incubus.

It was a specially cut red ruby engraved with the script of several interconnecting seals I'd designed myself. I'd had to trade in four whole services to get a dozen small stones like that, but it was worth it.

The demon was fully aware of the danger of this stone touching its skin. In a matter of seconds, the activated seals sucked all the energy out of the demon and locked it inside the ruby.

After that, the incubus lost its fine appearance and looked like an old man bent with old age. Not its actual form, but it still reflected the difference between what they are and how they like to show themselves to people. It can't be helped, but we often judge people by their appearance, and demons know this perfectly well, so they make themselves look as attractive as possible.

"And you, I see, are a real old-timer." I whistled and picked up the stone that had fallen to the floor and was now filled almost to the max with energy.

Somehow, I expected more resistance from such an experienced demon, or had this energy been acquired in a way that had nothing to do with summoning? Well, okay, it didn't really matter.

"I've been saving this energy for hundreds of

years!" the incubus shouted furiously, but then he hunched his shoulders and continued sullenly — "Are you going to taunt me now?"

"Why?" I raised an eyebrow in surprise. "Everything I wanted from you, I've got, so I'll just kill you."

"Thank you." The demon bowed unexpectedly.

"What was that?" I had to ask.

"Death is better than going back when you've lost everything," he replied with a sigh.

I thought it might be something like that. After Serby's stories about the existing order in their worlds, it's not surprising that upon the return of a previously quite strong demon, its own would've just killed it out of revenge and to elevate themselves, in their own eyes at least, at that more successful fellow demon's expense. If you look at it like that, then through death I was sparing it the fate of being a slave to those it considered weaker. You could argue that's what it deserved, but it's not for me to judge. The worldview of these creatures is different from that of humans, so trying to predict their reaction is a thankless task.

Not to drag things out, I created another small seal. It'd be enough to destroy the remnants of the energy keeping the demon from its eventual death. There wouldn't even be any pain... almost, well, maybe a little. I tended to cut out the noises coming from them, as I didn't really want to listen to an excess of foul language. It's very difficult to carry out the final destruction of a dark entity in a painless way — they cling to their life instinctively, even if, like this incubus, they've agreed to die and are prepared for it.

"Well, all that turned out easier than I thought," I said as I watched the flashing sparks disappear into the air — the only indication that there'd been a demon there recently.

But what next? I don't know how to knock a guy out, erase his memory or put restrictions on his activities in any way. And I've never heard of anyone managing that, either — it's far too fantastical. Which meant there was a chance the guy would want to do the summoning again, and the consequences of the next attempt could be a lot more serious. And there was the girl who was almost sacrificed... she was alive. Her magic may have been depleted, but she survived. What to do with her was also unclear.

Not my favorite MO, but I had to get rid of the kid so as not to put others at risk. Also, he'd seen me, which meant that, given half a chance, he might want revenge. The only thing I needed in my life to be completely happy was a commoner-avenger on my case. There was a stabbing pain in my heart, but I put all feelings to one side and began to draw a seal in the air.

There are other types of dark entity I can summon, but they demand more than just energy in return. They're much more bloodthirsty, but more effective in some cases than the ones I tend to use. Unfortunately, like that day's failed ritual, it requires a sacrifice.

In a way, it was karma. The guy wanted to use

the girl to summon a demon, and now he'd be playing the role of victim himself. Technically speaking, a summoning wasn't required, but, put it this way, it wouldn't have hurt to give something a good feeding — it'd make my work a bit easier in the future.

Finally, the last symbol was added, and the seal turned itself parallel to the floor above the body of the still unknown kid. Maybe it was for the best. The design began to glow green in the air and, for a fraction of a second, sank into the floor, leaving not a trace of the unsuccessful summoner's body. Everything was clean, not overly dramatic, but what they'd do with him in another dimension... That was another matter.

Now, I could finally turn my attention to the failed sacrifice. Despite her condition and the amount of strength extracted from her, the girl was still very attractive. I could only wonder how such a nondescript guy managed to get her back to his apartment, let alone involve her in a ritual.

After a brief inspection of the apartment, I found her clothes thrown haphazardly into a bag in another room, apparently ready to be disposed of as evidence. I also found a blanket, which I wrapped the girl in. I wasn't about to start fiddling around trying to get her dressed — that would've taken too long. She should be grateful to be alive and, well, not freezing to death, either. I could only imagine how many questions would be going around her head when she woke up and started trying to figure out what happened.

"You can destroy the seal," I told Serby.

I could've done it myself, but there was still some energy left in it that would've just dissipated into thin air. The dog, though, could absorb it for his own benefit, but for that he required my explicit permission. If he'd been so brazen as to try without it, a lot of it would've been wasted. It wasn't for nothing that I'd spent time studying ways to restrict those I summoned and to impose conditions on them.

"Now no one will know that anything happened here unless they go in there." Serby looked into the room where I'd decided to leave the girl. "What are you going to do with her?" He went up to the brunette and started sniffing her.

"Hmm, I think I can find a way to erase the diagram," I said. "As a last resort, I could just burn the floor. And her..." I looked thoughtfully at the serenely sleeping girl, who already had the color returning to her cheeks. "When I pulled her out of the seal, she was very pale. Maybe I'll leave her clothes here, too. She'll wake up and disappear by herself."

"Fine, only I thought you'd take her with you," Serby said.

"The last thing I need is to be messing around with her! She's not a trophy to take home with me," I protested. "Let's get out of here before anyone comes."

In the kitchen, to my disappointment, there wasn't anything but instant noodles and a wide selection of cookies. It wasn't surprising he was in the condition he was in. Not with eating food like that.

I summoned a fire spirit strong enough to burn the floor but not set fire to it. Otherwise, it would've all looked very strange in there, and I could do without attracting any more attention.

Half an hour later, everything was done, and I calmly continued on my way to Petrograd. Back home. At last.

CHAPTER 6

THIS TIME I MADE IT to Petrograd smoothly, without running into any trouble. Except that, in one of the towns, someone took it into their head to try to steal my bike, and now the unlucky thief is lying in their local hospital with serious burns. But he only had himself to blame. Even the police had no complaints.

I arrived in the afternoon, and my favorite place greeted me with just two random customers and Misha behind the bar.

"Gregor, hi," he said with a cheerful wave. He was studying the bottles and making some notes on a tablet.

"Anything interesting while I was away?" I asked, sitting on a stool and leaning against the bar.

"Some of your special clients came in," he said, emphasizing the word "special" and he pushed a list of their names towards me. "Also, a couple of local bands who want to perform here in the evenings got in touch." Misha pulled a small bundle of papers out from under the counter. "Here's what they play and where to hear it. I think these two are worth a listen." He found the corresponding papers and put them on top.

"Thanks," I said, picking them up. "Is that something new you're concocting?" I pointed to the tablet.

"Yep. I've come up with a couple of new cocktails. I'm just working out the proportions."

"Buy everything you need for the first batch, and this week we'll arrange a free tasting," and I smile at the guy, who, despite his outward indifference, was still waiting for my answer. It was something Misha wanted to get into, but, for some reason, he was afraid I'd say no. "I'll be in my office if you need me."

Opening the door to my office, I waved the guard-spirit away and, putting my sword on its stand on the wall, I collapsed contentedly into my armchair. It was only after being away that I realized how much I missed those four walls. When I'd found myself alone, the bar became my new home, and I loved it with all my heart. And, as a nice bonus — I'm much more powerful here than anywhere else, but I'd rather no one else knew about that.

Although I'd tried to settle all my affairs before I left, there were still some matters that couldn't be dealt with without me, as clearly indicated by the pile of papers lying on the desk. Within two hours, I'd finished the paperwork and was listening to songs from the bands wanting to perform here in the evenings. And, as Misha said, the first two really were worth listening to. I've always liked rock music, and those groups, well, rocked.

I hadn't originally planned on setting up a venue for live performances — quiet conversations at the bar and arranging rooms for meetings was more what I had in mind, but it was Misha who convinced me it wouldn't harm business and would, in fact, bring even more people through the door. So, we started inviting young, still little-known groups, so they could get some exposure and hopefully a generous tip from the customers (quite realistic given the prices for drinks).

It got to the stage where, after performing in my bar, three bands went on to the capital to conquer pastures new. All it took was to catch the eye of my "special" clients, who, it turned out, were no strangers to music themselves. Then a few hints and "random" phrases, and, hey presto, there was a buzz about them, and things, hopefully, went as well as possible for them. In any case, all kinds of exotic drinks and first-edition albums arrived at the bar from time to time. Nice when bands remember who helped them get to where they are.

This started the rumor about my place being a steppingstone to success, and then we no longer had to look for bands to perform: they laid siege to us themselves, begging us to give them a chance.

"You've been neglecting your training." Suddenly, the ghost of a Japanese in a kimono came out of the sword.

"Look who's talking," I said, pushing my papers aside. I'd have to give them to Misha so he could send them to the appropriate addresses. Perhaps I'd give him a raise as he really was already doing more than a simple bartender should. "Usually, you just look at me reproachfully."

"Student, show some respect." He frowned, becoming more material with each second.

"You forget. about the essence of our agreement," I raised the index finger of my right hand. "I give you the opportunity to carry on existing and developing your path of the sword or whatever you call it, and you teach it to me and protect me from danger. I don't recall anything about how intense training should be. I repent." I sighed and lowered my hand. "Back then, I dreamt about Japan and your art of sword fighting, but I have too much I can't leave unattended."

"I understand. Yours is a difficult path," Miyamoto said after a short pause. "But I can't calmly... exist, knowing that my school is not evolving."

"And what do you want me to do?" I raised my left eyebrow, trying not to appear too interested.

For a start, the swordsman's spirit was never particularly talkative and had accepted its current situation with a certain fatalism. It was more important for him to continue to develop his school, which, according to him, had changed a lot after his death. Miyamoto wished more than anything in the world that his teachings would progress rather than fading into oblivion. Maybe that's why the spirit of this strong-willed man had survived to this day.

"I want to set up a school where I can pass on my teachings," he wasted no time in saying.

"Do you understand the difficulties involved in that?" I wasn't saying no straight away.

"I can wait," the Japanese said with a shrug. "Gregor, in my time, people like you became either rulers or corpses. Setting up a school of some kind would not be a problem for you."

"Hah! I don't know whether to rejoice at such an assessment or not. Miyamoto, of course, I'm prepared to consider your proposal, but for now, honestly, I've got other fish to fry, and whether that will change in the next ten years... I can't promise anything." I threw my up hands.

"I'm already dead, what's ten years to me," he replied, then disappeared back into the sword.

By having the last word, the inspirited sword didn't give me the chance to change its mind. Honestly, it would've been better if it stayed quiet, and only reminded me about training now and then.

I mean, he understood I was curious as hell to see what would come of a martial arts school, where the instructor happened to be a ghost. Thanks to me, he'd already accumulated quite a lot of energy, which could've made him material and practically indistinguishable from a living person for quite some time, but, ultimately, a corpse is still a corpse.

Yes, it was definitely worth asking around Petrograd to see how many would be interested in see-ing such a school. Maybe it wouldn't turn out to be such a flop after all.

Looking again at the sheets of paper with the names of the bands on, I rang their lead singers' numbers and offered them a short one- or two-hour evening slot at my place. Both almost echoed each other with their words of thanks and prom-ised to make it an experience to remember for the customers. Well, we'd see.

I loved running my bar, but at first, when it was still a dream, I'd no idea it'd involve so much paperwork and keeping an eye on every little de-tail. Then, I somehow got sucked in, and what used to be a cause of panic seemed only to be a slight inconvenience. All those purchases, promo-tions, rental bills, and a whole lot more. All this hit my wallet hard at the start, but as soon as the meeting booths appeared, and I was able to prove how convenient they were to the aristos, word of mouth did the rest. The money started to flow in, not like a river, but it flowed all the same. Six months later, I was already making a steady profit and was able to expand the range of services on offer.

And, of course, there were the "services" in re-turn. The nobles initially perceived this as an ec-centricity of mine and were quite happy about such an exchange as it didn't require handing over any money. Everything changed as soon as I began to exercise my right to their "services" and showed several minor aristocrats what happened when they ignored my requests.

No, nothing terrible happened to them. Little accidents. One person would stumble and roll down a long staircase, another would have a flowerpot fall on his head. Small things you wouldn't pay too much attention to, but if they kept happening every day, even the most stubborn person would start to wonder what was behind them.

And I... I was just waiting for them at the bar, where we'd go back over the terms of our agreement. Also, I couldn't be accused of anything, since no one could see the summoned spirits playing tricks on those who'd broken their word.

So, all by themselves, began the rumors about me being someone who brought good luck in business, but likewise bad luck if the obligations towards him were disregarded. Since then, about half of the city's aristocrats were in my debt (not including those I dealt with outside Petrograd), and I was in no hurry to use up those "services" if there wasn't the need to. Gradually, others stopped looking on this condition as a "whimsy", but from time to time you still got someone who was particularly shameless.

That's how we have fun.

Aha, it was nine o'clock. Time to go down. It was after sunset that my main clients arrived. And no, these weren't some mythical vampires invented by fantasy writers, but simple workers, if that's what you can call people who aren't quite on friendly terms with the law. And what could I do if agreements where there could be no chance of any deception tended to attract members of the criminal fraternity? Incidentally, this meant no one touched my bar, although any place like mine is under "protection", one way or another. My place was hands-off where criminals were concerned and, so far, they'd stuck to that rule.

I greeted the regulars and went straight to the bar, where I helped Misha, who was snowed under with customers. I can't say I know much about mixing drinks but putting together something basic, like whiskey and cola, is something I can do. But that guy was a wizard and could put on a real show when he felt like it.

"Good evening, landlord." A hoarse voice attracted my attention.

It belonged to a somber-looking man in jeans and a leather jacket. My trained eye immediately took in the faded tattoos and demeanor, which clearly indicated his line of activity, in general terms at least.

"Room three's now available," I replied, mixing another cocktail. I put the glass down in front of a grateful-looking girl, and handed him the key. "Remember, there are rules here. Please don't break them."

"I've been told." He shrugged his shoulders and snatched the key from my hand.

"Don't forget, you've got to pay for the time when you're finished," I said after him, which made him stop for a second, but he then carried on walking.

I was in no way worried that the stranger

wouldn't pay. At the very beginning, when the meeting rooms first started, I was told who to contact if anyone gave me any problems. And there was no doubt they'd straighten things out very quickly.

"I don't like those types," Misha suddenly said, watching the man who, despite his direct manner, seemed reluctant to push his way through what was by that time a fairly sizeable crowd.

"I should hope not, they're not chicks," I retorted. "If they're prepared to pay for the bar's services and abide by the rules, then I see no reason to refuse them," I said, pouring a pint of beer for the next customer. I didn't like the drink very much, but a lot of people just can't live without it.

"Business is business, hey?"

"Exactly. Keep your mind on the job, there's a queue already," I said in a serious tone.

It was still quite quiet in that part of the bar, with gentle music in the background. But you only had to turn right and go down the corridor, and you found yourself on a dance floor and could do something else to let off steam other than drinking. Not a full-on disco, but the music there was a bit more upbeat.

Too much, maybe, but the customers liked it, and it was too late to talk about the inappropriateness of certain decisions when I'd already combined a bar with a negotiation zone.

Half of the rooms were still empty, but there was still a lot of time until morning and, I dared hope, the cash till would see at least an extra thousand imperial rubles by the end of the night.

Half an hour later, a call-light for the room where the recent somber-looking man had gone was activated under the bar. But the yellow color didn't mean my presence was requested — it meant that something was up.

"And I was looking forward to a quiet evening," I sighed and, putting back a bottle of rum, I headed for the problem room. "Why's everything falling apart?"

Before I could get to the room, I had to say a few words to some aristocrats I knew who could've taken it badly if I'd ignored them. There's no need to create problems where there aren't any.

"What's going on here?" I asked as soon as I crossed the threshold, and I quickly closed the door behind me before anyone could see inside.

There was the man I'd already seen, sitting in a leather armchair, and everything would've been fine had he not been lacking something as incredibly vital as his heart. A small detail, but one which put a different complexion on things.

"Looks like we'll have to close early," I said to myself, and I started dialing the number of someone who could help me out in such a situation.

*   *   *

"Mr. Vetrov, good to see you looking so well, albeit under such circumstances," said the man I'd recently called, and he tipped his maroon bowler hat in my direction.

He was no older than thirty and stood out due to the hat, which had earned him his unusual nickname. As for his clothes, he was dressed in a three-piece suit, and all in all, looked like an English dandy. If you ask me, he only needed a cane to complete the look.

The bar was already empty by then. I'd let all the staff go so they wouldn't get in the way. My mood had gone to hell and the last thing I needed was to lash out at someone.

"Don't," I said, gloomily. "What's your name anyway? I can't bring myself to call you 'Hatter' like everyone in your world."

"Address me as Ivan, Ivan Ivanovich if you prefer it in full." He gave a short bow and smiled.

Aha! I detected a slight accent. American, I reckon and, back home, he'd call himself something like Mr. Smith. God, what's with all the clichés? Anyway, best not get too involved with them.

"Don't tell me — the surname's Ivanov?" I couldn't help myself.

"How did you guess?" The Hatter's face was a picture of surprise, but almost immediately took on a more serious aspect. "Well, now we've finished with the introductions, perhaps you can tell me what exactly happened here, since this is the first time you've called me in many years?"

"Unfortunately, I had no choice," I replied. "I feel that dealing with what's happened without you is kind of... wrong. Yeah, maybe that's it."

"Right." Ivan scratched his chin. "I'm intrigued."

"This way, please," I said and came out from behind the bar to escort the person who'd been introduced to me way back as 'The Fixer', whatever that was supposed to mean.

"Very interesting," he mused, seeing the room where the dead man was sitting. "If I understand correctly..." He pointed to the wound.

"Yep, someone ripped his heart out. My rooms allow you to make an honest agreement, no deception, but protecting customers from each other..." I threw open my hands. "Never had anything this reckless. It'd be much easier if it was suicide, or a bullet or knife wound, for example."

"It's a very good thing you decided to call me. This is Yuri Rybov. He's the head of the squad... I mean, he *was* the head of the squad, the punishment squad for a very respected person. So, if you'd tried to get rid of the corpse yourself, they'd have come looking for you in no time."

"Looks like I'm in trouble now," I muttered.

"No," Ivanov replied. "Now I'll get on with straightening out this unpleasant incident. It's your frankness in this matter that speaks in favor of your non-participation in the murder."

"I'm a suspect?"

"I'm afraid so," he said without an ounce of sympathy. "Mr. Vetrov, I'm obliged to consider all possibilities, but you are trusted by people who people listen to. So, I don't think there'll be any problems."

"Maybe you know what he wanted to use the room for?" I asked.

"Rybov wasn't a fan of talk. In fact, as far as I know, he hated it. Action was much more his thing. Thanks to his talents and determination, he quickly made it to head of a pack of scumbags prepared to do anything the boss ordered," Ivan replied. "It's surprising he decided to use your services at all. This guy was more likely to eliminate the obstacle than negotiate with it. You have CCTV?"

"Yes. It only covers the entrance to the bar. There isn't any inside, and definitely not in the meeting rooms."

"Hah, I see. Discretion."

"I wouldn't have made it to this age, otherwise." I grinned. "Most people don't like noses being stuck into their business. So, what are you going to do with the body and the killer?"

"I've already contacted some people. Ivanov showed me the screen on his smartphone, where he'd been typing a message. "They'll take Rybov on the quiet and see to it that no unpleasant rumors about your bar slip out regarding this. You can safely forget about it, like nothing ever happened."

"And what didn't happen — does it happen a lot?" I asked nervously.

Well, what else was I to do? Despite my somewhat bold behavior towards this man, I still didn't want any conflict with Petrograd's shady underworld. Of course, it's hard to get to me at home, but you can't insure against everything, and it's not as if I never left the house.

"Why, is something happening?" Ivan asked

with a smile.

With that, our conversation came to an end. Half an hour later, a team of workers did come. They smartly bundled the body into a bag and silently disappeared, once they'd cleaned Rybov's blood off the chair. Quite a service, damn them all to hell.

Although I don't like outsiders in my bar, I couldn't not call "The Hatter" due to my old agreements with his bosses, and there was no good reason to attract the unwanted attention of various other people. I doubt the head of a punishment squad could just disappear without a trace, which means they'd get round to me sooner or later, and then there'd be a lot more questions to answer, and the conversation would be a very different one.

However, no one said that I had to be completely open with him. I did leave some details out, "by accident".

In the negotiation rooms there are several entities that guarantee no lies will be told during the conclusion of a contract, and they make it known in one way or another if this happens. Finding the right spirits capable of catching someone lying wasn't easy, but it was worth it. It was down to these efforts that the bar started to bring in its main source of income. But as well as these entities, there were also spirits capable of some very specific things.

One of these spirits could capture demonic energy, and that's exactly what it told me when I walked into the room. The poor spirit was very frightened, but still had to tell me about it because that was its function. True, it was one of the weaker ones and could only give me a vague picture of what happened.

Why do I always seem to attract trouble? First, I encounter someone performing a ritual to summon a demon, then this. So close to home, as well. What I did know for sure was I really wouldn't want to meet Rybov's killer, whoever they were.

"They've gone, finally." Snorting dramatically, into the room where it all happened came Serby.

"Huh, and you always manage to go AWOL." I turned my mind away from oppressive thoughts.

"I was asleep," came the dog's simple response. "What happened here?" He looked at me with idle interest.

"You tell me," I said, encouraging him.

Despite the spitz's outward appearance, I knew this demonic dog was curious as hell and couldn't just let such an event go. The most surprising thing was he hadn't shown up here before now.

"I smell blood and something like a demon, but not quite," Serby suggested a few seconds later.

"I think there was a demon that somehow managed to stay in our world," I added.

"I doubt there are many more madmen in your world who'd want to have a demon here for the long term."

"So, what's your opinion of me, then?" I folded my arms melodramatically.

"There's nothing offensive in that," Serby replied. "Usually, you humans see those like me as just a means to an end and, as a rule, no one considers long-term contracts. It was from you I found out it was even possible."

"Hmm. Amazing what you can learn about yourself from a simple conversation."

"Basically, it could be someone possessed — the smell of the killer is quite particular," Serby offered another explanation.

"How can that be?" I looked at him with surprise. "I've never heard of that."

"How?" The spitz shot me a quizzical look. "The subject often comes up in your films."

"Don't compare apples with oranges," I said dismissively. "Not everything people think up actually exists."

"But they were right about possession. There's a rare species of demons that, instead of creating a body for themselves in this world, prefers to use a human one as a vessel. That's not to say they are weak or strong as a result, they just are."

"And what's dangerous about someone who's possessed?" I asked.

There aren't many occasions when Serby has anything truly worthwhile to say, but, clearly, what had gone on here had really captured his interest.

"He's indistinguishable from an ordinary person and in rare cases may not even be aware of his condition, leading a normal life, but the demon controlling him can take him over at any time and do things which they then have to pay the price for," Serby replied in surprising detail.

"Do you think it managed to get in here without arousing anyone's suspicions? And so near someone who's supposed to have a developed nose for danger?"

"Anything's possible."

"And why do I attract all kinds of evil spirits?"

"That, I hope, is a rhetorical question?"

"So." I suddenly became suspicious. "It looks like there's something else you've not told me."

"Alright." Serby released a protracted sigh and shook his head in a comical way. "You're someone who took the risk of getting in contact with the energy of other dimensions and managed not only to survive, but in fact be successful at it. And despite all this, you didn't notice that in your bar you'd created the perfect dwelling-place for demons and other dark entities. It's also good that you figured out how to shield your... rods from the parasitic sucking of all sorts of strays, otherwise you wouldn't have been able to move for them."

"There it is, that feeling when you're raised up only to be knocked down again," I said.

"So what, it does you good sometimes. The less full of yourself you are, the longer you'll live."

"This from a creature with a vested interest in my not dying for as long as possible."

"You wrote the contract," said Serby turning his back on me.

"Like I could've done it any other way," I muttered in response. "What will we do with this possessed one, then?"

"Well, nothing. Either he won't show up at all, or he'll become a regular visitor. Either way, such creatures can breathe more freely here."

"And the city woke up to yet another serial killer."

"Then you can seal the demon up in a person or figure out how to get rid of it," Serby suggested.

"Okay, we'll think about this later. Enough revelations for one day," I said with a shake of the head, then closed the door to the room.

*   *   *

I spent the next three days reexamining the system of seals on the anchor rods so only those entities I'd given the right to would have access to them. It was bad enough having freeloaders pushing to get into my bar, let alone homicidal customers.

To my disappointment, it turned out Serby was right. No matter how hard I'd tried initially to take make sure the rods worked properly, they still leaked some energy, causing a slight increase in the background magic near them. I didn't think it critical at the time, so I just left it as it was, but if you believe what the demon said, for entities like that, my bar really was the equivalent of a breath of fresh air in a polluted city. I could only wonder how no one had wandered in before then... or maybe they had but, if so, they disguised themselves very well.

And why had I only found out now that entities, which in theory aren't supposed to stay in our world for long, were able to stroll around here? Something was always pulling them back, and only a contract could limit how strong that attraction was. After all, they were alien, and the world was always fighting them in some way.

Why was all this happening? The worst thing was — I hadn't felt the presence of anyone possessed, so there was no way of blocking them from coming into the bar, which meant the killings could continue, and that definitely wouldn't be good for business.

And, worst of all, I hadn't visited any of the capital's auction houses, where I might've found something like Miyamoto's sword. I'd already proved I could see what others couldn't among old bric-a-brac and find a use for it. From there, my less than joyful mood slid to rock bottom. No, this attitude wasn't going to get me anywhere.

Putting everything aside, I just headed to the embankment to get some sea air and clear my head. That usually helped.

As I walked by the water, I started looking at those who'd also come out here on this sunny day. Of course, I was looking more at the girls out running, but who could blame me?

I wondered how all this would've looked to people two hundred years ago, before the world knew magic existed?

I watched one of the joggers jump off the pavement onto the water and run across it as if it were a solid surface, only swaying on the waves occasionally. An easy trick no one looks twice at these days that any water mage could do, even a Novice.

Or, for example, a mock battle between two air mages buffeting each other with air currents so their opponent couldn't get close to them. It looked as if someone had taken them by the scruff of the neck and was tossing them around without mercy. It might sound like I'm exaggerating, but that's exactly how it looked. It'd attracted quite a few spectators, and the gamblers among them were betting on which of the magicians would be the first to start flagging as, apparently, both "air warriors" were of the same rank.

And these were just a couple of examples. People didn't pay attention to most of them as the sorcerers capable of doing anything truly spectacular were aristocrats — for anyone else it just added a little something to their humdrum lives. Of course, it was easier for any magician to get a job in a field where his gift would be of some help, but that was no substitute for a more intelligent and able person. And no one had sunk to those depths yet.

As I was looking at another girl who was on some of the outdoor exercise equipment, I didn't see a guy walking towards me, and we collided.

He quickly said "sorry" and hurried off.

I just shook my head and carried on walking. But I couldn't shake the idea that it was absurd, us bumping into each other when there were no other people within a couple of meters. When I patted my jacket pockets, my wallet was missing. Christ, that corny old hustle!

Making sure no one could see what I was doing, I created a small seal — and the missing item was back in my hand. A painful cry rang out in the distance. Don't steal other people's things, then! I'd been fitting small locator-seals on stuff I didn't want to lose for a while now, and using them to bring it back with a little help from some spirits.

Strangely enough, this incident lifted my spirits and, whistling the catchy tune that was stuck in my head, I carried on walking, admiring the girls in their sports outfits on the way. I must say, I do like it here in summer.

* * *

I wasn't going to attempt to deal with the possessed person, I mean, it wasn't my concern. Instead, I refined the anchor rod system so now nothing could get my outgoing energy for nothing. Anything that tried had a nasty surprise waiting — a vicious attack that would suck the energy back out of the intruder and make the anchors start operating in reverse.

So, I found out that several spoiled dark entities had become completely shameless, ignoring the rules and using my feeder for free. There wasn't much I could do about it — their greed led to a rollback of energy which just disembodied the demons, so I had to summon others to replace them. Fortunately, they weren't particularly strong, so it wasn't difficult to find fellow creatures of theirs who were willing to actually work for their energy.

Meanwhile, snowed under with paperwork, I finally came up with the idea of finding a manager. I didn't set up my own bar to spend all day pushing paper. Others could do that. I had thought about making Misha the manager, but he'd have been out of his depth, so I had to look at more suitable candidates.

There was a problem there, though. A lot of the time those with the right qualifications were servants of one noble family or other, and that wasn't what I needed. Of course, the aristocrats didn't take just anyone under their wing, but any commoner would be happy not just with the good salary, but also the status it brought, placing them much higher than the others. As for any experts belonging to one of the clans who might be available, there was no danger of them being loyal. The servant to a family was loyal to that family alone, which meant if they found out something they shouldn't, they might report it to that family's security service. I didn't want to attract too much attention to myself, although I knew that an establishment offering such exclusive services as mine hadn't escaped people's notice.

In the end, after weeding out more than thirty candidates, I found the resume of a girl who, for some reason, hadn't become a servant to any family yet, but who had more than one diploma and several business awards. As well as which, she was asking for quite a low salary compared with other far less remarkable candidates.

"Seems like she'll fit in well," I said with a

smile.

I either attracted such people, or they saw something in me. All my employees had a dark past, which they didn't want to share with everyone, and which made it hard for them to find a job. So, Misha, a Michelin-star chef, worked for me behind the bar, and Natasha, a master of several martial arts, worked as a waitress.

Yes, this girl will definitely fit in.

"Alright, Olga Kuznetsova, let's see what you're all about," I mused to myself, and I ran my eye over her resume one more time.

CHAPTER 7

AS PREDICTED, OLGA HAPPILY AGREED to the job and, not letting the fact that I was her boss put her off, she wasted no time in establishing her own practices and subjecting my past decisions to scathing criticism. And I couldn't object, since she demonstrated in fairly simple terms where I'd gone wrong and what I could've done differently. It was obvious the girl had seized the opportunity with both hands and was now using all her pent-up energy to prove to everyone and, to herself as well, that she hadn't studied so hard for no reason.

Olga didn't have what you'd call the "visual data" of a model. She had pleasant, average looks, but she had a certain charisma and inner strength that made people sit up and listen, whether they wanted to or not. So, if I ever found myself thinking this, it was best to clear out while I still had the chance, well, so I didn't get roped in to yet more activities. The main thing we managed to agree on was that the concept of the bar wasn't to change, and more or less important decisions were still not to be made without me.

The handover took two weeks (at least I had plenty for Olga to do so she didn't keep hanging around me) and now at last I could lie on the sofa in my office in peace and concentrate on my job orders, which, fortunately or unfortunately, were coming in more and more frequently.

It's widely believed that, apart from magicians of one kind or another, nothing else mystical inhabits our world. This is partly because during the Magic Wars of the Middle Ages, most magical creatures were exterminated, and the world's magic energy, depleted by the casting of spells of legendary proportions, finally finished off any survivors. It was only two centuries ago that the magic energy began to replenish itself, which is when magicians declared themselves once more, but this time as the only mystical power in existence.

I got the chance to read all about this in our family library before it burned down, so it was more or less true. Which made it all the stranger for me to discover my powers and learn how to summon creatures from other dimensions, because there was no information about summoners in the books at all.

A few years later, when doing some research, I discovered that all evidence suggested the magic in the world was gradually changing, and that there wasn't a fixed amount of it. Its acute depletion had affected the world greatly, which is why magicians like me started to appear. So, why couldn't demons be walking our streets, disguising themselves? Crazy, I know, and my hunch was impossible to prove, but, theoretically, that could be the case.

So, where was I? Oh, yes, about my jobs. My work is unique in that I am to some extent a private detective (as a child, I watched all the films, and I always liked Sherlock Holmes), who was called upon when someone wanted to have someone followed or to find information that couldn't be obtained via the proper channels. The spirits I summoned were able to do much more than that, so, for me, this really wasn't difficult.

So, from the outside it might've seemed I was spreading myself too thin in areas which didn't, at first glance, have much to do with each other, but back then I, like any teenager, was trying to find my place in the world, and things turned out as they turned out. I didn't want to give up the connections and reputation I'd already established, so I had to keep all the areas of my activity going. Not to mention, my private orders earned me a considerable amount of money, so I could afford to buy a bar and turn it into the place I'd always dreamed of.

I hadn't really been doing much of that in the last few years, but there were still occasions when something caught my interest.

Recently, requests had started to come in to investigate some strange incidents involving commoners, or rather, the servants of several clans. They'd simply begun to disappear without a trace. Understandably, no one was shouting about this — they didn't want it to become public knowledge — but when three families write to you at the same time about almost the same thing, you can't help but find it intriguing.

All these families were involved in maritime trade, and the missing servants were crew on merchant ships. If it'd happened while at sea, no one would really have panicked — any number of people can be swept away during a storm — but they all disappeared after coming ashore with the cargo. The clans could've suspected each other (they were in competition, after all), but they'd all had servants disappear, so they decided to turn to me as a neutral.

I could've not taken this on at all, but when Olga said she needed to go through all the accounts for the last few years with me... To be honest, I jumped at the chance.

I didn't need to go and meet the ones hiring me — their people had been warned I was coming, so it was only my motorcycle that might've attracted any attention. Security at the port entrance showed me where I could park my bike and escorted me to the manager of one of these companies.

"What can you tell me about the people who've gone missing?" I asked after I'd been given a general idea of what'd happened.

"Their only connection with each other is their

connection with the company," the manager said with a shrug. "They're all descended from generations of servants and hold various positions. True, none of them has risen through the ranks but they're all still quite new. Yes, maybe that's the only thing they have in common — they all started working at the port quite recently."

And that gave me what, exactly? Yep, absolutely zilch. I've never been a brilliant detective — the creatures I summoned always did everything for me — so my questioning was purely to keep up the appearance. No more than that.

I asked to be taken to where the last one disappeared and be left alone there. It turned out to be a warehouse where goods delivered by sea were stored before being taken away.

What all the missing people also had in common was they disappeared in the port area and, each time, to everybody's complete surprise. One minute you're talking to someone, you turn around for a second and, pfft, they're gone.

So, slowly looking around, I approached the scene of the last incident, where everything had been left as it was. Even the missing person's cap was still lying on the ground exactly where it fell. As I said, no one was in a hurry to involve the police in this, so there was no investigation to speak of — all anyone could only come up with was pure conjecture and no definite conclusions.

Squatting down, I found some stains that looked like dried puddles, but as far as I could remember, it hadn't rained for several days. When I ran my finger through one of them and licked it, I could taste salt. Seawater, but that didn't mean much, being so close to the sea.

Right, it was time to stop messing around and get down to business. And yes, rinse my mouth out later and stop pretending I'm a detective. Quickly drawing a seal, I fed it with my energy and summoned a bloodhound spirit, which appeared before me in the form of a cat.

"Why a cat?" I looked in surprise at the creature, which began to lick its fur, as if it really was a cat. "Oh, okay, then. Look for who attacked the victim."

Once it'd finished preening itself, the summoned spirit approached the cap and, giving it a gentle lick, headed towards the remnants of the puddles, this time limiting itself to sniffing around. After that, it stood listening to something and ran off.

"Wait," I said after it, but it pretended not to hear, although what do you expect from a cat.

Ultimately, the sniffer-cat led me to one of the containers there and pointed clearly to some drops of blood on the corner of it. It was entirely plausible someone had been hit over the head there. Further traces formed almost invisible tracks leading away to the right and stopped at the water's edge. It looked like the body had been dragged into the sea.

At least it was clear the victims hadn't been just kidnapped — they'd been killed. I reported this to the manager and ordered him to clear the port for a couple of days.

"You've no idea how much the downtime will cost us!" he shouted furiously as soon as he heard this.

"And how much will it cost if you have no employees left?" I asked with a grin. "Call your boss and tell him that because of you I can't do the job, which means people will keep on disappearing."

"Did you find out anything out?" He wasn't budging.

"You never know," I said with a sly smile and a shrug of the shoulders.

As expected, he didn't take my word for it and still called his bosses, only to tell me later, with a sour expression, that I had thirty hours, after which the port would carry on as normal. I did wonder how they were going to tell their employees they had an unexpected day off.

As a result of all this toing and froing, towards sunset, the port area was free of people and, therefore, any unwanted witnesses. Working in a warehouse that was more or less empty and, at the same time, closest to the open water, I began to create magic seals, this time using ordinary pieces of chalk, or rather, not quite ordinary, but that's what they looked like on the outside. Creating seals using energy meant expending at least a little of it on transforming them. I couldn't predict then how much energy it would take, so it was better to take a little longer over it and try to be sparing.

Now, all that remained was the final step. Standing on a part of the floor that was still clean,

I pulled out a small knife and cut my left hand with it. Clenching my fist, I stretched out my arm and waited for the dripping blood to cover a large enough area, and only then did I direct my energy through the blood towards the floor, and the small puddle was transformed into another seal that started to glow dimly. Now, I just had to wait.

The last seal made of blood was in this case designed to attract the attention of anyone hungry for human blood and flesh, which meant that sooner or later the mysterious kidnapper would reveal himself.

I'd already managed to doze off before I was awoken by a scratching, rustling sound coming from the far end of the warehouse. Where the exit to the sea was.

I didn't hide, looking with curiosity at who'd decided to respond to the call of the blood seal. And out of the shadows came the kidnapper who turned out to be some kind of freak covered in scales.

"And who might you be?" I asked in surprise, not really expecting an answer.

"Newt, mortal," unexpectedly gurgled this, I don't know what else to call it, creature. "Why have you disturbed me?"

"Oh, I am sorry, fishy," I chuckled, palms outstretched. "But you've started causing problems and I was asked to sort it out."

His bulging whitish eyes stared at me. Unfortunately, the physiognomy of this creature was so very different from that of a human being that I couldn't tell what his emotions were as he looked at me, or whether, in fact, he was experiencing anything similar to emotions at all.

"What can such a weak human do to me, descendant of the gods?" he pronounced haughtily.

How could that be? His mug told me nothing, but the intonation in his voice left me in no doubt that he considered itself superior.

"Huh, is it not shameful for a descendant of the gods to steal people like some kind of rat?" I asked. "Don't make me laugh, fish face."

Newt said nothing in reply, and just rushed towards me, his webbed mitt outstretched. At the same time, he crossed the zone controlled by my seals and, immediately, steel chains shot out of a dozen places and wrapped themselves like snakes around his arms and legs. Oh, and, his tail, too, which I hadn't noticed before. In the end, the creature was suspended in the air, able only to wriggle a bit.

"Who are you, mortal?" the newt asked, once he realized that trying to break free was futile.

"Wrong question," I said with a grin, going closer and running a knife over the scaly skin of this overgrown fish. "The right one is — how much will a newt go for on the black market?"

"How dare you?" He started to struggle furiously, trying to break free from his chains.

I stood and watched this curious spectacle for a couple of minutes. My spell had cost me a fair amount of energy and it was one no one had been able to overcome, so far. I'd also made sure beforehand that the creature would be cut off from the water, as it would probably have had the advantage there. This thing had managed to kill people. Who knew what its strengths were? So, it was best to be on the safe side.

"Although..." I said, musing and tossing my knife up into the air a couple of times. "Maybe you'd fetch more as fillets."

Thanks to another seal, which killed the sound around it, no one could hear the creature's screams.

* * *

I only managed to get everything done just before sunrise. I honestly thought that all three of the companies had simply ordered the murders themselves, and that they'd been carried out by a mercenary or a group of them. Even if that'd been the case, my seals could've worked and tied people up before the security service of the family which owned that area of the port arrived. But all my bold expectations had been surpassed by the appearance of such an unusual critter as the newt.

I couldn't have planned for any of this, so I was completely unprepared for transporting the newt, which is why I decided to cut it up into pieces. I had no experience of carving up carcasses to speak of (I did have to work in a slaughterhouse as a teenager so I could at least eat — not the most pleasant time in my life), so if I spoiled something, it wasn't critical in the grand scheme of things.

Scouring around between the shelves of the

warehouse, I found some airtight containers and, not really caring about what happened to the contents (everything could be written off thanks to this small fry), I emptied them out. They were just perfect for moving my priceless cargo. I had more trouble trying to fix them onto the bike, but, in the end, I even managed to do that, too.

The black market is basically an illicit zone, but it's the only place you can buy goods that can't be obtained legally. And exclusive goods appear there too, which may not have a completely clean past, but the demand for them is high all the same.

The black market also exists covertly thanks to the "blessing" of the aristocrats, who are the first to be informed about rare commodities or any product related to their sphere of activities. Few families want their secrets to be known outside to outsiders, which means they're prepared to buy these things before anyone else does so no one knows what they get up to. Situations vary, of course, but for the most part, everyone tends to adhere to this rule.

There were several zones located in Petrograd, divided both by area and activity. All designed so that not all the goods could be nabbed in the event of a raid. And, of course, there were separate establishments — but only for people who'd been checked out.

It was to one of these that I headed. Thanks to my connections with the shadow world and the fact that I offered them a small discount, over a few years I'd banked a certain amount of trust.

And, I'd also been a supplier of exclusive goods, albeit not very often. It was enough for me, after a superficial check, to be allowed into the parking lot of a club, which also doubled as a branch of the black market.

There, as in other branches, they strictly maintained customer privacy, and the check at the entrance only informed me whether I'd been granted access or not. To keep visitors incognito, everyone was given a cloak and mask at the entrance. I was also assigned an escort so that I didn't have to carry all the containers myself. And I could only marvel at the strength of the porter, since the apparently scrawny newt weighed just under a hundred kilograms, and there was also the weight of the containers... basically, I would've been bent double trying to haul them around myself.

The end point of our journey was the office of the manager, who was supposed to help in providing me with any services.

"Welcome to our establishment," the man smiled good-naturedly. Unlike me, he was wearing a half-mask, hiding only the upper part of his face. "Tea, coffee?" he offered.

The office was quite typical and not in itself particularly interesting, except for the security magic I sensed that could wrap itself around an intruder in a matter of seconds. Or at least try to detain him if he turned out to be too powerful.

The black-market man himself was dressed in a dark tailcoat with a silver trim on the sleeves, which, however, was devoid of any symbols so you couldn't tell which family he belonged to.

Opposite him was an empty chair which I sat down in.

"Thank you, but that won't be necessary," I replied, making sure the porter had put down all of the containers.

"Do you want to avail yourself of our services, or have you decided to offer something of your own?" the manager said, hinting at the containers.

"Yes, I have goods for sale, and I'd like you to evaluate them," I said, and I leant my elbows on the armrests of the chair and clasped my hands in front of me.

"Do you mind if I call the evaluator, then?"

"Please do," I said, once again observing that everyone seemed to have a communication bracelet, except me. A trend that was really starting to get on my nerves.

After five minutes of silence, a dried-up old man came into the room, the first in all that time not to be wearing a mask or hiding his identity in any way.

"Aristarkh Georgievich." He immediately approached me, and we shook hands. "And what is this intriguing thing you've brought us?" the evaluator asked. He looked over immediately at the containers but stopped short of opening any of them.

"Be my guest," I said.

First, he took out a hand... or rather what passed for the hand of the creature I'd killed, and began to examine it with interest. When they're alive, these otherworldly creatures can take themselves back to where they came from, but when dead they don't pose any threat and are, in fact, ordinary carcasses which can be sold for profit.

"Very interesting," Aristarkh said, breaking the silence. "Would I be right in saying that no more than an hour has passed since its death?"

"Possibly." I didn't give a straight answer.

"I can't determine what kind of creature this is," the evaluator offered his verdict.

"You mean it's not an animal?" It was the turn of the manager, who'd remained silent until then, to be surprised.

"Well, how can it be an animal with such a skeletal structure?!" the old man exclaimed to him irritably. "Look at these membranes and the structure of the hand," and he almost poked the limb in the manager's face. "This can only occur in a humanoid, native, unlike us, to an aquatic habitat. Maybe you can tell me what species it is?"

"As far as I can tell, it's a newt," I said cautiously.

"I won't even ask where you managed to obtain such a specimen." The evaluator frowned and turned abruptly towards the manager. "To make an accurate assessment, I'll need to take all of this to my office."

"Of course." He gave a peremptory nod. "But can you make a preliminary assessment at all?"

"Is it just one example of the species here?" Aristarkh clarified with me and, after a nod in response, he continued: "At the lowest, about four hundred thousand due to the rarity of the product and that little is known about it. I'll only be able to give a more accurate figure after a detailed assessment of all its parts."

"Thank you." The manager punched a message onto a holographic display. Two seconds later, there was a knock on the office door and two men came in. "They'll help you move it."

"Do you not have anything else like it?" the old man asked me unexpectedly and somewhat hopefully.

"Sadly not," I said, hands spread.

"That's a shame because such interesting specimens don't come along very often," the evaluator said with a heavy sigh, clearly disappointed by my answer. He promptly turned his attention to the men called by the manager with redoubled energy. "Why are you standing there like dummies? You think I'm going to be carrying these?"

Without waiting for an answer, he simply opened the door and disappeared down the corridor, muttering something under his breath. The men quickly picked up the containers and rushed after him.

"I must apologize for the behavior of our valuer," the manager said, taking the floor as soon as the doors closed. "But he is really one of the best in the business, and if he said that what you brought is worth four hundred thousand, then it is."

"Could I take that much right now?"

"Of course," the man said, smiling. "Given that it's such a large amount, what would you like to purchase?"

"I'm interested in books on ritual magic, including those that are banned or considered lost. There are also a number of materials I'd like to purchase."

"As for the first part of your request, I need to contact the management to come up with at least a rough idea of what we can provide. As for the second part," he put his hand under the table and pulled out a tablet. "You can have access to our marketplace and everything you select will be delivered to this office or a place of your choosing."

Taking the tablet, I started familiarizing myself with the trading platform program, which turned out to be surprisingly intuitive. Everything was divided into different categories, which, in turn, had a large list of filters. So, it wasn't difficult for me to find what I needed. It was, of course, a pity to part with such a huge amount, but until I could see it, it was still only virtual money to me, which is far easier to spend.

First of all, I went to the precious stones section, where I selected two dozen gems of various cuts. Whatever materials I'd tried, gemstones, especially those with the right cut, were the best at absorbing the energy of other worlds, and it was much easier to put seals on them than on wood, which you could only use once.

The prices for the stones were slightly higher than on the open market, but they hadn't been registered anywhere, and that cost, too. Otherwise, there could've been questions as to why I needed so many jewels — questions best avoided.

As well as those, I ordered a couple of rare magic materials, which I didn't yet know how to use, but once I saw them on the general list, I simply couldn't resist. They could always be sold on as a last resort — luckily there was always a demand for such things.

In total, all this pleasure cost me forty-two thousand imperial rubles. Yes, the amount was considerable, but I'd also selected stones with a certain purity, which pushed the price up even more.

Accidentally catching sight of my watch, I was surprised to see it'd been almost two hours since I'd picked up the tablet.

"I'd like to buy everything on this list." I handed the tablet back to the manager, who'd been working at his computer all that time.

"Ah, very good," he said once he'd taken in all the details. "Please wait ten minutes, and I'll provide you with all the information on the first part of your request. In the meantime, I can offer you some tea or coffee."

"No, it's okay." I waved my hand, half-covering my eyes. It was nighttime out there, and I hadn't been to bed.

In the end, the manager sorted things out even quicker than he said.

"I picked up seven copies for you for within the agreed price," he said, displaying all the details on a screen that appeared from behind his desk. "There's a separate list for books on this subject, which either have a higher price or exceed the one set."

"You're tempting me to spend even more," I chuckled.

"You could say that." He wasn't denying it. "So, take a look at the list while I find out what our evaluation is."

"Okay."

There were only seven books, but I wouldn't have been able to buy them all at once anyway — the total price was too high, and the money too easy to spend... it would've been too much. So, I had to study each volume separately. For the most part, they weren't one-off editions, but still, as a rule, no more than a hundred of them had been produced.

All these books had survived the Magic Wars and up to this day. Only what was gnawing at me was I doubted, in our age of digital technology, that no one had thought of producing electronic versions of these books. It was quite possible that such copies had been made from the black-market archives, but no one was going to make them available as it was much more profitable to produce your own copies of books and sell them like that.

An interesting situation in general had developed around these books. All the magic in them and the ways of using it, which had been widespread before, were considered obsolete and gradually became just relics to read about, while their uses were... dubious. They'd been superseded in the performing of magic by willpower — it was faster and allowed you to attack almost without having to redeploy, assuming you had the power.

However, due to the peculiarities of my gift and its area of focus, the full effect of willpower wasn't accessible to me. So, it was also good I was able to adapt and create seals using pure willpower and energy, without the constant need to make drawings or waste time on coming up with yet another design.

Ritual magic was the closest field to mine, and if I wasn't ever able to apply the schemes and rituals from these books, then I had long got the hang of the general principles and interpreting them for myself. It was a pity though that I couldn't read the books beforehand to see how useful they'd be, but, on the other hand, our ancestors didn't write that many of them for the information in them to overlap.

Not only were the descriptions of the books not particularly detailed, but their prices varied, and I wanted to buy as many as possible. So, I had to sort them and look regretfully at the ones that got away, and, of course, with even greater regret at those I couldn't have because of the cost.

Something else interesting. This type of magic isn't used by anyone officially, yet the prices were as if the demand for them was huge. So much for reform in the magic arts.

Finally, after much thought, I selected four

books, which, together with the previous list, left, from the hefty sum of four hundred thousand, some five thousand imperial rubles. Well, easy come, easy go. And when else would I have dared spend so much on books? I can't imagine when I would.

Two minutes later, the manager came into the office, and quickly took a seat. "Sorry for the wait. The evaluation has just been completed and, as a result, we are prepared to pay five hundred and thirty-two thousand for your product. Part of this amount will go to pay for the list you chose. What would be a convenient way for you to pick up the balance?"

"Can I set up an anonymous account and transfer it all to that?"

"Yes, we can set up such an account at the preferential price of two thousand imperial rubles. Naturally, with an account like that it's impossible to track where the money came from and where it went to. We have many clients who use such a service," he whispered in confidence.

"Then let's put this on the main list," I said after thinking for a while. A separate account, and one that can't be tracked (bearing in mind the amount used to open it is relatively small), couldn't do any harm.

"All the goods will be waiting for you at the bank in a safe deposit box." After a few minutes on his computer, the manager gave me a printout, with the bank and box number on it. "The box opens to the bearer of this key," and he pulled out a small flat metal key from his desk drawer. "Please don't lose it, or else you won't be able to open the box."

"Thank you," I said, and I tucked it away in my jacket pocket.

"I do hope you have enjoyed your time here with us, and that you will have recourse to our services on another occasion," the manager said with a smile, accompanying me to the door. "Someone will see you to the exit."

"I'll be sure to look in on you again as soon as a new product or more money turns up," I replied, and I followed the escort.

By the time I'd seen to all my business, it was almost the morning when the manager at the port was supposed to allow his employees back in.

"You can tell them it's safe there now," I said before he had a chance to say anything.

"And the missing persons?"

"Get a team of scuba divers ready and check the nearest body of water. You might find them there," I said, shrugging. "It's no longer my concern. The threat's been eliminated."

As I uttered those last words, I turned around, leaving a somewhat confused man alone with all those problems. And he hadn't even seen what inside the warehouse yet. Let him work it out for himself what to do and, more particularly, how to explain it all.

Just to make sure, I summoned a small observer-spirit, which, for the next two months, was to patrol the area nearby and inform me of anything unusual. I wasn't about to allow my reputation to be damaged by taking my eye off the ball.

Just as I was riding into my garage, I received a message on my phone saying that money had been received in my account, which was a joy to see. Always love it when that happens.

"Mr. Vetrov, where have you been?!" Olga's exasperated cry rang out, almost making me trip over myself, but luckily the wall saved me from looking like an idiot.

"Olga, you'll give me a heart attack like that!" I muttered. "And how many times do I have to tell you, call me by my first name. I'm not a fan of formality."

"But how can I?" she asked, flustered. "You're the boss."

"Yes, I am the boss and I'm ordering you to call me by my first name. You can address me formally in front of the customers, if you must," I said, willing to compromise. "Did you want me for something?"

"Yes." Olga nodded more decisively than usual and was, as always, a bundle of energy. This all suggested a person who has finally found an outlet for their talents. "You've been quite haphazard in your accounting, and I need you to clarify some points."

"I see." I said with a sigh. "Come to my office. I get the feeling this could take some time."

"First of all, I don't understand how the bar can afford to stay afloat," Olga came out with it as soon as we sat down in my office. "It makes a profit, but not enough to put on events on this scale."

"The source of income is no concern of yours," I said somewhat rudely.

"I don't mean that." Olga waved dismissively. "I need to know what funds I can count on so I can make plans for developing the business."

"Just show me all the options, and I'll find the money for them," I replied much more calmly this time.

"But I need at least a ballpark figure!"

"Okay," I drummed my fingers on the table. "Let's set a limit of ten thousand imperial rubles. You can plan everything based on that being the absolute maximum I can give you each month."

"That's more like it." Olga looked satisfied with my answer.

"Anything else?" I asked, not really expecting an answer I wanted to hear.

"Yes," she came back immediately. I was hoping for the opposite. "What do you think about the idea of redesigning the bar?"

"Oh, Christ!" I exclaimed, leaning back in my chair.

"They'll be changes for the better," she said quietly.

"As I said at the very beginning, the concept of the bar won't change. I can be as flexible as you like regarding anything else."

"So, what do you think about food, then?"

"People come here to drink, not to eat," I slapped my hand on the desk, but this didn't frighten Olga in the least.

"But we can offer light snacks, and salads, and fairly simple dishes would do for the daytime."

"And turn my place into a snack bar?"

"We just won't serve food without any alcohol." Olga shrugged her shoulders. "We just make it a new rule — a lot of people do it."

"Okay, you convinced me," I said, heaving a heavy sigh. "Suggest a few options and some menus you think would work. I'll take a look later and pick one."

"I've got it all here," Olga replied straight away, taking out some papers from the folder she was always carrying around with her.

"So, you already assumed I'd agree ?" I looked at her with skepticism.

"But you have, Gregor," she said, emphasizing my name, then got up from her chair. "I won't bother you anymore. I'll go and get on with my work."

"Go already," I said, waving her away.

Just what had I done, taking her on?!

CHAPTER 8

"THERE YOU ARE!" I exclaimed joyfully, finally finding Serby wandering around on the first floor. "I was beginning to think you were avoiding me."

"Oh, yeah, hiding from you," the dog muttered, knowing escape was futile. His legs were short, and he couldn't run fast on them. "What did you want?"

"You recently demonstrated remarkable engagement in issues which I, as it turns out, don't know everything about," I began in a roundabout way. "So, tell me, how can a dark entity stay in our world, apart from through a contract?"

"Can you not drop it?" Serby requested, somewhat doubtfully.

"No, of course, not."

"Okay," the spitz sighed, shaking his shaggy head. He made himself more comfortable and continued: "It's not like it's a secret, but they try not to broadcast it."

"And why's that?"

"Don't interrupt, or you'll have to find out for yourself," he snapped. "Right, where was I? In general, strong demons, spirits or, as you call them, entities, may well break into this world, but to do so they have to expend a lot of their stored energy, and it could all be for nothing. No one has yet been able to identify what makes for a successful or unsuccessful transition. So, we don't risk killing ourselves. But if you're lucky, you can find yourself in this world and make up for everything you've lost relatively quickly, or even become stronger, strong enough to go back later, if that's what you want."

"Hmm so, how did that newt end up here, then?" I dropped the question in.

"The newt?" Serby cocked his head to one side. "So that's why you're asking? And how did your meeting end?"

"Huh? Oh, it ended with him being cut up into pieces and sold for a tidy sum."

"Gregor." The dog hiccuped nervously and recoiled. "You scare me."

"He started it! Anyway, it's irrelevant. How likely is it we'll start being infiltrated by various creatures?"

"On the one hand, as I said, transiting here on your own is quite risky, and for everyone who's used to another world, here is a bit... disorienting. On the other hand, your world is very rich in energy, which we don't have enough of. And, well, of course, we mustn't forget about such incidents as with the incubus — humans themselves can summon a demon from beyond," Serby said with a grin.

"Well, I hope I don't meet anything else. The last thing I need is to have to deal with all sorts of evil spirits," I said with a heavy sigh.

"Why don't you become a demon hunter?" The spitz's grin grew even wider, which, on his face, looked rather unsettling. "It's a fairly common job with us. Everyone wants to eat."

"Damn you. I don't eat just anything, you know."

Serby only snorted at this with derision, as if to say I'd be missing out, and trotted off somewhere to carry on with his ever-important activities. I was just thinking about going to my office to take a nap (I'd stayed up over my new books), when Misha came upstairs with a perplexed look on his face.

"Hi, you're not due to come in yet," I said.

"I got out early," the bartender said. "I'm here about something else. There's a girl hanging around down there who insists on coming up here."

"Well, get rid of her, whatever she wants," I said with a wave of the hand.

"But she looks as if she walked here all the way from Moscow."

"Like we don't have enough of our own crazies." I shook my head. "Okay, I'll be right down."

Letting Misha go, I went into the office and locked my books away so no one would open them accidentally. I'd completely forgotten to do it when I woke up. When I went downstairs, I didn't immediately go to the girl Misha had been talking about, deciding instead to take a look at her from a distance.

The stranger was tall with dark hair which she left to tumble halfway down her back. Her clothes were kind of sporty and would've looked more appropriate on a hike than in the city, although some people go for that look. From the scuffs and dust on her clothes, it wasn't impossible that the girl had indeed been walking for quite some time. It was strange that she did, given all the different transport options and that there is such a thing as hitchhiking.

As if sensing my eyes on her, the girl turned around abruptly. Several curls of her hair at the front were completely gray. The stranger put her hand to her chest and sighed with relief,

"Found you, at last," A weak, timid smile appeared on her face.

Only then did I realize where I might've seen her before. It was the victim in the incubus summoning ritual. How did she find me? She couldn't have seen me as she was unconscious the whole time.

*   *   *

"So, you're saying you woke up naked in a strange apartment and don't remember a thing?" I asked the girl when she'd raced through her story up in my office.

"Yes."

"And you were led here by a feeling you didn't understand, which only left you when you saw me?"

"Yes."

"So, what's your name?" I asked wearily.

"Lena Petrova," the girl said with a timid smile.

"So, you can remember that?" I asked, surprised.

"Well, everyone has to call themselves something," she said, embarrassed.

"And what am I to do with you, Lena?" It was more a rhetorical question than one addressed directly to her.

The girl shrank at these words and looked away.

From what she'd said, it seems that after I left, she woke up in a room and couldn't remember who she was. She quickly got dressed and looked around the apartment but couldn't find anything to explain why she was there. Then, she had the overwhelming feeling she was being summoned, a feeling which brought her here. She had a little money in her purse, so after buying everything she needed for the long trip, she set off. Lena didn't describe her entire journey, but judging by what she left out, she got into a couple of scrapes but somehow managed to extricate herself.

What I was most concerned about was this incomprehensible summoning. Why did it lead her to me?

"Okay, you can stay here until I figure out what to do about all this," I said after a long silence. "We have to sort it all out, once and for all."

"I won't get in your way," Lena said happily, ignoring my muttering. "Thank you."

I gave the girl the keys to one of the empty guest rooms on the first floor. So, you could say, I put her out of sight for a time, but I still had to do something about this.

I spent the next two days going through my books looking for any clues. But I couldn't find anything like the call Lena had described. This made me terribly angry. I've never been one for mysteries.

"There he is, absorbed in his, what are they again...books." Serby came into the office. "What's so interesting about them?"

"Huh, they're a way of conveying information," I said without looking at the dog as I put another book aside.

"Everything we need to know, we learn by living an extra day, and not rummaging through useless pieces of paper," the spitz scoffed. "What are you looking for?"

"Have you ever heard of a connection between two creatures, where one of them can find the other even many miles away?" I dared to ask, not really expecting an answer.

"Of course." Serby nodded solemnly. "Ours means I can find you anywhere. And you had to read books for that? Pah! It's obvious."

"I'm so stupid!" I exclaimed.

"For once I agree with you."

"Right," I said sternly. "Sit there and don't go anywhere, I have to check something. And, for God's sake, keep your mouth shut!"

"What's your God to me?" Serby retorted with contempt, but one look from me, and he decided not to expand on the subject.

I know that our God is something incomprehensible to a creature from another dimension. And if you can't feel the influence of something, then you can't be afraid of it. Sometimes it's very difficult to get across to a demon that there are just certain phrases that shouldn't be taken literally.

"Come in, I have to check something." I brought Lena into the office, and she suddenly jumped with fright and hid behind me. "What are you doing?" The girl silently pointed at the dog. "Are you scared of dogs?"

"It's not a dog," she said, shaking her head. "It's something else that has taken on its appearance. It's dangerous."

"Well, of all the impertinence." Serby forgot what I'd said about keeping quiet. "Calling me 'it'!"

"What did I tell you?" It was my turn to be annoyed.

"And the point in being silent if she already knows I'm not a dog?" he protested. "Especially as she's already connected to you."

"What do you mean?" I didn't understand.

"Oh, I keep forgetting you're a dropout," Serby snorted. "There's also a connection between you and me, just of a different kind.”

“So, enlighten me about this connection, as you’re so smart,” I snapped.

“If I’m not mistaken, it’s something like a teacher-student connection,” the demon replied, cocking his head to one side.

“Okay,” I took Lena’s hand and made her take a seat. “How could this happen if I only saw her once before she showed up at the bar?”

“Saw me?” Lena butted in.

“Later.” I waved my hand.

“Could be a farewell ‘gift’ from the incubus,” Serby replied after a few seconds of reflection. “Maybe it couldn’t find another way of ruining your life, or it didn’t have enough oomph. Just be glad it’s you who’s the teacher, and not the other way round. That would be amusing, though.”

“That really is bad luck,” I said.

“Is anyone going to tell me what’s going on?” Lena asked timidly.

I had to tell her briefly the story of our acquaintance, if you can call it that. And tell her a little bit about who Serby was.

“Don’t worry, I’ll be sure to get rid of this connection,” I said as I finished the story.

“Don’t!” The girl jumped up anxiously, looking at me imploringly.

“I can find your relatives, don’t worry. They’ll help bring your memory back,” I said, trying to put her at ease.

“I don’t want to go back,” Lena replied quietly, lowering her head. “Judging by your words, I should've died, but thanks to your intervention, I didn't. Let it be so. The old me died, and this is the new me."

"That's right," the spitz interjected. "Especially as it's just stupid to refuse a student with such a strong dark gift as yours."

"Why do you always have to speak in riddles?" I shouted at the dog, unable to contain myself. "What do you mean — a dark gift?"

"Well, it's hard for me to explain," Serby said, somewhat surprised. "It's like a scent. That's how I know she's like you. You even have certain notes in common."

"That's the last time I intervene in an active ritual!" I leaned back in my chair and put my head in my hands.

I could guess how Lena got what Serby called her "dark gift." During the ritual, she was the conductor that pulled the incubus from its world into ours, but the process didn't go to plan, and it seemed that some of the energy from another dimension merged with her own abilities, creating something new.

There was no way I could just sweep all this under the carpet. And, since there was a connection between us, if the girl did anything, others could find her and come after me. Then I'd end up being responsible for her recklessness! No. Better she stuck around — then at least I could try to keep an eye on her.

"Okay, so you'll be my student," I said, looking at Lena, who was patiently waiting for my answer.

Her face lit up with joy, but she then tried to adopt a neutral expression. As if that helped — all her emotions were practically written on her face. "And the first rule is — don't tell anyone that Serby can talk. He doesn't usually behave like this, but it seems today he's got a flea in his ear."

"Hey, I don't have fleas!" The dog was appalled and gave me a menacing look. "They'd burn if they tasted my blood."

"Shush, don't talk back."

And that's how, from nowhere, I ended up with a student.

*   *   *

We spent the summer months trying to get to the bottom of Lena's gift. The problem was, although, like Serby said, our abilities were similar, she wasn't able to use the same methods as me. She'd already been quite powerful to begin with, then, however, with the addition of rogue energy that she somehow managed to integrate, Lena was about the level of Senior Master, which was not so far off my own. A magical energy meter, or MEM, would've told us more precisely, but we didn't yet have the right paperwork and going through official channels wasn't an option. And the black market would still have been rather expensive. I knew this from when I had to assess my own powers while keeping a low profile.

Lena's gift was something I knew nothing about, and I'd never come across anything remotely like what was happening to her. People didn't survive such an influx of alien energy, and that was that. Scientifically speaking, the girl was unchartered territory.

Meanwhile, I'd finally managed to sort out her papers, so now my student was no longer a non-person but Elena Nikolaevna Petrova, a girl from a small village in Siberia which had been deserted for ten years, so it was impossible to prove her origins. I wasn't expecting anyone to go that deeply into it, but it was still better to be on the safe side.

But everything boiled down to my just not knowing how to teach Lena how to use her magic without inadvertently harming herself or those around her. She easily understood many of the simplest diagrams and could reproduce them, but she only had to power another seal with her energy, and the whole spell went out of control, and the outcome was often unpredictable. Also, I didn't know any other magic except creating seals, so I couldn't suggest an alternative.

The only thing I succeeded in teaching her was how to rid her body of any excess magic which could have a negative impact on her health. Storage devices couldn't always withstand such an influx, so we had to try various precious stones until we finally arrived at obsidian, which was surprisingly good at collecting the surplus magic. So, soon my student got herself a whole set of jewelry, which, with her dark hair and almost black eyes, made quite an impression. She also began to dress mainly in black and silver, which only went to accentuate a certain gloominess in her. All the same, she felt quite comfortable looking like that and couldn't understand why people sometimes shied away from her.

During all this time, I was moving further and further away from hands-on control of the bar. This was perfectly dealt with by Olga, who made more and more small changes that really did attract new customers. I never thought adding snacks to alcohol would have such a positive effect on the daily takings, but the girl was right again, so after that I mostly went along with her suggestions.

The demand for meeting rooms didn't decrease, but recently no one had required my presence to conclude a contract like Lazarev had. It was enough for everyone that lying during the negotiations was an impossibility, which meant anyone who came here had already decided to come to an agreement.

I occasionally provided my services in exchange for payment, but searching for ways to help Lena took more and more time, so I rarely agreed to do any work, which, thanks to the fairly decent amount of money I'd accumulated, had become more of a hobby than a way to earn a living.

Although applying my know-how to Lena turned out to be no use to her, things were a little different for me. For the most part, I intuitively understood what changes needed to be made to a seal, and where, for it to work. My attempts to explain this led to delving even deeper into questions of magic, more particularly — ritualism. As a result, I reworked some of my seals, so they operated more economically and effectively. But like I said, this didn't make things any easier for my student.

The most memorable, perhaps, was the first experiment when I decided to show her one of the simplest summoning seals.

"Look, this structure allows us to direct the energy of our world to another dimension with a clearly defined search criterion," I said as I finished drawing a small pentagram with a pair of control symbols at my desk.

"But what kind of creature is defined by this search? How do you determine what'll respond to this summoning?" Lena asked.

"I've taken a lot from the ritual magic used in antiquity," I explained. "Our ancestors used the energy of the elements to tear the fabric of the universe and explore other realities. This required heaps of energy, so preparing for any such ritual took a very long time. All this came about because they hadn't yet worked out a system and, you could say, wasted most of the energy they put into it. Using centuries-old experience and my intuition, I developed my own system of symbols, circuits and seals, which allow me to do with a relatively small pulse what took our ancestors several weeks. I had many unsuccessful attempts until I found the patterns I use now," I said. "Look." I pointed to three symbols, one after the other. "These symbols are responsible for the selection criterion, since I don't need everything that just wants some free energy answering my call. The first is responsible for the strength of the summoned creature, the second is responsible for the area it is strong in, and the third is to lure it into our world. One of the simplest seals in my arsenal."

"And what does this seal summon?" asked Lena who listened carefully to me until I stopped talking.

"I call this creature Firefly," I said with a faint smile. "It helps to illuminate the room at night instead of a flashlight. Let's try channeling your energy into the seal and you'll see for yourself what happens."

Following my instructions, my student touched the seal and directed her magic energy into it. The initially slow process then sharply accelerated and, suddenly, the seal that had been glowing faintly with a silver light started to blaze with a crimson fire, and a burning creature tried to get through the gap in space.

It was also good I carried out this first summoning experiment in a room in the basement which was specially designed — although not for results like these. Supplying a small pulse of energy launched a whole chain of seals to block the summoning, and a clawed hand that had already managed to stretch into our dimension was cut clean off.

"Hmm, the creature that answered the call was too big." I scratched the back of my head, perplexed.

Lena's only response was to give me a slightly

frightened look, but realizing that I wasn't about to admonish her, she carefully went over towards the hand. It was still convulsing, as if trying to grab whoever it could, but eventually it calmed down.

"What was that?"

"Hah, no idea," I said, kicking the limb left by the unknown creature. "There are so many spirits, demons and, well, downright monsters out there that it'd take more than one lifetime to learn about all of them. So, I don't even bother. Okay, let's try something else."

But no matter how many seals I suggested, none of them worked properly. The energy flow generated by my student was too unstable. But even this kind of thing, which went beyond the constraints of the seals, simply shouldn't have happened. I was baffled.

The worst thing of all was that, despite the negative result, Lena continued to believe in me and listened to me as her teacher in everything. And how, after that, was I to tell her that I couldn't help her? It was with such thoughts that I spent a week moping around, keeping myself to myself.

I was distracted from my musings by the sound of a message on my phone. It was a notification of another email from Christopher Lazarev, who, for several years, had been sending me a blank invitation form to the Academy of Magic under the patronage of the emperor. The patriarch of the family of healers still wouldn't let up with his idea of luring me there, as if it would be any use to me with my abilities.

Wait a minute... A sudden thought made me leap off the sofa I'd been lying on, and I quickly powered up my computer.

The Academy of Magic had its own website, where it posted all its documents, including its charter, which was what interested me then. Studying it took me most of the evening, but afterward... afterward, a potential plan of action began to take shape.

The point was the Academy's statute was drawn up with the specific nature of aristocratic family life in mind, and there was something that had been a tradition, but not used in modern times, that had also passed into it. A teacher could, for example, accompany his student to the Academy to determine how useful the education would be or whether homeschooling would be better. As I understood it, this was done to wean students off this preferred form of education within the family circle gradually, so they'd start to have some contact with their peers. Of course, no one did away with homeschooling completely, but the children of aristocrats still spent most of their time at the Academy, which meant it had a certain influence on them. I'm simplifying, of course, as behind any such action there are another dozen hidden motives, but I mention only something which it looked like I could use.

Maybe I'd like to go to the Academy, but straight away there were several things to consider.

One was that Lazarev had offered me the chance to study there almost from the very start of our acquaintance, but I'd politely refused. Otherwise, everyone would consider me his man, which I wouldn't want at all. It was enough that I was no use to anyone when I became the last member of a junior branch, but to then become a servant to someone else. Maybe it was a matter of pride, but I just couldn't do it.

On the other hand, there was the issue of money — it still cost a lot to study, and getting a grant, when I'd barely gone to school, would be something of a problem. And giving away what I'd developed myself to get a place as a student... I hadn't suffered so much and taken so many risks just to hand over a ready-made solution to somebody else.

So, while in principle I could get quite a lot out of being at the Academy, it would also receive no less from me in return. And to become bound by obligations... throw away the independence I'd worked so hard to attain...No.

Also, I was getting older every year, and I really would stand out among the young aristocrats for that reason alone. I would've much preferred to stand out in a different way.

So. Because Lena was my student — but, more to the point, because our relationship had been established by a magic connection — this meant that I could attend classes with her. But more importantly, I could access the Academy of Magic library, which was rightly considered one of the most extensive in the world.

For Lena, it was an opportunity finally to understand her gift. There had to be someone among the teachers who could fathom it, seeing as I couldn't. And, I have to admit, the teacher in me is not all that. I mean, I developed all my current magic using a gift particular to me, and explaining the principle of the seals to anyone else was quite challenging, as I just couldn't find the right words.

"Lena!" I called out loud to my student who came into my office a few seconds later. "Get ready, we're leaving."

"Where to, teacher?"

"You're going to enter the Academy of Magic, and I'm going with you."

"But it's really expensive!" Lena's eyes were wide with surprise.

"Oh, you don't need to worry about that," I said, brushing it off. "I've got a blank bearer form, so you'll get in for free with one of the grants."

"But how can I? I can't control my magic at all."

"Which is why you need to go there, so we can find a way of controlling it." I gave her a smile of encouragement.

"You said 'we.'"

"Yes, we," I confirmed. "The Charter of the Academy allows a teacher, even more so as a result of a magic connection, to accompany his student until he is sure that the knowledge imparted to them won't be to the detriment of homeschooling. This was used at the time the Academy was founded and has never been rescinded, which means that we absolutely can use this loophole to get me in there."

"Ah," Lena said timidly.

"Yes?"

"But I don't have anything to wear. As far as I know, there's a dress code..." she finally found the courage to say.

"I must have forgotten about that," I said, scratching the back of my head. "So, we need to go shopping, then, and get a uniform made up for you. We still have three weeks before the official induction, so we should have time."

"Okay."

*   *   *

You could ask, why have anything to do with the Academy, especially as, for several years, I persistently ignored all Lazarev's attempts to get me installed in there? Well, I got bored.

I used to devote a lot of time to my bar, but after hiring Olga, she somehow quietly took everything over, and I had to sign some papers once a week, and then once a month, and occasionally set aside money for her new projects. As I already mentioned, I was accepting fewer and fewer jobs from clients as I didn't need the money, so I could pick and choose what to take on without compromising the relationships and reputation I'd built up.

So, if Lena hadn't turned up at my bar, I might have decided to enter the Academy myself, but in the standard way. But with her magic being incomprehensible to me and the consequences it had had for my seal... The best way to solve both problems was indeed the Academy.

And why hide it? I was also curious to see what educating the Empire's future magicians involved.

Broadly speaking, all studies at the Academy of Magic were built upon the principle that aristocrats were the shield and sword of the state and had to be ready for action at all times. I don't know how it is that states didn't fight each other over the magic when its existence was announced to the world, but for the last two hundred years there'd been agreements not to wage all-out war over it.

This didn't mean there weren't clashes, though. There were so-called Free Zones, where the principle of "might is right" was in full effect. The zones themselves weren't very large — they were rarely any bigger than a minnow European state — but this didn't stop many trying their hand in these places. At first, these zones were seized by mercenaries, whose presence meant any attempt to take the land back would prove to be far too costly. Instead, the Free Zones supplied the world with the best mercenaries, and there were still groups prepared now and then to pit themselves against these outlaws. And not always without some success — after all, an aristocrat is not one of your self-taught magicians.

And not to forget the ever-dangerous African zone, where things weren't great before, and when local magicians began to appear there with a vengeance, then basically... Basically, most of Africa, despite its rich resources, was considered fit only for those who had some kind of death wish.

I got distracted.

The shopping trip didn't take too long, although we did spend two days over it since it turned out that Lena needed more things than I thought. I mean, Lena was also a commoner, with no memory of the past, yet she'd already bought more than five different outfits. "For the first time" too, as she put it. I shudder to think what kind of wardrobe the children of boyar families haul around, because with them it's not just about looking good — they don't want to fall flat on their faces in front of their classmates.

Making up the uniforms took two whole weeks, and I was glad I'd decided to embark on this odyssey in early August, and not towards the end, when we definitely wouldn't have had time to fit it all in. There was so much stuff in the end that taking it on my bike was not an option, and I've never gotten around to buying a car as I'd never needed one until then.

"Can we fly, then?" Lena suggested, looking at all her luggage with dismay. She clearly didn't want to leave even a small purse behind.

"I'm not keen on public transport," I said with a nervous twitch of the shoulders. "So, you can fly without me but take Serby along."

"Hey, why me?!" The dog, who was also present, was horrified.

"Because you'll protect Lena," I answered.

"What kind of guard am I in this body?" the demon snorted disparagingly, hinting at his small size.

"Don't worry, you can bite a finger off, at the very least," I said with a smirk.

"Someone here will be missing their fingers soon," Serby growled menacingly.

"Don't argue. Accompany Lena and make sure she doesn't get into trouble, and I'll make my own way there."

"You're going there on your motorcycle again?" the dog scoffed.

"Yep," I nodded. "Also, there are certain things they just won't let you take on board a plane, and I can't not take them either. So, it's not the best option for me either way."

As there was no point in any further discussion, we called a car which took my student and Serby to the airport, and for the first time in a long while I was able to take a break and stand at the entrance to my bar for a minute.

"So? Got rid of your burden, then?" asked Misha, coming over to me. There weren't many customers at the time, so he could take himself away from the bar for a while.

"Hah, just temporarily. The important thing is you don't wreck the bar while I'm gone."

"Everything was fine last time," he said in mock indignation. "And Olga won't let anything happen." He started rubbing the back of his head.

"Got that from her?"

"Yeah," Misha said. "A good swing on her for

such a delicate girl. Okay, back to work, otherwise she'll notice and come at me again."

"Go already." I laughed at his lame joke. Well, he did cheer me up, at least.

After standing on the street for a while longer, I went upstairs to my office, where I'd already packed a bag with everything I needed and calmly waited for the sword, which I'd decided to take with me this time. Who knows what lay in store for me in the capital, not to mention surrounded by nobles. It'd be better to have it with me than regret not bringing it later.

As soon as I took the sheathed blade from its wall-mounting, I heard Miyamoto's voice: "A warrior must always be on the path to self-improvement."

It was as if he hadn't said anything. Sometimes the old swordsman liked to throw phrases out there, and it was up to you to work out what he meant.

"That's a warrior, but I'm an ordinary dark magician." I grinned at my reflection in the mirror, taking the sword more comfortably in my other hand. "Well, then, it's time to go. Let's hope my student hasn't got into any trouble without me."

CHAPTER 9

IN THE CAPITAL, I was greeted by endless gridlock and... police checkpoints at all the entrances to the city. It was only when I got to one of these checkpoints that I managed to find out what'd happened.

"So, what's going on?" I asked, handing my documents to a policeman.

"Routine check," he said

"Come on." I smiled. "I'm interested."

"Someone robbed the Rothstein Bank," the man muttered, all while checking my documents against his database.

"Who dared to break into that clan's property?" I whistled with surprise.

"If we knew that, we wouldn't need any check-points," the policeman grumbled, handing back my documents. "You may pass."

I nodded to him and moved on along the now

not so busy road.

You really had to wonder who managed to rob such a famous bank and how. They had a security system that could pretty much withstand Armageddon, but there you go. Judging by the sheer number of checkpoints, it wasn't just a couple of thousand they stole, either. Most likely that kind of information wouldn't be made public, however — it would've been bad enough that anyone found out about the robbery, as it would've hit the reputation of that wealthy family very hard.

I remember how for some TV channel, the bank employees conducted a guided tour where they showed how sophisticated their security systems were, and that depositors shouldn't be afraid of their valuables being stolen. To back this up, there was a demonstration of what would happen to a robber if he entered the restricted area.

The journalists were impressed by the cloud of ash — all that was left of the dummy-thief. This was all quite legal, as the Rothsteins had built their bank on their ancestral lands, which meant that they could do whatever they wanted with any offenders.

I wondered how they were going to explain all this to their customers now.

As soon as I cut through the outskirts of the city, I headed towards the hotel, where I'd already booked a room. Naturally, the Academy provided a dormitory for its students where they basically all lived, but it wasn't open to those who hadn't enrolled yet. We had to find a place to sleep in any case. This meant picking from among places that were far from cheap, but better to pay more there than try to get halfway across the city to the Academy through all the traffic jams.

To be honest, the owner of this particular hotel owed me, so there was no problem getting my penthouse. It wasn't like I'd come to the capital for the hell of it. And I liked to be comfortable.

"How are you settling in?" I asked, going into the communal part of the hotel room.

Lena, who'd been lying on the couch, reading some magazine, beamed at me and put it aside. But typical Serby just gave a half-hearted flick of the tail, not even deigning to open his eyes.

"It's so interesting here!" exclaimed Lena before immediately complaining, "Except he won't let me go anywhere."

"Huh, quite right, too. There are places you can't go with a dog, and you are too tasty a morsel for many."

"What do you mean?" Lena looked at me blankly.

"You're a commoner, not from any of the families, but also a powerful magician." I explained. "In theory, you should've been invited to become a servant a long time ago, but they missed you for some reason. Now they can be much tougher on you whatever you might think. I hope I don't need to explain how?" But judging by the girl's puzzled expression, she didn't understand what I was hinting at. "Powerful children are born from powerful magicians, and if this magician is a girl and a commoner, then what she wants doesn't come into it."

"So that's why you sent Serby with me?" Lena had worked out the real reason behind my decision.

"Yes. Becoming a mother is wonderful, of course, but not like that."

"So, what's stopping them from doing that while I'm at the Academy?" she asked, not particularly frightened by such "prospects".

"Well, officially, all students are in the same situation while they're studying." I threw my bag down on the floor and went and collapsed in a soft chair. How nice it was after a long journey. "Of course, some are more equal than others," I said with a smirk, "but basically, no one wants to be expelled from the Academy, let alone have rumors circulating about them. It's easier to use your own servants, who can also have the gift."

"But how can you enroll with your servants?"

"It's not expressly forbidden in the charter, but the old clans have a habit of sending a couple of them with their children to provide a "decent" standard of living while they're away from home. Not to mention that a lot of people live in Moscow, and a young and handsome nobleman can easily find a date for the evening. Another thing is that once you graduate you may start receiving proposals, but you'll be a qualified magician by then, and that's already a different kettle of fish." I shook my head. "Alright, let's leave it there for now. We've got a couple of days before the official admission ceremony. Anywhere you'd like to go?"

"An exhibition of antiquities of the Magic Wars era opened at the Tretyakov Gallery this week... I'd like to go there," Lena concluded meekly.

"Okay, let's go. They won't be showing anything major there, but there might be a couple of interesting exhibits."

"Thanks." Lena smiled and ran off to her room.

First, I took a shower and changed my clothes. Only then could I feel human again. Although I like riding my motorcycle, there are still some unpleasant aspects that can spoil the overall experience (especially over long distances).

Once I'd unpacked, I did what I always do in a new place and engaged in some summoning. I limited myself to the already familiar set of creatures and spirits that would turn the hotel room, if not into an impregnable fortress, then at least into somewhere that'd give me the chance to retaliate in case of attack. Although I'm not paranoid, I still prefer to plan my security in advance. It's a pity you can't bind the spirits to yourself, but then in the magic sense I'd be lit up like a Christmas tree, due to the constant outflow of energy or the presence of so many storage devices. Binding an entity in a stationary way is much more reliable.

Just an hour of doing this makes me feel much safer. And with that thought, I went to sleep.

* * *

I was awoken not by the rays of sunlight that were meant to illuminate my room in the morning, but by the sound of muffled cries somewhere in the distance. Not yet fully understanding what was happening, I jumped out of bed and ran into the living room. It was only then that I realized that the sounds were coming from Lena's room, so I ran there. The door, as luck would have it, was locked, and there was no time to create a seal to break in, so I just knocked it down — I'd rather pay for the damage later than listen to a girl in pain.

As soon as I was in her bedroom, I had to duck, or a bolt of raw energy would've taken my head off.

This was another problem with Lena that I didn't mention. She hadn't had time to adapt to the alien energy in her body. So, at night, when she had less control over her mind, any nightmares were accompanied by uncontrollable emissions of raw energy, which the spirits I'd summoned were now feeding on voraciously. Had they not done so, there would've been nothing left of the room.

I basically crawled on the floor like a commando, moving towards my student, ready to activate protective seals at any time in case she suddenly directed any magic at me. I'd had some fly at me once — it wasn't too painful, but it was annoying.

After a few long seconds, I finally reached

Lena's bed and gently placed my hand on her stomach, activating a seal to pacify her. I didn't really expect it to work at first, but it seems my seals can affect the dark energy from another dimension, as it succeeded in stopping this chaos. Another nuance preventing me from properly identifying Lena's abilities.

By the time the seal had finished its work, Lena was already breathing calmly, and she peacefully turned over onto her side, resting her head on her hand.

There, there.

After making sure she was okay, I went back to my room to catch up with what was left of my dreams.

When I woke up in the morning, I felt completely done in, like I hadn't slept a wink.

"Good morning, Gregor," said Lena, who was finishing her breakfast. "Did you not get any sleep?" she asked anxiously, peering into my face.

"Don't worry." I smiled softly at her. "A strong cup of coffee, and I'll be fine."

"Did I have nightmares again?" she asked, biting her lip.

"I already told you." I went up to the student and squeezed her shoulders gently. "You don't need to worry on that score. By the time you enter the Academy, I'll have finished the emission-absorbing system, and you'll be able to sleep without the risk of blowing it up. And you'll be expending magical energy when you're studying, which means there be less chance of any surges."

"Thank you," Lena whispered softly, clutching my hand. "You always come to the rescue."

I said nothing in reply, afraid my voice would give me away. I'd treated this girl like a younger sister from the beginning. And, well, I did feel slightly guilty about her current condition. That said, when there's such a beautiful girl in front of you all the time... it's difficult.

Sure, it'd be nice to go out for the evening to unwind and release any built-up tension. I didn't think that Lena would turn down the opportunity, but I... I, basically, felt confused, and I was tired and didn't want to make things worse.

"I am your teacher, after all," I laughed and moved away. "As far as I remember, the exhibition opens at eleven, so we don't have much time."

"Oh," Lena groaned. "I haven't decided what to wear yet."

And quickly clearing the table, she rushed to her room. Well, that distracted her. Now I could have a spot of breakfast in peace.

Life in a hotel does have its charm — there's no need to cook. You only have to place an order — and everything's brought to your room. Lena had taken care of this beforehand, so all I had to do was choose a sandwich and decide what to save for later.

As I sat down at the table, I almost stepped on the dog asleep under it.

"There you are, Serby!" I exclaimed, staring at him.

He kept trying to pretend he was fast asleep,

but once again he was betrayed by his tail that began to twitch nervously.

"What now?" the spitz asked reluctantly, realizing that there was no way I was going to leave him alone.

"Where were you last night? Lena had another nightmare, and we agreed that you'd absorb all her emissions."

"She put me out of the room," Serby grumbled. "And, unlike you, I prefer to sleep peacefully at night."

"What did you get up to this time? I raised a quizzical left eyebrow.

"Your student completely forgot who I really am and treated me without the requisite respect."

"Aha, and you behaved like a regular dog. Left her a little present, did you?" I asked with a grin.

"Where do you get such ideas from?" Serby almost growled. "I just kept her awake, and then I went to another room and went to sleep. You always make stupid jokes when you've had no sleep."

"Yes, I know."

Leaving the dog be, I finished my breakfast and, to wake myself up, took an ice-cold shower, which made me shiver like I had exposure. But finally, I was awake and able to get my head together.

In the meantime, Lena had chosen her outfit for the museum, so I didn't have to wait for hours for her to come out of her room. I've met girls like that and it's not something I have the slightest desire to go through again.

To go out, Lena chose dark trousers and a light-colored tunic, and, of course, heels. While she was shorter than me, in them she was about the same height. I went for the suit I'd had made up back in Pushkino, deciding to try it on for size.

Glancing at the full-length mirror, I made sure again that everything fit perfectly.

Looking back at me from the mirror was a dark-haired young man whose hair was untidy (I was always too lazy to comb my hair, and just cut it from time to time). Gray eyes shone, if you looked closely, with an otherworldly light — the only feature I inherited from my family. Quite an attractive guy, in my subjective opinion, even if not a paragon of male beauty. Never had any complaints from the ladies, mind you.

The tailored suit consisted of dark gray trousers, a white shirt and something similar to both a jacket and a blazer (I don't really know much about clothes, I don't need to). That member of the Lamanov family did a great job — you couldn't tell the suit was made of magic material, and I hoped no one else would realize, either.

Lena came up to me unexpectedly and straightened my shirt collar. It was slightly crooked, and I hadn't noticed.

"That's better," she said with a nod and a smile and, picking up a small purse, she hurried to the door. "The exhibition is open already, so let's go."

Grumbling inside, I picked up the tube I hid my sword in, and slowly followed her. She wouldn't be going anywhere without me anyway. I needed the tube to hide the weapon from prying eyes. I could manage without it in Petrograd, but in the capital, I still didn't feel comfortable going out without back-up.

The elevator from the penthouse led directly to the parking lot, so we headed straight for my bike, which gave out a contented roar when I started it up. Lena flinched slightly at the noise but tried not to show any emotion. It was still hard for her to accept there was a dark entity inside my motorcycle. Yet, she looked upon Serby quite normally. Maybe that was to do with the fact he could talk.

Sitting on the bike, I winked at Lena, who was still hesitating to take the next step. Frowning slightly, she clenched her fists and sat behind me, holding me very lightly around the waist.

"Hold on," I said once we'd taxied briskly out of the parking lot, and we took off. To Lena's credit, she almost let out a squeal.

We made it to the Tretyakov Gallery without any problems, primarily because we could maneuver on a motorcycle much better than in a car and could go where cars couldn't. Not many dare to get in the way of a magician, something which I took full advantage of, so I threw caution to the wind. Being stuck in traffic doesn't really do it for me.

Leaving the bike in the parking lot, we went straight to the main entrance. I'd paid for the tickets online so we wouldn't have to queue up for ages.

"So many people," I said, shaking my head, as

we tried to get into the building without bumping into anyone.

"Exhibitions like this don't come along all that often. Going by the reviews, there were even more people here in the first two days. Most of the crowds have died down, now," Lena explained.

"Hmm, I still doubt there's anything worth seeing, though."

"Which is why it's attracting mostly commoners, since for us... I mean, them," Lena corrected herself after a short hesitation, "there's quite a lot here compared with what's told about the real history of the world. And this time they're presenting a collection of ancient artifacts belonging to several families. People are allowed in to see them in small groups and there's tight security," Lena said, looking at me knowingly.

"Hah, maybe it won't be as boring as I thought," I replied.

By this point, we'd reached the front of the queue, and I gave my name. It's a good thing it's often near the top of the list, otherwise I fear the little old man checking for it would've been fumbling around for quite some time before he found it. So, it all took about a minute — much better than standing in line, and then having to do so again at the entrance.

"Right you are," he said with a nod. "You can go in."

When inside, the first thing I did was turn away from the general flow of people. I've never liked crowds, and you don't really need guides at such events as there is a plaque next to every exhibit which tells you all about it, including its history. Lena was rushing to join a group, but I took her by the hand and led her away.

"Let's find out where the aristocrats' exhibits are, and we can have a look around the general exhibition afterward," I said by way of explanation.

I couldn't really see any of the clans wanting to display anything that would be of interest to the public but, in any event, this was still better than looking at the remnants of staffs or magic crystals. And looking at sorcerers' clothing from those days is completely absurd — what could be so interesting about ordinary robes?

After wandering around the building for a time, I finally found a part of the hall that was cordoned off by a screen and security guards dressed in suit jackets. People were allowed inside in groups of five, and the next group could only go in once the previous one had come out. When we approached, there was a young couple standing at the entrance and no one else waiting.

"Do you know when we can go in?" I asked the guy who'd just been having a lively conversation with his companion.

"We were told to wait five minutes until the tour is over," the cheerful young man replied enthusiastically. "You also can't wait to see what the aristocrats could display that's so unusual?

"You could say that."

Our conversation petered out by itself. The couple were only really interested in themselves, and I had no intention of continuing the conversation.

"There are so many interesting things here!" Lena said excitedly.

She couldn't wait to see these relics of the past close up. She gave the impression that she'd definitely have tried to pick them up if they hadn't been behind glass.

"Huh, most of the stuff here is just garbage no one needed any more but which, for some reason, this generation seems to find interesting," I said, unable to share her enthusiasm. "Like I said, anything truly valuable is always kept in the family and used by them. It's incredible that anyone decided to display their collection at all."

Our conversation was cut short by one of the security guards.

"Before you go inside, please hand over your weapon," he said, turning towards me without so much as an introduction, and he pointed to the tube behind my back.

"Well, you'll have to pay for the damage if anything happens to it." I handed it over with a grin. "Oh, yeah, don't even try opening it."

"Don't worry," he replied coldly, refusing to rise to it. "Your belongings will be safe and waiting for you at the end of the tour."

We went and joined the couple, and a young woman with light-brown hair, glasses and a tablet in her hands came out from behind the screen.

"Only four?" She looked at us in surprise.

"The main group only set off recently. They've

not reached this part of the exhibition yet," the guard nearby explained.

"So, these are the most impatient ones, then?" She smiled broadly. "Let's go now, then, before the next group turn up."

As we went in, we could see a small gallery divided into several areas.

"There aren't many artifacts in this part of the exhibition, but they all have their own history and are still active, so please don't touch anything," the woman warned us. "Our establishment is not responsible for injuries resulting from the unauthorized operation of relics. As indicated on your tickets."

"I thought that was a joke." The female half of the couple looked at her in surprise. "Who reads small print anyway?"

"Don't worry, there hasn't been a single case yet," said the tour guide, smiling. "It's just the management covering itself, so it doesn't get sued. So, come on, then."

While this may have spooked the couple, hearing this only served to cheer me up. Maybe there was something of interest here, after all.

"Our first exhibit has been through a lot but made it to our time intact." The woman pointed to a quite ordinary, albeit expensive-looking, piano. "The magician who made this piano was a huge fan of Ludwig van Beethoven but couldn't play at all. So, he made it so that anyone who sits down to play anything by Beethoven will do so like a virtuoso, whatever their actual standard. Unfortunately, this magician made a mess of things, and anyone who played it couldn't stop until their fingers started to bleed."

"Killer tunes, eh?" I chuckled.

"You could say that," agreed the gallery employee. "So, unless anyone feels like playing it," I detected a hint of a challenge in the way she looked at me, which earned a faint smile in response, "then let's continue." We went over to a stand, where there lay a nondescript-looking dagger in its scabbard, with several chains wrapped around it. "The famous dagger that killed Gaius Julius Caesar. It was given the name Brutus after what happened."

"What's so magical about it?" asked the guy, doubtfully.

"In the time of the Roman Empire, the priests of the gods performed rituals over the ruler Julius Caesar to prevent anyone from killing him. All the same, the conspirators found a way around this and were able to make an enchanted dagger to overcome the priests' protection. It's also believed to contain the spirit of Marcus Junius Brutus, who briefly survived Caesar. Therefore, it's better not to touch the dagger unless you want to turn into a bloodthirsty killer," the guide warned us.

I was skeptical about this at first, but when I took a good look at the dagger, I saw a barely noticeable dark haze, and, at one point, it seemed to me that it twitched. I heard the chains rattle, in any case. And the thing really was possessed, but not like with my sword, where it had come about voluntarily, but forcibly, by the looks of it, which was why the spirit living in it was, most likely, if not crazy, then clearly not a paragon of virtue. And, after so many years spent inside a murder weapon, it wasn't surprising. Someone had come up with a very original way of taking revenge on the emperor's murderer.

"Is there anything here that's not so sinister?" asked the girl, who was a little scared after hearing the story.

"Of course," said the guide. "Remember the story of Penelope, Odysseus's wife, who wove a burial shroud and unraveled it every day? Well, in our exhibition there is a similar artifact that makes it possible to weave any fabric, but at night it begins to unravel itself, so that by the morning it's back to the way it was before. It seems, the magician who made this was a fan of the Odyssey. The next exhibit," and she led us to an old full-length mirror. "This is an ungaikyo." The guide pointed to its surface, which seemed to reflect anything but the actual room we were in. "In Japan, it's believed that any fairly old object can be inhabited by a demon or, as they call them, yokai."

What the guide didn't mention is that the older the object, the stronger the powers of the yokai can become. Did I mention I was interested in all things Japanese? Well, I was hardly going to skip the subject of their spirits and demons.

"Can I take a look in it?" I asked the woman.

"Yes," she said, "as long as you don't go closer than two meters. It's very old, after all."

"Don't worry," I said with a smile. "I know how to handle these things."

Going as close to the mirror as I was allowed, I stared with curiosity at its surface, which finally stopped depicting a riot of flashing lights and began to go misty. Sneaking a look at the other people on the tour, I realized from their faces that they couldn't see anything like that. Well, so much the better.

I surreptitiously sent a small bolt of energy into the mirror to give it an extra shot of vigor, and tuned it in with my magic. My research revealed that such objects can't absorb magic energy from the surrounding world themselves. Their capabilities are limited to the maintaining of their "life", if that's what you can call it. So, the ungaikyo hungrily devoured my treat.

A few seconds later, my reflection appeared in the mirror. Another amazing ability of these yokai is they can reflect the true essence of things, even when concealed by spells. If they weren't such a rarity, these "reanimated" mirrors would be a wonderful way of detecting illusion.

So, it was me I saw in the ungaikyo, but there were also differences. A blue mist was emanating from my eyes, petering out around their edges, lending my appearance an otherworldly quality. A dark haze swirled around me, originating from the left side of my chest, where there was my heart and... the mark left by my grandfather's experiment. Instead of my usual clothes, I was wearing light chainmail, with the familiar sword hanging from my belt. Although it's strange to describe a deadly weapon I hardly ever use like that.

How interesting. I suspected I'd see something like that, but it's one thing to assume, it's another to know for sure. Thought-provoking.

"Lena, come here," I said, and, without asking why, she came and stood next to me. "Now look in the mirror and try to make yourself out."

As I said this, I stepped back a little, stood right behind her, and put my hands on her shoulders. Looking over her shoulder, I could see her in the mirror. She was wearing a dark red dress decorated with her own obsidian. Instead of being free flowing, her hair was in an intricate kind of arrangement, set with black stones. She was enveloped by two opposing fires — one consisting of normal-looking flames, and the other of what could only be described as darkness in its primordial form. There was a certain predominance of reddish-orange fire, but it was hard to say long it would stay like that.

Feeling that the ungaikyo might not be able to take much more, I gently squeezed Lena's shoulders and pulled her aside.

"How was it?" I whispered, ignoring the others' curious glances.

"Beautiful," Lena replied, unexpectedly. "What was it?"

"Your true essence. It's made me think of a couple of things, but I still need to confirm them."

While we were talking, the couple approached the mirror, but judging by the disappointed expressions on their faces, they didn't see anything interesting and were already urging the guide to show us the next exhibits.

Maybe there was something else here worth looking at, but I was too distracted by my own thoughts for that. Well, Lena had been truly delighted with what she saw, at least, and I couldn't help but be pleased for her.

"Sadly, that's the end of our tour," said the gallery employee, bringing proceedings to a close. "I do hope you enjoyed it all and that you'll come back another day to see what else we have on display."

After thanking the woman who clearly loved her job, we headed over to the security guards, where my tube with its sword was returned to me safe and sound.

And, of course, even after what she'd seen, Lena didn't want to miss the rest of the exhibition. So, I had to accompany her and answer questions about certain things. After all, I was from a junior branch of what was still quite an old family, and we'd been taught the history of the world from a different perspective from commoners.

As I saw it, the most remarkable exhibits there were the living paintings, the inhabitants of which sometimes behaved quite vulgarly, which couldn't but attract people's attention. Unfortunately, the secret of creating such paintings has been lost, and so far, no one has been able to develop a complex of spells capable of recreating it. The modern approach to magic has also made that difficult.

The last Magic Wars weren't without their consequences and much knowledge was lost simply down to the completely new circumstances our ancestors had to adapt to. It was partly because of this that I didn't like going to such exhibitions — they reminded me only too well of what the magic community missed.

In the end, we went around the whole exhibition, twice even, since it was impossible to get to some parts because of the crowds. Lena was enraptured by what she saw, almost jumping up and down with excitement.

There was someone who could enjoy life — unlike me, who moaned all the time. I do wonder if there's something wrong with me.

Just for the sake of variety, my chopper wasn't surrounded by a gang of teenagers, for once, and you don't tend to see criminals in the capital on a main street. Not at this time of day, anyway. This time there was just one man standing next to it. He was wearing a brown coat (perverse given the hot weather) quietly smoking a cigarette and looking up into the sky. He might have appeared to be just standing by it, but my instincts told me that it wasn't that simple.

Ignoring him, I approached my motorcycle and fastened my sword onto the side of it in case I needed to pull it out in a hurry. It was unlikely I'd be attacked, but still.

"Do you know it's against the law to use so many spells on a vehicle?" The cloaked stranger eventually turned his attention to me without discarding his cigarette.

As he turned to face me, I could see the man had bright blue eyes, probably a week's worth of stubble, and a few small scars on his face. Indeed, there was a very prominent one, running all the way back from the temple, like it'd been done with a claw or, well, a knife (although the mark isn't really typical of a knife).

"Yes, I know." I nodded and gestured to Lena that everything was fine, and she should get on board. "I have permission to use this mode of transport within the city and outside it."

"I still recommend refraining from using your motorcycle in the capital for purposes other than it was intended."

"Is that a threat?" I narrowed my eyes.

"Hah, no, just a warning."

"And who might you be?"

"Konstantin Skuratov." The stranger took out the badge of an organization that was quite well-known around the Empire. "The Imperial Magic Security Service."

"And what have I done for your service to dispatch a nobleman after me rather than a regular employee?" I asked.

"We watch all the magicians who come to the capital, and you're famous enough in Petrograd to be allowed in," he said quite openly, although he left the second part of my question unanswered. Or he was just giving me the official version, which was far from the truth.

"Huh, watch all you like," I replied. "Just don't

get in my way."

Without waiting for the officer to respond, I got on my motorcycle, started the engine, and went off to join the traffic. I could still see him in my mirrors for some time, but, eventually, I turned down another street and disappeared from his field of vision.

I'd have to check the bike for bugs and tracking devices. I didn't believe this functionary was just hanging around my motorcycle, and all those things could be done without attracting attention. But then again, he did want to talk to me for some reason.

What was worse was he was from a boyar family, which meant he might be pursuing not only his official interests, but those of his clan, too. And in light of this, our "meeting" was more like an inspection, where they were just keeping an eye on me for now. But when would this "for now" end and aggression from the Skuratovs begin? If it began at all. Or was I getting too paranoid and the man meant what he said?

Why can't anyone be straight with me and just tell me what they want?

CHAPTER 10

THE DAYS LEADING UP to Lena's induction into the Academy of Magic just flew by. All the necessary paperwork had been prepared and sent to the Registrar's office by then. Lena passed the theoretical exams with flying colors. Fortunately, despite losing her memory, she could remember everything I'd told her, pretty much straight off, and she herself buried her nose in the textbooks to consolidate her knowledge. Ignorant magicians aren't much use to anyone, and the Academy is, after all, a higher educational institution. They teach magic theory there themselves, so no one asked her to.

Of course, as well as the theory, there was also practice, but assessing the candidate's strength was all done using an MEM. The threshold for admission was five hundred conventional units of magic, which, in turn, was equal to the rank of "Senior Apprentice". I had no doubt Lena would easily surpass that despite her not really being able to control her powers.

This time I went against my principles, and we arrived at the Academy gates by car. I had to shell out on renting a magicar (as much as five hundred imperial rubles for a couple of hours), but it needed to be made clear from the start that my student was no ordinary commoner, and that she had someone behind her. Otherwise, bullying would've been inevitable. And while it can't really be avoided, at least she'd have time to start adapting to her new community, which was more than enough to be going on with.

I chose a time near the end, when most of the students would already be enrolled, and the welcoming committee would be pretty tired.

"Welcome to the cloisters of our Academy." As soon as we walked through the door, a young girl immediately sprang towards us, beaming. Apparently, each newcomer had been allocated an individual who'd help to explain everything. "Your documents, please."

"Here." I handed her a folder with all the relevant papers and certificates. The most important thing was a grant form in the name of Lena Petrova.

"There aren't many grant holders this year," the girl whispered to me. "So, I think I can get them to let you jump the queue."

"I'd be grateful," I answered in a similarly hushed tone, quietly slipping fifty rubles among the documents and, judging by the look she gave me, she got where I was coming from.

"Please follow me." With another smile, she led us along the winding corridors, circumventing most of the other applicants. "In the corridors where all the students are is a lot of information about the magic aspect of the world, but you can catch up with that later," she said, deeming it necessary to explain the route we were taking. "Here we are."

The girl showed the way, and we left the corridor to find ourselves in a spacious room, in which the enrolled students and their support groups were milling about. Many people knew each other, so it wasn't surprising they were gathering in cliques. There were several anonymous-looking corridors, like the one we'd come out of, leading into the room, with one central wide and well-lit one. In the center of the room was a blue crystal, stretching in jagged shards towards the ceiling, and very nearly reaching it.

"Spectacular," I drawled, using my magic vision to look at it.

There was so much energy in the crystal that it would've been enough for several spells at the rank of Archimage, at least, if, of course, someone knew not only how to draw all that energy out of it, but also direct it.

"This is our pride and joy," the attendant said. "Every year the crystal grows a little bigger and its energy is enough to power many magical systems, but it's a secret," she whispered softly, putting her finger to her lips. "It is also a magic energy meter."

The academy employee pointed at the table standing next to the crystal, which was essentially a large tablet.

"Is there not a… simpler way?" I asked.

"According to our rules, the student must boldly present themselves to find out their level. And then the teachers will help to develop their initial potential," the girl pronounced solemnly.

"It's okay," Lena gently squeezed my elbow. "I'll pass," she continued, but not very confidently.

"Of course you will," I said with conviction. "How could you not?"

Giving her a smile of encouragement, I nudged Lena towards the crystal. She took a few hasty steps, but then slowed down as she neared the crystal. Our attendant stood to one side of her and activated something on the table (to record the test, by the looks of it).

When Lena was one step away from the crystal, she slowly exhaled.

"Now touch it and let out the maximum magic pulse you can manage," the Academy employee said, gently encouraging her.

My dark-haired student with several gray curls looked round at me, and I smiled warmly at her, gesturing to her not to hold back. Nodding to me, she turned to the crystal and put her palm on it.

A sharp exhalation — and for a moment it seemed as though out a strong gust of wind emanated from her. It lifted up her hair for a few seconds before gently lowering it back down again. Simultaneously, two lightning bolts — orange and black — seemed to shoot from her hand, constantly colliding with each other as they hurtled into the blue depths of the crystal, before they disappeared, dissolving without a trace.

I only noticed all this because I was watching what would happen. It seemed to me everyone else completely missed it, although, they were now looking at my student and whispering to each other.

And it was all because the hi-tech table next to the crystal not only recorded the test but was also clearly displaying the results. Four digits shone brightly above the table — one thousand two hundred and twenty. That's how many magic units Lena's pulse emitted — the level of Senior Master, extremely rare for her age.

It was also good no one knew about her past, otherwise there would've been even more problems. Due to her being a commoner, but anyway.

"Con...congratulations." It took our escort a little time to get over her surprise. "You passed."

The Academy of Magic could hardly turn down a Senior Master, who over the years may well develop into a Magister, or more.

"What now?" I asked, coming over towards them. Lena was trembling slightly having realized what'd just happened but, standing next to me, she tried to get a grip of herself and not betray her emotions.

"Now you must wait with the rest of those who've been tested and their guides until the groups have been put together. Then it'll be announced who's going where."

"Thank you," I said, and, giving Lena a little hug, I stepped aside. "How are you feeling?"

"My hands are still cold," Lena admitted. "Like you said, I didn't hold back. I had no idea I could produce anything like that."

"Well, yes, when the threshold for admission is the rank of Apprentice... you've upstaged most of them. Be proud of yourself."

"Without your instructions, I'm afraid I wouldn't have succeeded." Lena sighed heavily and wouldn't look at me for some reason.

"What kind of teacher am I?" I batted away the compliment. "Just showed you a couple of tricks and how to get in touch with your power. I wasn't in a position to teach anyone. On the contrary, I could learn a thing or two from you on how to set a goal and smash it."

"Come on, now..." Lena tried to object as I was speaking, and at my last words she blushed to her roots. "Thank you. I'll try my best!" she said fervently, finally bringing herself to look me in the eye.

"I didn't doubt you for a second." I squeezed her shoulder. "Now, take a breath. There's still a lot to do."

Contrary to my expectations, no one came over to us, although everyone kept looking in our direction. The next applicants couldn't boast of any equally good results. Only one arrogant guy emitted nine hundred conventional units of magic and, nose upturned, went off to a group of his acquaintances who quickly brought him down to the earth again, and he shot a somewhat malevolent look towards us. As if we didn't have enough offended youths already!

By the way, despite most of the applicants being aristocrats, not all of them passed the test and left the room distraught. As far as I remember, they'd still have two more chances before being turned down for good. Or they could just pay, but all the years of teaching would cost so much it'd be better to study everything independently than to try to smash through your magic ceiling.

Not everyone is lucky enough to have a powerful gift. Hmm, reminiscing again.

One of the last candidates was a guy I already knew — it was thanks to him I made a decent amount of money at that race. His result was literally at the lower end of the threshold for admission, yet he was as pleased as if he'd had the same figures as Lena. Our eyes met and we nodded to each other, but neither of us approached the other — Mstislavsky had his cohorts, and they pulled him aside straight away, talking about something very animatedly.

In the end, just over an hour after Lena's test, they began to announce the results. The entire intake was divided into groups depending on their abilities. It didn't make sense to teach those who could make a wall of fire with those who could only produce a tiny fireball. They required a different approach.

Thanks to her powerful gift, Lena got into the

top group. The way her eyes widened with surprise showed she hadn't expected more than half of the students in her group to be, not just on her level, but even stronger.

"Don't be so surprised," I said, feeling the need to say something. "Just take a look at their names. They're almost all from old noble families which have been magicians for more than a dozen generations. So, even the level of Master would be low for them."

"But how's that possible?" Lena asked incredulously.

"Marriages between strong magicians, as well as the long and painstaking work of eugenicists, who also work out when such a union will strengthen the family gift, and when it'll weaken it. Each old clan has families of servants whose function is to make precisely those kinds of calculations. True, there are sometimes, so to speak, "political" marriages, but even in those cases they try to make sure the children aren't weaker than their parents," I said with a chuckle. "Better to bear in mind that you're the only commoner in the group, and that you're going to find it very tough."

"I can handle it," Lena said firmly. "And I'll become a student worthy of my teacher."

"You've really got that fixed in your head, haven't you." I sighed heavily. "I already told you it was just chance that I saved you, and the connection between us is my mistake and the demon's revenge."

"Anyway," Lena shook her head furiously. "If

you hadn't been there that day, I'd be dead now."

I didn't get the chance to respond as the girl who accompanied us to the hall came over again.

"Congratulations on joining the top group. Your sister has the honor of studying with the heirs of ancient families," she said with great enthusiasm.

"She's not my..."

"I'm *not* his sister," Lena said, loudly interrupting me. For some reason she was incensed by this.

"Oh, I am sorry," the Academy employee lowered her eyes. "I must've misunderstood."

"It's fine," I said, reassuring her.

"Then, Lena, follow me, and we'll get acquainted with your classmates and mentor," she said. "You'll be able to meet up with your... escort in the evening when the introductory sessions are over."

"Wrong again," I chided her. "I'm Lena's teacher and, according to paragraph three hundred and forty-three of subparagraph two, I have the right to be present at all of my student's classes at the Academy."

"But... how can that be...?" She hesitated, before hitting upon a solution: "Wait here, please, I need to speak with the administrators."

"Now she'll run after someone from the rector's office," I observed as our helper disappeared down one of the corridors.

"Why haven't you enrolled here yourself?" Lena asked, taking advantage of the lull in proceedings.

"It's not worth the hassle," I said with a vague wave of the hand. "You're a different matter — they can help you here much faster than I can. And since there's the opportunity, why shouldn't I take advantage of it? And I think it'll be easier for you with me around."

"Thank you," Lena replied quietly, thinking to herself.

We waited for about ten minutes for our attendant to come back. During this time, almost everyone had left the hall, and we were, basically, alone. Well, I hoped Lena wouldn't miss much. There shouldn't have been anything in the introductory classes she couldn't catch up with later.

"Good afternoon, my dear fellows," a portly man in a mantle greeted us and introduced himself: "Nikon Izvekov, teacher of magic history. I was told there's some kind of problem?"

"Gregor Vetrov," I said, introducing myself in turn. "And this is my student, Lena Petrova. She entered your college today, but they don't want to let me in."

"Teacher, eh?" He looked at me with surprise. "I hate to ask this, but do you have any proof?"

"Here." I waved my hand, directing a drop of energy into my bond with Lena.

"A magic contract?" The man looked at us with more interest. "You don't come across such an archaism very often these days. And you, as I understand it, won't tell me how it came about?"

"You've understood perfectly," I said, eyes narrowed. "So, now can I carry on as her teacher?"

"Of course." Izvekov nodded. "I can't go against what's in the charter, but I can't help but point out that you are probably the first person in the last twenty years to take advantage of this clause."

"There's a first time for everything," I said with a shrug.

"Take these young people to the auditorium, otherwise they'll be late," the man asked our helper.

The girl bowed to the teacher and gestured to follow her. Of course, I assumed there'd be more resistance to accepting me as Lena's teacher, but apparently, my demonstration of the magic contract had a profound effect on the man's judgment. In any case, the less they bugged us the better.

Despite its antiquated appearance, the Academy made full use of advances in technology. So, now we were going up to the fourth floor not by stairs, but by elevator, in which soothing music was playing.

The Academy employee tried to keep quiet all the way, apparently fearing to get into an awkward situation again. While we... we were just immersed in our own thoughts.

I wondered what was going through Lena's mind then. Her pretty face was very thoughtful at the time.

Eventually, we were taken to a pompously furnished classroom designed for a group of no more than thirty people. There were just over twenty students in the class, so there were plenty of free places.

"And here is the last member of our group." Drawing attention to us was a thin man in a mantle (it seems this is the standard look for teachers at the Academy), who until then had been holding forth from his desk. "Don't stand in the doorway. Have a seat," he said to Lena. "And you, young man, if I'm right, are not one of my students?"

"Correct," I said, "but I will be attending the class."

Without waiting for a reply, I gave Lena a nudge and we both went and occupied the last row of the small amphitheater, sitting high above the rest. This attracted the others' attention, but the newly admitted magicians simply couldn't bring themselves to turn their backs on the teacher to get a better look at us. Not on their first day, anyway.

While we were taking our places, the Academy employee who'd been accompanying us jumped up to the teacher and began to explain something to him. He asked a couple of questions and then dismissed her.

"Well, now that all the members of the group are present, then, perhaps, we can continue," the man said as if nothing had happened. "Before we were interrupted, I was going into the reasons why our empire founded the Academy of Magic, and why there are educational institutions of this kind in the first place. Maybe Mr..." He stopped short, scrolling through something on the graphic screen built into his desk. "Vetrov can tell us what the purpose of such institutions are?"

Hmm, I'd been added to the main database and attached to that group already. Smooth operators, you have to say.

"Are you sure I'm the one to answer that?" I asked with a grin.

"I'm interested in hearing your point of view, and I'll be sure to correct you if you make a mistake," said the teacher with a weak smile, but his whole demeanor suggested he was really hoping I'd flunk it. What could I do? No one likes an upstart, and that's what I looked like to them all.

"Huh, well, then, after the last Magic War, when the world's energy was depleted, many families lost their power and authority. Once powerful sorcerers who'd become weak were saved only because the magic community carefully concealed its existence, and ordinary people simply didn't realize that anything had happened. Unfortunately, not everyone believed that our world would someday recover after such events, so many took advantage of their opponents' weakness and killed them. After the ensuing bloodbath, many layers of knowledge accumulated by our ancestors were destroyed. Now that magic energy has returned to its previous level, a need to train the younger generation has arisen. For the most part, the surviving ancient families retained their unique methods, but many of them had to change theirs to fit the current reality. As this problem was common to the entire magic community, various magic institutions were created in each major state in order to gather all the remaining knowledge together and develop more. Some old families have still not accepted these changes, and their heirs undergo traditional schooling at home."

"And what about the fact that, studying together, you learn not only to control your gift, but also to establish contacts, make friends?" the supervisor wanted to know, listening to me attentively.

"Oh, please! Friends, here? Connections, yes — they're a big deal in aristocratic society, but friends..." I shook my head. "Not so easy to find friends in a snake pit like this."

"How dare you?!" A girl in the second row jumped from her seat angrily.

"I dare." I turned towards her with a smile. "Imagine a situation where you have to make a decision on which the life and honor of the family depends, but as a consequence, your friend may die or be slandered. Which would you choose?"

"I... I..." The girl didn't know what to say.

"You'd all put your family and its interests first, otherwise you wouldn't be aristocrats. So, what kind of friendship can there be here?" I pressed the point. "Yes, alliances are possible between you if your families' spheres of activity coincide, but friendship between people at the summit of authority is something, well... magical." I laughed.

"Nevertheless, our current progress would've been impossible without the founding of such institutions," the teacher chipped in, indicating to the student that she should sit down.

"All this progress is not down to the students studying at the Academy, it's down to people who are fanatical about their work," I said, throwing out my hands. "I doubt anyone from this group will want anything to do with the magic sciences in the future — the most you can expect is the improvement of family techniques, techniques which will stay private. By contrast, commoners can come to magic science and live it, create something.

"A bold speech for a commoner," said a blond-haired guy quietly from the front row, but in the silence following my words, everyone heard him distinctly.

And there, it seemed, was the first test of my strength. The guy, narrowing his eyes slightly and folding his arms across his chest, stared at me intently waiting for an answer.

"According to the statutes of the Academy, all students are equal until they graduate," I said, grinning. "So, at the moment, there are no aristocrats or commoners here — we're all students of the Academy of Magic under the patronage of the emperor."

"Then maybe we should settle our differences like students do by sparring?" he suggested.

"According to the very same charter, only students or teachers can participate in sparring if it is in the interests of learning," I recited. "Unfortunately, I'm not a student of the Academy nor one of its teachers. I'm not against the idea, provided your esteemed mentor gives us permission."

"I am against it, and will not allow you to conduct this fight," the group supervisor said sternly, but as soon as the murmuring began, he raised his hand, and everyone fell silent. "I propose it be held in two months' time in preparation for the academic tournament."

"If I don't have to participate in your tournament, then I'm not against the idea," I said, shrugging.

"In that case, I declare that this man has insulted my honor, and for that I demand a duel," said the blond guy, getting up from his seat. "To first blood, naturally." He smirked in my direction. "As such, there's no need to wait for the start of the tournament — everything can be resolved here and now."

"An aristocrat challenging a commoner." I grinned. "I wonder what they'll say in tomorrow's papers. What if that only serves to enhance your honor?" I said, and I chuckled quietly for greater effect.

Come on, come on! A bit further and there'll be no stopping us.

"You are all witnesses!" The blond guy said, addressing his classmates more loudly this time. "Will you allow us to use one of the training areas?" He'd remembered his manners and asked the mentor's permission with a bow.

"Children," the teacher sighed wearily. "What's got into you all?!" He slid his palm over his face, but pronounced all the same: "Okay, but only in my presence and under my supervision, otherwise you might do something stupid."

Almost everyone in the auditorium broke into a smile — with some, one of malevolence, with others, one of anticipation. And for the rest, this was just a chance for some entertainment.

It wasn't, in fact, my intention to insult everyone there — I was telling the truth. A truth that not everyone brought up in a noble family can stomach. All I needed was to find one such quick-tempered fella. It was a good thing it wasn't that girl who'd come up with the idea, otherwise, if I'd ended up fighting her, it wouldn't have had quite the same effect.

Only Lena looked worried.

"What's all this about?" she asked quietly once everyone had gone off after the supervisor.

"Honor, dignity... take your pick," I replied. "But, in fact, in your group, where there are only aristocrats, a lot is decided by the right of might. It may not be your own personal power, but that of your family, but either way... this is a factor which the hierarchy in noble society is built upon and which changes how people are perceived." I paused for a while until the students walking in front of us were a bit further away. "We're commoners, and we don't have a powerful clan behind us. And, if that wasn't enough, I also exercised my right as a teacher, which must raise a lot of questions. Most people will think we cheated so that one enrolls and two get to study. So, I need to make it clear I'm not as easy a target as they think. Of course, there's the risk that afterward they'll want to make me their enemy number one, but that will also divert attention from you and let you just get on and study.”

“But what about you?” Lena asked.

“Hah, have a bit more faith in your teacher,” I said. “To be honest, I could do with a bout of sparring to stay in shape.”

I hadn’t really had many direct encounters with other magicians, but enough for me to come up with a few tactics. And that I’d be revealing my abilities — well, I’ve never really hidden them. Just that now they’d be there for all to see.

As Lena needed to talk to me, we found ourselves bringing up the rear, and as we entered the training area, the rest of the students had already taken their seats in the small stand and were now just waiting for us to appear. The guy who challenged me had already managed to change into an outfit reminiscent of medieval leather armor, but where, in keeping with the times, it was all made of magic fabric and leather. The result was a set of clothes that could already withstand quite a lot and protect the wearer from serious injury.

As far as I know, such kits are given to all students at the Academy and aren’t anything out of the ordinary. As for how much something like that would cost outside the Academy... No, my suit is definitely more expensive, since it’s designed primarily to hide its properties, but such kits for training well-heeled kids are a very expensive indulgence.

Also, this was the minimal, so-called “light” kit. There are more serious versions, but they’re intended for clan warriors and the special units of various agencies. A "heavy" kit, for example, can take an ordinary person with no gift to about the same level as a Senior Mage and enable them to engage in hand-to-hand combat with them. Not that anybody would, but to be able to withstand the attacks of a magician of that level and be able to get down to business with him — that doesn't come cheap.

"Get changed, Vetrov, and go out into the arena," said the teacher, pointing to another similar set of clothes.

"No need. I don't intend to get my suit dirty."

My opponent's eyes flashed aggressively at this, and he just about managed to hold back an angry outburst. Fine, the more he lost his cool and forgot what he was supposed to do — the more chance I'd have to get everything over with quickly, without it taking too much out of me.

"You're not my student, so I'm not responsible for your safety," the supervisor warned me, pointing out that whatever was about to happen wasn't his fault.

Well, I wasn't expecting anything else. After all, my status in the college was all rather ambiguous.

"I'm well aware of that," I replied, and putting my hands in my jacket pockets, I walked past him and onto the training area.

That part of the field was strewn with sand and enclosed on all sides by a protective dome, which not only prevented the spells of the fighters from getting outside, but was also strengthened by them, so the dome could withstand a lot, and overloading it... I'm afraid that would take the powers of top-ranking magicians (although there are always exceptions to the rule).

Moving a few steps away from the edge of the arena, I could feel the magic of the room working, strengthening the dome. Well, there was no going back now.

"No one likes upstarts here, you know," the blond guy suddenly took it upon himself to inform me. Well, that was only playing into my hands. "Especially when they're also commoners."

"Funny, that, because I don't like big-headed aristocrats," I said, grinning. "Want to chat a bit more or shall we just get on with it?"

The guy gave a malicious smile and waved his hand, whipping up a scythe made of wind that headed in my direction. So, your specialty is wind? Okay, fine.

I threw my hand forward, and a red cut ruby flew towards my opponent. Except it flew, God forbid, only a couple of meters — I'm not much good at throwing. But I didn't need to be. A small pulse of structured energy towards the stone — and everything around was obscured by dust, and you couldn't see what was happening inside the dome. I needed to hide a little what I'd just done and, to be honest, I wanted to do something flashy, and that should've looked spectacular.

Meanwhile, my opponent didn't lose his bearings and, using the power of the wind, cleared the area around him and enlarged it with the help of a miniature tornado that sucked up all the sand that had been scattered.

"You're dead," I said when he could finally see me.

"I'm not even hurt," he exclaimed.

"Turn around," I said, sighing heavily like I was trying to explain something to a child.

This contempt annoyed him even more, but he turned around all the same.

"Well, isn't he an idiot?" I asked loudly, addressing the audience, who didn't understand what was going on.

"You take me for a fool!"

"Well done, you finally worked it out." I clapped my hands sarcastically, which pushed him over the edge.

My opponent completely forgot he was a magician, and ran at me with clenched fists, although, to be fair, he wrapped them in air magic techniques which them look like improvised drills. Just as the distance between us was halved, something shot out of the sand and at the same time, the guy, even though he managed to shield himself from the blow, flew a few meters to the side.

Now the audience could see some kind of creature crawling out of the sand, something like a scorpion, but a very large scorpion with six pairs of eyes, which were now intently watching their prey.

To summon such a demon, I'd need a fairly large seal and a massive amount of energy, but fortunately I'd stuffed almost all my rubies to the max with energy, and it was difficult, but still possible, to introduce summoning circuits into them. How I did it, don't even ask because some would kill you to find out. One drawback of such a quick deployment of the seal was that the summoning still took time, so the sand turned out to be a very handy way of hiding the creature's appearance and making its stage entrance all the more impressive.

And it was this demon, by the way, that took the impact of the air scythe before hiding itself in the sand.

Getting up from the ground, the blond guy shook his head. He was no longer assessing the situation rashly and he set his sights on the creature I'd summoned, considering it to be much more of a threat. To some extent, he was right, but it was still going to be a shame to disappoint him.

The guy attacked the scorpion with astonishing zeal, performing one air magic move after another, forcing what was not a small creature (four meters from the head to the start of its tail) to recoil, and even throwing it aside. I don't know where this demon came from, but it kept rushing towards my opponent with amazing perseverance, not giving him a moment's respite.

I put my hand down to the side, and under it a glowing red seal began to appear on the ground. A couple of seconds later and it was complete. Out of it came the head of a dog, blazing with fire. No less than a fire hound, straight out of the books about demons. I remember this creature's appearance surprised me when I first managed to summon it — a fire hound like all the descriptions. And yet, it turned out to be surprisingly peace-loving and just loved being stroked.

This time, though, I wasn't going to be playing with it. Instead, I ordered it to go around my opponent's side. I didn't need to say it out loud since, thanks to an additional circuit in the seal, summoned creatures could not only receive a predetermined set of actions, but also hear commands directed at them, and if they wanted to get their energy, they had to execute them without question.

The hound tore forward and was behind the blond guy for a couple of seconds, then, with a yelp of joy that made the protective dome seem to quiver, it rushed at him.

The scorpion was pretty tired by this time and had expended all its energy, so I brought it back. My opponent could've used this opportunity to attack me, as air technicians, luckily for them, are quite fast operators, but, as I expected, he got distracted by the summoned demon. What I didn't expect, however, was that he would protect himself against the hound with an air sphere — they're usually used against heavy objects. It seems even the hound was confused when the tongue of flame it released towards him was drawn into the air sphere, instantly turning it into a fire sphere.

I had to save this idiot and order the demon to draw all the fire into itself, which wasn't a problem because fire was its native environment, and the demon could completely control its own flame, even if it'd been intensified by an alien technique.

I had to move from where I was standing, although I initially wanted to stay there to make the outcome of the battle look more theatrical, but this guy might have needed medical attention, and there was no point hoping someone else would provide it any quicker.

By the time I approached my opponent, the sphere of fire had gone out, and he himself was standing looking dazed in the middle of an area of burnt earth. He was gasping for breath, but the air around him was red-hot, and he started to cough incessantly.

"What was that? he asked, wheezing, eyes fixed on me.

"It was incorrect assessment of the enemy..." — I began to count on my fingers — "...incorrect use of air techniques and incorrect tactical decisions. So, basically, I'm the winner." I showed him three fingers.

"But I'm not wounded," he replied drowsily. He was still in shock.

"Christ," I said with a sigh. I mentally give the hound a command. It grinned and whipped the fella's leg with its spiked tail, leaving several long cuts on it. "Happy now?"

Just then, a signal sounded, and the energy to the protective dome was shut off. The rest of the group swarmed onto the arena, looking in astonishment at the fire hound, which started to disappear as I sent it back. To their credit, several guys went up to the blond one and started helping him.

One of the girls even went to the trouble of using healing techniques.

"I do hope there won't be any more questions for me now?" I asked cautiously, casting my eye over the group.

"Who are you?" asked the girl who was the first to be outraged when I answered the question from the group mentor.

"I'm her teacher." I pointed to Lena. At the time, she was standing on my left, looking as unshakable as a queen.

"Can I spar with you?" some guy asked.

"Yeah, me, too," rang out from the other side.

"I won't be sparring with anyone!" I said, exasperated.

"Do you have a girlfriend?" suddenly asked the girl standing to my right, looking at me with a twinkle in her eye.

Jeez, where have I ended up? And this is the future of the aristocracy, the flower of the nation? Such children!

CHAPTER 11

IT WAS A COMPLETE SURPRISE the group didn't keep their distance from me — on the contrary, everyone seemed to want to get to know me better. But most annoying of all were those who wanted a sparring match.

This flood of questions was interrupted only by the appearance of the group supervisor, who first of all made sure that everything was fine with the blond guy, and then gave me a thoughtful look.

"Vetrov, you may attend the group's classes," he said eventually. "I'll arrange all the necessary documents myself."

"Thank you."

As it turned out later, without the help of this man, whose name I didn't know, I'd have had to run around the Academy, collecting all the necessary signatures. After all, I wasn't a student, but I needed a pass to get in, since I didn't have a student card. And getting a pass... well, to do this I'd have had to fill out a whole stack of papers.

Meanwhile, we were all going back to the auditorium assigned to our group. For one reason or another, Lena and I were the main topic of conversation, and even the blond guy I defeated was trying to squeeze some details about my magic out of me. But I kept silent, and Lena played the ice queen to a tee, to the extent that even some of the guys next to her started to take on the appearance of shy little boys.

The first day at college had flown by and surrounded by the other girls, Lena went back to the dormitory, where she was allocated a separate room. I only just managed to warn my student not to let her guard down and get into conversation with these cunning foxes before they took her to one side and started whispering something. From the sneaky looks in my direction, it was obvious what they were talking about, but I couldn't do anything about that, nor was there any need. It was best Lena was accepted into the team, and revealing a "secret" about me was quite a good way of bonding with her classmates.

I, however, had to vacate the college grounds as my documents would only be ready the next morning.

I thought I'd be spending the evening quietly in my room, bickering with Serby as usual, but waiting for me when I got back was a very unexpected visitor.

* * *

"My dear nephew," someone I didn't expect to see there smiled warmly at me. "You have no idea how surprised I was when I heard you were in Moscow."

A beautiful woman of about forty was standing at the door to my room, smiling at me like we'd only seen each other recently. Her tight-fitting dress and overall appearance would make most men want her, but her charms didn't work on me, and she wasn't attempting to exploit them. Anyone witnessing all this would be very surprised at how I could react to such cordiality with so severe an expression.

My visitor was Katrina Voronova, my aunt, a member of the senior branch of the family. Katrina wasn't her real name. My aunt, so they say, was difficult in her youth, and to spite her parents went from being ordinary Catherine to Katrina — in the Western style. Apparently, a serious scandal even resulted from this, but they didn't change anything, and only the members of the Voronov family really know what happened.

"Mrs. Voronova." I said, addressing her formally, "I thought we straightened everything out last time?"

Whatever my attitude towards this woman, I didn't forget my manners and invited her into the living room, quickly arranging some tea and snacks, which thankfully just required a call downstairs.

"Come now, Gregushka," she said, smiling sweetly. To be fair, she wasn't using the form of my name I hate the most on purpose. "That was so long ago. You were young and didn't really understand everything."

"Huh, from where I'm standing you told me in no uncertain terms that you didn't need 'weaklings' in your family. And that you offered me a place with the family if I shared all my grandfather's discoveries, which, as I understand it, you couldn't find?

"Nephew, dear, you got it all wrong. You must've misunderstood me," Katrina said and began to laugh. "Anyway, you're completely different, now. You're so grown up."

"Interesting, and how did you know I was here?" I asked, ignoring what she'd said.

"Oh, quite easy," she said, waving her hand. "Your second cousin is in the third year at the Academy — you've probably never seen him. But he realized straight away who you are and told me you were there."

"Is that so?" I folded my arms. "Let's say it really is my cousin, although I don't actually know all the members of the family. But it's not like I went into hiding, so, out with it, why the interest in me, almost four years after we last spoke?"

"Am I not allowed to want to see my nephew?" Katrina looked at me resentfully.

"Drop it, Aunt. You never gave a damn about me. At first, I thought when you saw what I could do without any support from the family you'd welcome me back, but your attitude towards me destroyed my last childhood hope. It wasn't me you wanted, it was my family's secrets, all along."

"Which belong to us," Katrina said firmly with a smile on her lips. "The junior branch is the junior branch and is supposed to support the main family. That's how it was, is, and always will be. The last time we met, you showed yourself to be an enterprising young man, able to start your own business without any capital, but this is of no interest to us. We have a hundred servants who are much better than you in that regard." My aunt wasn't concealing the crux of the matter from me. "So, yes, dear nephew, you became of interest to the family again after showing what you're capable of."

"I didn't really go out of my way to hide it," I said, shrugging.

"I admit that," Katrina said, bowing her head slightly. "Those who reported on you have already been punished for their oversight. In their defense, however, it's worth pointing out that while you didn't hide your abilities, no one could really say that much about them."

"I'm just modest," I said, grinning, watching my aunt's movements closely.

An ice mage of junior rank can do a lot of damage at short distance. I didn't really think she was about to take more decisive action. However, the conversation was going in a completely different direction, so it was better to be safe than sorry.

"And brazen," my aunt didn't neglect to add. "And I almost believed you when you convinced me you didn't know anything about your grandfather's findings."

"You may not believe it, but I don't know anything."

"You're right," she sighed. "I don't believe you, so best of all would be for you to bring us all the surviving records of your grandfather's research as soon as possible."

"Hah, sorry, but I can't. They were all burned in the fire. You know, the one that killed my family."

"Well, in that case, I'll have to take you away and work out how to repeat the experiment they carried out on you," Katrina said coldly. At the same time, it felt like the temperature in the room had gone down by ten degrees and was still dropping. "Dearest nephew, it would be better if you came with me willingly".

"And if not?" I asked, eyes narrowed. I wasn't disconcerted by this threat at all.

"No matter how strong you've become over this time, you can't outmatch me," my aunt said contemptuously, as she rose gracefully from the sofa.

"Oh, I know that perfectly well," I said and smiled at her for the first time that evening.

"Then will you be a sensible boy and come with me?" she asked, although she made it sound more like an assertion.

"No." I shook my head.

"Oh, well, I'll have to get tough, then." She raised her hand and started to perform a technique of some sort.

"I wouldn't be in such a hurry," I warned her, staying exactly where I was. I picked up my cup of tea theatrically and took a sip. I immediately regretted it, however. "God, I hate cold tea."

"Don't test my patience," my aunt said. Out of nowhere, she created an icicle almost half a meter long. That, and what she was saying, and things were looking dicey already.

"You were absolutely right — I might not outmatch you, but you asked for it." I smirked and clicked my fingers. In response, magic seals lit up on the floor, ceiling and walls of the living room, and began to move around in a captivating dance of lines and symbols. "And I've prepared in advance for visits like these."

"What's all this?" Katrina asked, looking around warily.

"This, dear aunt, is what you so wanted to see." With these words, out of the seals shot chains made of energy which wrapped themselves around her arms.

She didn't have time to react and found herself suspended by her outstretched arms, unable to break free. The icicle she'd created with her magic fell as expected, smashing the glass table with the tea and cookies on it.

"You're so going to pay me the cost of cleaning this room." I shook my head as I watched the already cold tea seeping across the fluffy carpet. "I wouldn't try moving again, or the chains will pull even tighter," I warned her.

"Let me go, boy!" Katrina said venomously, finally showing her true colors.

"And it was all 'nephew' this and 'nephew' that," I said, laughing.

"Let me go," my aunt said once again, more calmly after she'd been hanging there for about a minute.

"Okay." I smiled at her, and with a gesture the chains went back into the seal. "Just don't do anything stupid." I wagged my finger at her. "The chains can come back any moment."

"What kind of magic is this?" Katrina asked, rubbing her wrists. It was clear she wasn't about to sit down again.

"Would you believe me if I told you it was something I developed myself?" I said, grinning. "Of course you wouldn't," I second-guessed her. "It doesn't matter. The main thing is you came to the decision that I'm no longer one of your family a long time ago, even as a member of the junior branch. So, please don't take it the wrong way if I don't tell you anything."

"You do realize you can't resist us?" my aunt asked, looking at me in a very strange way.

"Oh, don't worry," I said with a wave of the hand. "I'm well aware of my strengths and capabilities. Better believe me this time." I paused for a moment. "I really wouldn't make me angry. On this occasion, we can part on good terms. I haven't held a grudge against you for a long time, because to some extent," taking in the room with my hand I continued: "All this I owe to you not helping me. If I hadn't been in such a deplorable situation then, who knows where I'd be now?"

"Just words."

"The words of someone you used to consider a 'weakling'. If that turned out not to be true, who knows what else you can expect from me?"

Now I was really interested in what my aunt would do.

"Okay." Katrina looked pensive and sat down opposite me. "Perhaps I was mistaken about you, but what's done is done and there's no going back. And it'll look stupid if I suddenly go back on my decision to banish you from the family."

"I'm not coming back."

"I also heard you provide services for money or in exchange for similar services. Is that true?" she asked unexpectedly.

"It is," I replied cautiously, not knowing what she was driving at.

"And if I offer you money for your grandfather's work?" my aunt asked bluntly.

"Why are you bringing all this up again?" I frowned. "I don't have any information about my grandfather's work. It was basically a miracle I survived his last experiment."

"His successful experiment," Katrina added.

"Relatively," I agreed reluctantly. "Are we going to keep on and on about the same thing or..." I waved my hand in a vague way, giving my aunt the chance to continue.

"Or I can offer you a return to the family," she said, testing the water.

"I'm not interested," I replied straight away.

"I've already had enough of talking to you, aunt. I have no desire to return to the clan that exiled me, or, basically, do any business with you. I don't need money or help from you, but if you need my services, hah, we can go over some of the payment options," I said, hinting they wouldn't come cheap.

"Don't bury your head in the sand, nephew, dearest," Katrina said coldly once more. "Maybe you really have become more powerful since our last meeting, but you are a commoner, and you have no family behind you."

"Don't threaten me," I answered in the same tone. "I've not been the person you knew then for a long time, and I'll counter any threat a hundred times over. Let's just forget either of us exists, and things won't get ruined for you," I said, emphasizing the last word.

"Just like your grandfather," my aunt said unexpectedly. "An arrogant type with an unbearable character."

"Well, I didn't take after my father," I said, recalling his weak character, which was partly responsible for our family's downfall. "Let's pick up where we left off," I said, nodding towards the seals. "Otherwise, we won't get to wreck the place."

"You really are sure of yourself." Katrina looked at me strangely. "Either you're too self-confident, or you really hope to wriggle out of this."

"Want to find out?" I gave her a provocative look.

"Perhaps not," she replied a few seconds later. "You surprised me and so be it, we won't argue any more today. Just don't forget the family is still interested in your grandfather's research."

"Ask him, then. However much I 'theoretically', — I emphasized the last word, — might want to annoy you, I don't have the records of my grandfather's last experiment. And, as you mentioned, he wasn't the most warmhearted soul, and he didn't really share his thoughts with my father, let alone with me."

"Very funny." Katrina gave a dry laugh. "Your grandfather's been dead for some time."

"Sure about that?" I asked. "I never actually found his body."

"You mean..." she said in a hushed tone. I could see the cogs whirring in her head. "Why not? It's possible... He always was a wily bastard."

At these words, my aunt jumped up from her seat, and, muttering something along the lines of a farewell, she bounded out of the room. That's how she upped and left — completely possessed of the idea that my grandfather could've faked everything.

"Great," I said with satisfaction. "You've earned another reward." I turned to the small spirit that was barely visible against the background of the active seals.

The spirit had been carefully influencing my aunt's mind all that time, nudging her towards making the decision I needed her to, otherwise, I'm afraid, she wouldn't have believed me so easily. And so, the summoned creature had fulfilled all the terms of its contract.

I was very lucky I'd been able to summon it the other day, as I'd only managed to find a creature like that a couple of times before. Another thing that worked in my favor was my aunt herself must've been considering this a possibility, otherwise, to change her mind, the spirit would've had to be much more forceful with her, which it simply wasn't capable of.

And to be honest, it was a downright bluff. My grandfather's body wasn't found, since it was difficult to make out any people among the rest of the debris. There were grounds for the reputation he'd earned among our relatives, which is one reason why I went looking for him for two years, not to mention my aunt's interest in obtaining the documents on our family patriarch's final experiment. It was a pity they really didn't survive the fire — if they had, I can't even imagine the price I'd be able to put on them.

There was something else that interested me more — how did my aunt find out about my grandfather's research when my family kept quiet about me having so little of the gift that I could quite easily be considered bereft of it? For so many years, no matter how hard I tried, I couldn't find an answer to this. I can, of course, use my gift to summon the spirits of deceased people, but only those with quite strong personalities who something kept here. And the outcome of all my efforts was I only managed to summon those who were long-dead — the rest for some reason were deaf to my magic. So, I couldn't ask my grandfather directly what he did that day, and whether the destruction of the entire family was worth it.

There were too many unfathomable things about my family, which I didn't notice then because of my age and which it was too late to find out about now.

So, I had a few weeks or months before my aunt gave up trying to find my grandfather and showed up here again. And however well-prepared I might be, I can't stand up to a whole clan. I had a lot of debtors, of course, but no one would defend me without getting something hefty in return, and I wasn't prepared to go there. It seemed that, however much I didn't want to, I would end up having to engage with my relatives.

If they really wanted to get me, then there wouldn't be any polite chit-chat — I'd just be rounded up by one of the clan's combat groups and delivered to the patriarch. And no one would say anything to them about it because I'm a former member of the family, which means some details about me could've surfaced years later which justified such a use of force. I still liked to hope that, despite their rather disdainful attitude towards the junior branch, they wouldn't stain themselves with the blood of their own family. And I'd make sure that in the worst-case scenario the Voronovs would suffer considerably.

My aunt's visit only brought my plan forward, so I got to work a little earlier than I was going to. Right up until morning, all I did was create one summoning seal after another, making agreements with various demons, which would not only allow me to call them faster, if necessary, but also tell me how to respond in a given situation. Admittedly, I always had several contracts on the back burner, but I was by no means going over the top with these new ones.

In the end, I'd had no sleep, had almost no energy left, and was standing in the kitchen drinking a strong cup of coffee.

"Just try it," I warned Serby, who'd condescended to join me at breakfast, and was clearly itching to say something cutting.

For the long duration of our contract, the demon had already learned when it was best not to cross me, so I didn't hear a peep out of him. Or maybe he was more interested in the sliced ham in his bowl? Whatever.

The alarm clock on my phone sounded, telling me it was time to get moving, and so I ruefully took the last sip of my invigorating drink, and headed downstairs. Twenty minutes — and there I was at the gates to the Academy.

At the entrance there was a kind of checkpoint from which a gray-haired old man came out, heading towards me with a faint smile. He may have looked completely defenseless, but as far as I knew, this "gatekeeper" was Klim Bukreev himself — veteran of several minor military conflicts (if you consider any of those in Africa to be minor) earth mage, and one of the few commoners who'd made it to the rank of Master. To some extent, this job was a decent pension for him, since he couldn't fight after several serious injuries, yet it was hard to think of a better line of defense than him, with his ability to erect stone walls and create golems in almost the blink of an eye.

"Good morning." I nodded to him, handing over my documents. "I believe a pass and all the associated documents have been made up for me."

"Vetrov?" Bukreev asked after checking the documents. "Heard about you. How did you manage to impress Khodkevich? It's the first time I've seen him advocate a student like that."

"Khodkevich?" I looked at him in surprise.

"Yeah," the old man said. "The supervisor of your group, Arkady Khodkevich. All the documents are signed by him. You've not forgotten what the supervisor's called?" He squinted at me. "At least try to remember before the exams, otherwise you'll be out on your ear."

"Ah, I'm not a student," I said.

"What, then?" Bukreev frowned.

"I'm the teacher of one of your freshmen," I explained to him.

"That can happen?"

"Old law. Tradition," I replied briefly.

"Well, that figures. There's always been a strong belief in tradition among the aristos," the old man mused.

"It doesn't always do them good, but that's for another time." I smiled slightly.

"For sure, for sure." Bukreev grinned and then looked at me with interest. "And you, I see, recognized me?"

"How could you not recognize a mercenary with the call sign 'Golem.'" I threw out my hands. "No rumors about you among the commoners, of course."

While I had no particular interest in such issues, personalities like Bukreev were widely known, thanks to their origin. They kind of showed others that you can achieve a lot with hard work and perseverance. True, in such stories they forget that the gifted among the aristocrats are much more powerful than a commoner whose gift suddenly awoke one day, and most often the naturals among commoners are the bastard children of some ancient family, which is why their gift is so strong.

"But most of the kids don't even suspect that I am a strong gifted, and more," the old man said, giving me a sly look. "So, you're not a student, you say?" he asked again, and I nodded. "That means the student rules don't apply to you, so I'll have someone to talk to of a night," he said. "You'll keep an old war veteran company, won't you?

"It'd be an honor," I replied. "On one condition — you tell me the truth about your adventures."

"What, not a fan of tall tales, then?"

"You can hear tales in any bar, but the unembellished stories of a famous mercenary can be a wonderful transfer of experience to the younger generation, so it doesn't screw up out of ignorance," I said with a chuckle.

"Are you off to the Free Lands, then?" Bukreev asked with interest.

"Not now," I answered honestly. "But who knows what the future may hold."

"Fine approach," the old man said, nodding and stroking his chin. "So, come down. It's been a long time since I reminisced about the old days."

"You can count on it," I promised, and I took my documents.

The old man opened the gate, and I rode into the grounds, heading to the parking lot, some distance from the main driveway of the Academy which covered quite a large area.

To be honest, I was still a bit shaken after talking to him. It might've looked like we were just having a nice chat, but his request was more like an order, and resisting someone who could literally bury you alive isn't the best way to go. Passing through this gate every day were aristocrats who may have been too arrogant to realize they'd offended the old man. I'm afraid even to imagine what would happen if you rubbed this veteran of magic battles up the wrong way.

I'd definitely have to pick up a nicer than usual bottle to help him remember the "old days" and mellow out a bit. I tasked Misha with this by phone message — he knows drinks better than anyone and he'd be able to find something that fit the bill.

I left the chopper in the parking lot and walked towards the main building. Given the time, everyone should've been in the middles of classes, but the Academy was far from deserted. Students and academy staff scurried through the rooms and corridors, paying me no heed, which was fine by me.

That day I was on my way to the library, which occupied almost five floors at the far end of the right wing and contained both ordinary textbooks and priceless volumes. I wouldn't have access to the latter, for obvious reasons, but even so, there should still have been some rare editions not otherwise available, and I've already mentioned the black market. It'd be easier to sneak in here than blow a fortune on books that could prove to be useless.

The library was surprisingly deserted. The entrance was on the first floor, and was itself a reading room, so you could say you could see all the book lovers from the door. Out of over three hundred seats, only a dozen or so were occupied by students bent over their hefty tomes. Most likely this was down to it only being the beginning of the school year, and the freshmen didn't need any books yet.

"Good morning," A man with glasses sidled up to me. "I'm the library archivist," he said by way of an introduction. He was probably about forty. He was wearing a gray tuxedo and looked more like a butler than a librarian. It was only his long blonde hair pulled back into a ponytail that shattered the overall image. "You can come to me with any questions. And just call me the Archivist," the man said with a smile. "Most of the students have difficulty remembering my name properly."

"Thank you," I replied. "I'm interested in books on old magic, ritualism, and the magic of signs and symbols."

"Are you studying the history of magic?" he wanted to know. "Commendable interest, but I'm afraid most of the books on this subject are on the fourth floor, and access is only with the permission of your group supervisor, signed off by the rector. If you don't have that with you, then I can't take you up there," he said apologetically.

"No problem. For this first time, the books on open display will be more than enough."

"In that case, it's this way." He pointed off to the right, and I followed him. Eventually we arrived at a small cubbyhole with a dozen computers towering along the wall. "All books that are open access are in our database. We improve and add to it every year, so you can search for key phrases, and a list of books and their location will be displayed," the Archivist explained. "And I must warn you now — it is prohibited to take any books away. Forgetting could get you expelled," he concluded sternly.

"Understood. Thank you."

The Archivist looked at me deep in thought for a couple of seconds, and then turned around and disappeared. I sat down at the nearest computer and began to get to grips with its interface.

There wasn't, however, much to get to grips with. There was only one input line on the whole screen for entering text with a touchpad. The best thing, of course, would be to find books on demonology and occult sciences, but they'd definitely be in a restricted section, and I'd have to figure out how to get in there. Meanwhile, I could make do with more accessible manuscripts, which, quite possibly, could give me a clue as to what to look for next.

From outside, it might have appeared I was essentially spending my life doing everything for Lena. But the reality was slightly different. Yes, I saved the girl and was partly to blame for her condition, as I could've checked on her straight away and possibly have prevented what happened to her gift. Yes, I'd already managed to become attached to her and consider her one of my own, which meant I wouldn't give up, but the start of it all was our teacher-student relationship.

Magic connections in general aren't that common, but one established by a demon was completely out of the ordinary. I tried to study it using my sketchy abilities, but there was that much to it that... Well, touch even a small part of this connection — and it could backfire so badly for both of us that it was better not to attempt it.

It was precisely to deal with this that I needed all those books. And where else would you find such specialist literature but the Academy of Magic? There are, of course, colleges abroad, but getting there for a Russian is even harder than getting in here.

There was too much to this magic connection for me not to fear for my life. The issue becomes especially acute when you consider it was created by a demon unlikely to harbor any warm feelings towards me. Like a time bomb that could explode any moment.

So, it was only the desire to stay alive that'd brought me here, otherwise I'd never have run the risk of turning up here, flaunting my abilities and basically shining in front of my ex-relatives. All this was not like me at all, but I couldn't see any other way of achieving what I needed to.

As I was contemplating all this, I slowly picked five books from the main list that best suited my requirements. I'd need to look at the rest, but those would definitely be enough to be going on with, as almost every book was a rather large volume of a thousand-plus pages. A quick look would let me know if there was anything worthwhile in them or not and inform my further choices.

The library itself was quite hi-tech. For example, I could print out the selected list of books or send it to my phone, which is what I did. The books were on different floors and sections, so I had to wander around the library finding them. Fortunately, there were signs everywhere, and terminals dotted around the place, which not only helped to find the right book, but also showed a floor plan with a route to the relevant section.

The sections were divided not only by subject, but also by the age of the books. Also, each section was enclosed in transparent plastic and kept at certain temperature. If you ask me, with all the trouble they'd gone to over the equipment, it would've been easier to convert all the books into electronic ones, but, clearly, reading the primary source in its original form was a strong tradition at the Academy. It was also good that all new editions were provided both in printed and electronic format, but even the electronic ones could only be read inside the library.

Half an hour later, I was sitting at a table in a corner of this peculiar labyrinth, which I'd chosen straight away because it was quite far from both the elevator (yes, there was one here, too) and the stairs, which cut down the number of people who would see me. A comfortable chair and a window were just the icing on the cake.

Unfortunately, these were reprints of much more detailed books that you could bet were in the restricted section and, even with my knowledge, I could see they'd been written by light, if you can call them, magicians.

It wasn't that dark magic was forbidden or restricted at all, it was just more complicated and much more dangerous than any so-called light magic. Even mind-bendingly complex healing spells couldn't do anyone much harm, and any mistake could be put right. But try to correct a curse that's been eating a person alive for years. So, they didn't like black magic, and, because of this, it remained the preserve of individuals and small groups. Just try to find a really good book on dark magic, when there weren't many of these magicians around compared with the other ones.

In fairness, of course, it's worth pointing out that ritualism and runic magic are "colorless", that is, they were once used by everyone, so there was comparatively more material on these disciplines, but too much was lost after the last Magic War.

So, you could only hope the old books had survived, and develop your own methods, which is what, for my part, I was doing. Another reason was that with my gift being unusual, rituals from the books sometimes reacted unpredictably to it. A headache, but not a hopeless situation.

I sat alone, it felt like, until lunchtime, when I was interrupted just as I was onto my second book. I'd felt an unobtrusive magical presence just before then, so it wasn't hard to work out who was searching for me like that.

"I thought as you've been in here since morning, you must be hungry," Lena said, smiling sweetly as she put a few containers wrapped in foil down on the table in front of me.

"Won't the Archivist make a fuss?" I put my book aside, ripping the foil from the one nearest.

"The strange man who looks like a butler?" she asked.

"You thought that, too. Mm." I bit into a sandwich with sausage on it. I was immediately presented with a thermos which, judging by the smell, had tea in it.

"Uh-huh. He warned me right away that you can eat here, but if you get anything on the books..." Lena shuddered. "He said it in such a creepy way — all I could do was nod like a dummy and agree."

"Ignore him," I said, reassuring her, and I took a sip from the thermos. "I reckon the staff at this Academy are a right bunch. I wouldn't be surprised if this Archivist," — I made quotation marks in the air — is actually some retired mercenary and murderer, or someone who's decided to go straight."

"You think?"

"Hah, anything's possible." I'd finished the sandwich by then, so I moved on to the next one.

"Find anything interesting?" Lena asked, looking with curiosity at the books laid out on the table.

"Unfortunately, nothing so far," I replied, sighing. "But two books mention a primary source, which, most likely, can provide answers about my magic connection with you."

I'd told my student a long time ago how dangerous the magic that bound us could be, but to my surprise she wasn't afraid at all, and just doubled down on what I could give her. I had to push myself by comparison.

"How are the classes, by the way?"

"Nothing special so far, but my classmates are already starting to get bored with all the questions about you," Lena said, narrowing her eyes mischievously. "The girls, especially."

"Don't try to distract me," I frowned demonstratively. "Better find out just who your supervisor is and why his signature is enough to let me enter the Academy without any obstacles."

"Could they have not let you in?"

"Not really," I explained. "But they could've dragged it all out for quite a long time. Basically, I thought I'd be here in a month at the earliest, but it seems not."

"Okay. I'll try to find out, but..." Lena looked at me craftily. "I'll have to tell them something about you to get that information."

"As long as it's nothing important," I said, dismissing this as insignificant.

How wrong I was.

CHAPTER 12

I HAD TO LEAVE THE LIBRARY earlier than planned because of the promise I'd made to the Academy's gatekeeper. The good thing was that Misha had dealt well with his task and sent me several choices of suitable bottles, and even attached a list of the nearest places where I could buy them. Interestingly, almost all these places were literally a ten-minute walk away.

Slipping out with the others leaving the grounds, and without catching the eye of Golem, was a piece of cake as the old man was distracted at that moment by some boneheads who'd decided to have it out elsewhere other than the training ground. It seemed that as well as manning the gate, Klim Bukreev also kept order in the surrounding area.

I decided, out of all those on offer, to go for a store which didn't sell the usual brands, but what you'd call moonshine, except it was high-quality moonshine that had been properly matured. I remember one of my customers wanting to pay me with a crate of something similar, but I preferred money at the time. But, when I told him what I'd been offered, Misha cursed for quite some time as the bar could've made a lot more from it. Since then, I try to consult with him on such matters whenever possible.

Having bought the necessary, I didn't turn down the pack of snacks to go with that bottle. The man behind the counter smirked as he gave me the black opaque bag (it seems he took me for another student). It was just what I needed so that Bukreev didn't see straight away what was inside.

Thanks to this, I didn't raise any questions from the gatekeeper and could just go back to the library and finish reading the remaining books. Unfortunately, while there were some interesting points in all these books, which I'd definitely adapt for my seals later, there was nothing substantial in them. As I already told Lena, all the books made references to much more ancient primary sources, but any query on the library computers returned an error as if they weren't there. All I could hope was that they were there in the restricted section, but it seemed nobody was going to tell if that was the case.

All I had to do was figure out how to obtain permission to access the fourth floor or get in without it. Either way, I'd have to work hard for it, and at that point, unfortunately, I didn't even know which of the two options was the easiest and, critically, the quickest.

Looking out of the window with surprise, I realized it was already late in the evening, which meant that it was time to go.

"And there was me thinking I'd have to sit here on my own," the old man muttered as I approached his kiosk or whatever you call the place he inhabited.

"But I want to talk to you," I said, shrugging. "How could I pass up such an opportunity?"

"And I see you've come prepared." Bukreev was alluding to the package in my hands, which made an unmistakable clinking sound as I carried it.

"Goes without saying," I muttered back to him.

"In that case, let's go to my cubbyhole and get settled in," the old man suggested. There was nothing for it but to follow him.

What Bukreev called a cubbyhole turned out to be living quarters attached to a warehouse where all the household stuff was stored. As the old man explained, he asked the Academy to build this room, since he had nowhere else to go, and this way he could be on site all the time with little chance of any students dropping by unexpectedly. So, it turned out to be quite a quiet little spot.

His place was furnished quite austerely. A couple of wardrobes, a bed and a small kitchen with an oak table, and a TV on the wall. But what stuck out most of all was the gun cabinet with transparent doors and a combination lock. It housed the entire kit necessary for urban combat.

"Are you about to go off and fight?" I couldn't resist the question.

"If you want to hear my stories, remember the golden rule," the old man replied, putting my offering down on the table. "No matter how strong a gifted is, he can still run out of magic energy, and then only his combat skills give him any chance of survival. That's why it's so important to practice martial arts and, if you can't do proper weapons training, at least go to the shooting range. And most important of all — they've never found a single magician who can't be taken by a bullet."

"Well, what about, for example, stone armor using earth magic?"

"Yes, with that technique, you can hold out longer than in military kit, but you can just throw grenades at a gifted. That's why, although magicians are more powerful than commoners, they went the way of politics, not war. Otherwise, I'm afraid, they'd simply have been exterminated."

"Well, yeah. The Inquisition of the Middle Ages is a graphic illustration of how one gifted can't stand up to the mob. They only caught weak loners, but still."

"That's why Africa is such a hotbed," Bukreev said with a frown.

"So, what exactly is going on there? They report such horror stories in the news sometimes, they're hard to believe," I asked, tearing open the packets of snacks and putting them on the table.

The old man, meanwhile, took out two glasses from the cupboard and poured a little into the bottom of them from the anonymous-looking bottle I'd brought. One of the gimmicks of the store where I'd bought it.

"To the fallen." Bukreev picked up his drink with a stony face and knocked it back. I quickly did the same and promptly grimaced — it felt like I'd drunk burning liquid and everything inside me was on fire. "Where did you get hold of this?" The old man looked at me in surprise.

"There are places," I replied mysteriously.

"It really reminds me of the stuff we used to make with the fruit there on our campaign in Africa." Bukreev rolled his eyes dreamily. "Those were the days. Oh, yeah." He looked at me and smiled. "I have to say you've really surprised me."

I just chuckled contentedly. I'd have to show Misha my appreciation for the tip.

Carrying on as we'd started, we'd completely emptied the bottle in a couple of minutes, and Bukreev just heaved a heavy sigh and fetched a much bigger container from the cupboard. All I could do was to mentally pray I'd be able to take such a huge amount of alcohol. After a while, Bukreev started reminiscing so much that he stopped checking how much to pour into my glass, and just filled it to the brim, so I didn't have to keep drinking it all in one go.

Over the course of that night, Bukreev told me so much about the situation in Africa, I was just amazed. Everything was presented in a completely different way in the media and, as it turned out, a lot simply wasn't covered at all.

It's not for no reason that Africa is described as the cradle of humanity. It's also the place most saturated with magic energy. It was there, after the currents of magic returned, that the real devilry began.

Whole cities appeared and disappeared there — places where you could see the people who'd lived there in different eras, people who'd vanished from the face of the earth forever. They'd have been like ghost towns, if the inhabitants hadn't been quite real and able to interact with the locals. The "lifetime" of such cities varied, and it was never possible to predict when they'd disappear again. Anyone who stayed in the ghost town disappeared along with it. So, the first research parties perished until they worked out ways of dealing with these cities and stuck to the basic rule — don't stay there overnight because by dawn it could've melted away like the morning mist.

Also, in southern Africa they discovered ancient necropolises which, according to all the historical chronicles (by which I mean our chronicles, which were much more detailed than those known to mankind) simply couldn't be there. No one knows exactly what happened, but the official version is one of the locals decided to try and profit from the ancient buildings that appeared, hoping to find treasure. What exactly they did, no one knows, but the next day all those buried there woke up from their eternal sleep and exterminated practically everyone in the surrounding area — only the rapid deployment of combined forces was able to keep the necropolises within certain boundaries and prevent them from swallowing everything up.

As if this wasn't enough, the Egyptian pyramids awoke and, with the help of ancient magic, not only brought the pharaohs back to life, but also the surrounding desert. There's now so much greenery around the pyramids, you'd never suspect it was mostly sand before. And another conflict arose. With the help of the priests who'd returned to life, wielding their own brand of magic, the pharaohs went and expelled from their lands anyone who didn't want to serve them. Since then, the Egyptian government has spoken at almost every summit about the infringement of its rights and has requested troops be sent to destroy the pharaohs, but no one wanted to sacrifice people by coming to their defense.

So, the area was in turmoil, with them having to redraw the borders of the Egyptian states almost every year. And the old man told me about the places he visited, and from what he said, much stranger things were happening there.

Although he described certain operations in quite a lot of detail, Bukreev omitted any specifics from his stories, so you couldn't tell where and when they took place. Apparently, all mercenary units sign a non-disclosure agreement, and even though he was now retired, he couldn't name the actual places or the names of the people he worked for.

But none of that mattered. I can say I listened

to the adventures of this famous mercenary with childlike enthusiasm, and at the same time I tried to commit everything he told me to memory. I understood that, not being the unit commander, he couldn't share strategies for fighting in different conditions, but he repeatedly encountered other gifted ones, so I asked him to tell me more about that.

Sure, all this was related in the words and through the perception of someone who was, let's say, not quite magically educated, but the gifted mostly use the same techniques, as they are quite common and easy to use. Hearing how magicians begin a fight, from someone who confronted them, was of no little importance, and in different circumstances, would be worth a lot of money.

* * *

Morning greeted me with a massive headache and the total mystery of how I ended up back in my hotel room. Flopping out of bed, I crawled to the minibar and was relieved to take a glug of chilled mineral water, which did very little to quench my thirst, but did enough for me to collect my thoughts a little at least. This helped me make it to the bathroom.

Half an hour later, I finally got out of the shower with only a mild migraine in comparison. At least the room was no longer floating before my eyes — so that was something.

"Oh, you finally woke up," Serby said as soon

as I entered the living room and, being the plague that he is, he rounded it off by barking, which started off the humming in my head again.

"Shut up!" I gave a muffled cry and headed for the refrigerator, where I remembered there was more mineral water, as well as plain cold water.

"You shouldn't drink so much," the spitz continued more quietly. "I can smell the fumes from here."

"How did I even get here?" it took me a huge effort to say.

"You made it back by yourself," Serby snorted. "You were also shouting incoherently until you fell into bed."

"Our nocturnal get-together obviously went well." I laughed hoarsely and winced from a shooting pain in my head.

"I hope it was worth it!"

"Definitely." I nodded carefully, not wanting to cause another bout of pain. "The stories from a man with more than a hundred successful encounters with the gifted... Not everyone will tell you such things, least of all in such detail."

"What good are stories without real experience of combat," Serby scoffed.

"Sure, but thanks to what he passed on to me, I'll be able to work out my enemy's next move, meaning I'll be able to react in time. My magic isn't really made for one-on-one combat, anyway." I finally found the mineral water and clamped myself to the neck of the bottle. "Phew, that's better."

"People are strange." The dog shook his head.

"Voluntarily poison yourself... And you consider that recreation."

"Hah, better eight hundred and thirty imperial rubles than a few tens of thousands."

"You use money as the yardstick for everything."

"Hmm, but it is the yardstick for everything. In our world, you can get almost anything you want with money."

No longer paying attention to the dog, I opened the freezer and threw some ice into an empty bottle, then applied it to my head.

It was already way too late to go to the Academy, and I was in no fit state to sit poring over dusty tomes. The best thing I could do was to get myself together and finally do the rounds of the capital's hotspots. I mean, I hadn't had any fun for a long time as I'd been too busy with work or research.

I took another cold shower, shaved, and generally made myself presentable. As I walked past my bed, I caught sight of my phone lying there. When I unlocked it, I saw a dozen messages from unknown numbers and a couple from Lena apologizing. To get some information on the group supervisor, she had to tell a little about me and give my phone number to a couple of girls. Only there were messages from far more than two numbers. Yet another problem to deal with.

I'd have to discuss this with Lena later, but then I was more interested in the file thrown together on Arkady Khodkevich. At first, there was nothing in his biography that stood out — he was an ordinary nobleman, like many others from the far reaches of the empire, who no one had ever heard about. All that set him apart was he had a strong thirst for knowledge and no fear of experimentation.

The young aristocrat somehow ended up in Egypt and managed to get out alive, even though most of the magicians in the kingdom of the pharaohs perished. He also entered one of the ghost towns and got out literally at the last minute. There were several similar events in his biography, but the main thing was Arkady was the first person in years to succeed in negotiating with those who'd previously annihilated anyone with the gift, and he also managed to bring with him invaluable knowledge of their life and culture.

As a result, a couple of years later, Khodkevich successfully defended several works on the magic of Egyptian priests, especially on the emergence of the ghost towns. He believed studying all this was better than constant aggression, which only evoked the obvious response. He built his argument not only on words, but also on the techniques he learned from the priests and the ghost towns' residents.

It was evident from all his works that the supervisor of Lena's group believes it's only by studying all the African anomalies that we'll be able to take magical science further than ever before. Unfortunately, his approach had many detractors, but despite this, Arkady was still the biggest expert in this narrow field, and he was often turned to when difficult situations arose. Thanks to this, he carried a certain weight among magicians and had gained the reputation of being an adventurer.

It shouldn't be forgotten that he was assigned to lead the top group in the year, which showed he really was in good standing at the Academy.

I wondered how he managed to learn from priests who pretty much looked upon sorcerers as the enemies of their gods. Such a valuable employee would really be listened to, and his requests wouldn't be ignored. There you go, a black magician is a black magician, however engrossed he is in studying the cultures of other peoples.

I have to say I was surprised when I read that Khodkevich is not only a Master, but also a specialist in curses, which, combined with other techniques, is truly lethal. It's hard to protect yourself from something when you don't have the first idea how. But he seemed to me to be a rather quiet and reserved person. Which meant — his appearance was deceptive.

While I was reading the file, I got several more messages on my phone from people I didn't know wanting to meet up, so I just turned it off, got changed, and went out to paint the town red.

* * *

Waking up this time was way more enjoyable. Well, how can it not be when snuffling next to you are two raven-haired vixens, who only left me alone when it started to get light.

I have to admit, it had been quite a while — too wrapped up in business somehow. So, after saying goodbye to the cheerful and adventurous girls who, like me, had been looking for a bit of fun, I was in a great mood and felt refreshed, despite such a stormy night.

"Respect," Serby said suddenly. He'd been pretending to be asleep. "The nighttime is supposed to be spent with females."

"Uh-huh, dominate, humiliate, rule," I chuckled.

"Huh, you don't understand anything. In our packs, the alpha male is always with several females simultaneously. It makes the pack stronger."

"And how long does he enjoy such favor for?" I asked.

"Until he's killed by a pretender and his females," the dog said, grinning.

"Listen." I suddenly got carried away by an idea. "Maybe I should set you up with a little bitch of your own breed?"

"Don't push it!" Serby growled.

"Well, don't compare human relations with what goes on with you, then. But look, it's been a long time since you were with anyone... of your own kind," I said, searching for the right word.

"That's what you think," he scoffed.

"Aha gotcha." I went over to the dog and quickly activated a restraining seal so he couldn't escape. "And now you're going to tell me the whole truth about how demons can get into our world, and not that all baloney that it hardly ever happens."

"Drop it," Serby said wearily. "I was going to tell you, but later."

"I'm listening," I answered, sitting on a chair, not even considering removing the seal.

"Okay, your world is the base-world for many others. When your ancestors waged total war, there was a powerful eruption of magic that scattered the magic creatures across other worlds, making them adapt to new conditions. You were left virtually without any magic, and that's probably the only reason your world is still intact."

"And where did you get this from?"

"In every family..." Serby broke off as I looked at him. "Well, let's say we also have a structure similar to your family one. But it's more like one species... Basically, in each family there is an elder whose duty it is to preserve their history and pass it on to the next generation, so they remember where they came from and don't mess up. Funny, I know, but the way your world was described to us is the same way you describe hell. Well, it's hard to judge those who survived a global cataclysm and were torn from their native world."

"And why this long, although interesting, introduction?"

"You wanted me to tell you everything, so I'm telling you. As I was saying, in the worlds we inhabit, there is much less magic energy than there is here. And the transition here runs the risk of losing everything, including your life. Your world just rejects us if we don't acquire an 'anchor'".

"Let me guess — in our case the anchor was the contract?" I asked.

"Yes." The spitz nodded. "I serve you and protect you, so the world leaves me alone and lets me feed off energy for free."

"Hah, you talk about it as if it's a living creature."

"And it is," Serby replied frankly. "Every world is alive and can respond to a threat to itself, just not everyone can hear it or understand it. Your world is very old and can behave almost like a human being in some cases, eliminating a threat to itself with a surgeon's precision. But no matter how capable the world is of defending itself, there is always the possibility of avoiding its 'eagle eye'."

"Okay, we'll go back to that later," I said, deep in thought as I took in this new information. "Go on."

"Any demon or other creature that has got through to your world can, if it's accumulated enough energy, invite fellow members of its species here by opening up something like a corridor between the worlds. In this case, the chances of success are much higher, but there is still the issue of anchoring yourself in this reality. So, I, in fact, called up some females to help me relax." Serby grinned in a somewhat undoglike way.

"And only those that are from your species can come here through such a corridor, or can something else also slip through?"

"Your world is too tasty a morsel to share," Serby replied. "So, they avoid this method if possible."

"But you use it for your own selfish purposes, eh?"

"Let's see what you'd look like after a few years without female company," Serby muttered. "And your dogs, as you joked, aren't the same thing — it borders on perversion."

"Alright, alright." I put up my hands in a conciliatory way, deactivating the seal. "Why did it have to come to this? Couldn't you have told me right away?"

"And you get mad? It was better to keep it to myself. And I didn't take the opportunity very often — it still eats up a lot of energy."

"Yes, but other demons may well start an invasion like that," I retorted.

"To start, as you put it, an 'invasion,'" Serby said sarcastically, "a demon would have to be so powerful that it would cause a whole heap of problems all on its own. And as I told you before, no one's prepared to share a free feeder, even with their own species. By the way, aren't you going to be late?" The dog pointed to the digital clock that showed it was coming up to ten o'clock.

"Ah, I'm in no hurry."

After a pleasant night, my head felt a lot clearer than after that bender with Bukreev. During our chat, we not only talked about his adventures, but also somehow touched on how I couldn't get up to the fourth floor where the most useful books were. His advice was to take part in the Academy's annual student tournament. Although I wasn't a student, I could coach a group of them — and if they finished high enough, then my application to visit the fourth floor would be much more likely to succeed. The best books really were on the top floor, and they weren't about to let just anyone read them.

I wasn't keen on this option because it meant I'd have to assemble a team and somehow train them to work together, something I had no experience of. You could argue that even Lena was only my student because of our magical connection, as I hadn't actually given her much.

Meanwhile... meanwhile it was still worth going to the Academy. It was getting on for noon, and I had lined up two dozen books which might contain some useful scraps of information.

*   *   *

"Gregor, how's the head?" Bukreev asked with a smile as I rode the chopper up to the gates of the Academy.

"As you see," I spread my hands, leaning slightly. "I'm not used to it, so I had to miss a whole day to feel normal again."

"A day, eh? Still not bad," the old man said with a chuckle. "After the hooch I gave you, others had to rest up for a week. And you're fine. Resilient."

"Thanks for the praise, but I have to go."

"The library again?" Bukreev raised a quizzical eyebrow.

"Again." I wasn't about to deny it.

"Hah, and you say you're not a student. You spend more time there than some of them do."

"Nothing else for it. They're otherwise engaged, and I don't need to sit in class, so why not take advantage of the Academy of Magic's bountiful library to expand my knowledge?" I took my leave of him and slipped through the opening gate.

"If there were more students like you, maybe there'd be fewer dropouts," Bukreev said after me with a heavy sigh, but I didn't turn around.

The library welcomed me with just a small number of visitors again, so, once more, I picked out a few books and got settled in my favorite spot. This time I'd decided to do things slightly differently and selected books on general subjects, like the history of the world.

I had a similar book in my parents' house, but this was an expanded edition and told you about the most significant events in our history in much more detail. It was interesting to read it again, especially given that you see everything differently as a child.

"Gregor, is that you?" A familiar voice next to me sounded surprised.

I tore my eyes from the book and looked with mild amusement at the patriarch of the Lazarev family's niece.

"And that surprises you, does it, Miss Arina?" I asked, cheekily running my eyes over her figure, wrapped tightly in her Academy uniform.

It's only girls that can manage to take fairly standard clothing and create a real masterpiece, each in their own way. It's not just about the clothes, either, but also the way they're worn. And now, intentionally or not, Arina exuded such sexuality that, if I hadn't recently had that pleasant experience with those two girls, I could've done something stupid and invited her out for a good time.

I'm sure we'd have both liked it, but the consequences… not worth it for a fling unlikely to result in anything serious.

"Gregor." Arina put her hands on her hips indignantly. "We agreed not to address each so formally!"

"Okay, okay." I laughed quietly. "It's just you're so cute when you're angry."

"Oh… thanks." Arina was embarrassed all of a sudden but tried to pull herself together. "But you said you weren't going to enroll here!"

"Really?" I looked at her with surprise, not remembering that I had said anything of the sort. "And I thought you said you wanted to escape college."

"It doesn't matter." Arina shook her hair. "The reason I'm here is because my uncle insisted I finish it and not skip class." At this point, she started thinking about something, putting her finger to her cheek. Then she looked at me, her eyes wide with astonishment. "So, that's what he was talking about!"

"What do you mean?"

"Uncle said there was a surprise waiting for me," she said quite openly.

"I don't look much like a surprise," I said, frowning, and then started to laugh.

"You're right." Arina joined me in laughing. "The bow's missing."

"Now, come on," I said in mock indignation.

"But really, how did you get into the Academy?" She wouldn't let up. "I mean, this place is expensive for commoners."

"Who said I can't afford it?" I raised my right eyebrow.

"You must've spent a fortune!" Arina exclaimed in a hushed tone.

"I don't remember giving you reasons to doubt my financial situation," I answered somewhat rudely, but then she had overstepped the mark. "If I'd wanted to pay for my studies, I would've done, but I'm not here as a student."

"I'm sorry," Arina said, lowering her eyes. "It's just that I wouldn't have taken the opportunity to study here if I'd known how much it costs, but my uncle paid for it all without telling me."

"Since when did the Lazarevs start counting the pennies?"

"We may be rich, but it doesn't mean we can afford to waste money. It'd soon run out," Arina said firmly, shaking her hair in ridiculous fashion for added emphasis. "Wait." She suddenly gathered herself. "Did you say you're not a student?"

"Precisely." I nodded and enjoyed watching the

whole gamut of expressions play across her face. She displayed them all quite clearly. "I'm here as someone's teacher..." I briefly explained about the charter and the clause everyone had forgotten about that allowed me, technically, to be at the Academy of Magic for free.

"I didn't even know the charter had such a clause," Arina muttered pensively.

"That's why you should read all contracts carefully," I said in a teacherly tone. "I'm telling you as a professional in this matter."

"Can anyone do that?" Arina asked.

"No, there are specific criteria, but that's secret." I spread my hands apologetically. I wasn't about to talk about the magic connection, otherwise it would've led to more questions, the answers to most of which I didn't have.

"There we go, secrets again." Arina pouted ostentatiously, but then smiled. "How are you finding it here?"

"The library contains some very interesting books," I replied after thinking for a while. "And I've not been to enough of your lessons to judge. I don't see the point as general knowledge isn't any good to me."

"Gregor, I thought you'd be here..." Lena came up beside me unexpectedly and fell silent when she saw Arina.

"Arina, this is my student, Lena," I hurriedly introduced her to Arina. "Lena, this is Arina Lazareva."

"So that's what you are," Arina said pensively,

looking my student up and down, who, in response, maintained an icy calm and pointedly ignored her.

"I brought you some food." Lena showed me the packages, and before anyone could react, she started laying the containers out on the table. "I'm afraid I didn't reckon on a third person, so I suppose we'll have to share."

"Oh, don't worry. I'm not hungry. I'll just sit here."

"As you wish." Lena bowed slightly.

"Lena, you read the Academy statute." I looked at her reproachfully. "All students are equal, so if you're talking to someone who's not a teacher, then you don't need to stand on ceremony."

"Yes, teacher," Lena said, bowing politely to me.

"How interesting," Arina drawled, watching this with a sly look in her eyes. "And what is it you're learning from him?" she came out and asked Lena.

"Gregor taught me everything I now know about magic, and he saved my life," she added at the end for some reason.

"Ah, is that so?" Arina shot a glance at me. "So, you, sire, are a knight in shining armor."

"Hah, no." I was getting tired of looking at the unopened containers and so, not feeling inhibited, I began to eat. I was starving. "I was just passing by, and it somehow turned out like that."

"Oh, so you're not a knight," Arina said, shaking her head. "You're a downright hero!"

"Most definitely not," I scoffed and carried on eating in a way that let everyone know I was busy.

"That's exactly what a hero would say," she said with a smile. "And how do you find Gregor, overall?" she said mischievously, waving her hand vaguely. Lena, who'd remained calm until then, blushed desperately and couldn't utter a word. "I get it." Arina gave knowing smile.

"Are you going to keep gassing or are you going to eat something?" I intervened before Lena had the chance to say anything. I mean, I hadn't given any reason to think about me in that way and look what'd happened.

"Eat, of course," Arina responded heartily, pulling the nearest container towards her. "Mm." Her eyes widened with surprise as she tasted the first mouthful. "You cook almost as well as the chefs at my house! Tell me honestly," Arina said, turning towards me. "You took her as a student because of her cooking skills, not because of anything else?"

"You discovered my secret," I said, putting my hands up in surrender, although I put them down again almost immediately to carry on with my lunch.

"Will you take me as a student if I cook something, too?" Arina asked unexpectedly, which almost made me choke.

"No." I shook my head, and gestured towards Lena, who looked like she was about to lose her cool. "That position is filled already."

"Fine, I'll find another way, then." Arina wasn't

backing down.

"As you wish," I said, sighing with resignation.

It felt like she wasn't going to leave me alone, but maybe that way she'd calm down for a while.

CHAPTER 13

FROM THE MOMENT ARINA FOUND ME in the library, the get-togethers over my books lost their privacy. It's hard to be alone when two girls are constantly fussing around you. And if Lena could come at lunchtime or towards evening because of her studies, then it was if Arina didn't have any classes at all, and she just came when she felt like it.

I have to admit, delving into boring books in company was more enjoyable than doing it alone, and only the Archivist hovering in the background reminded us that we shouldn't make too much noise — it was a library, after all.

In the meantime, I got through more and more books, which enriched my knowledge, and thanks to them, I revised many of my seals, making them less energy-consuming, and contemplated several new kinds that still needed to be tested out. And I started thinking about the nature of my abilities, which, I thought at first, came under the category of summoning.

But after reading several works of famous researchers, I came to the conclusion that my restraining seals, and even those chains I'd shown my aunt, were never anything to do with the magic of summoners. It was something new, a deviation from the norm.

I'd actually been imposing extra conditions on contracts that had already been concluded as part of the summoning, but, according to these researchers, this was impossible. Almost every one of them lamented that summoners are so rare precisely because they can't think everything through for their first experiments and simply die at the hands of a creature that interprets its duties and restrictions far too liberally.

Whatever you say, I was lucky the creature that appeared with my first major summoning was Serby. He was too curious to attack me straight away, and, after regaining my strength, I imposed new conditions on him so that he definitely couldn't harm me.

There was also the summoning of items such as chains, which I'd initially considered an aspect of restraining seals. But, according to the books, when I summoned chains, I was imposing restraining features on them, and they weren't themselves the result of this method. Messed up, I know. My head was bursting from these thoughts and having to rethink everything I'd done up until then.

All my seals were created based on the knowledge I had. Also, I understood intuitively which symbol should be applied next, and which combination of characters and designs would be successful, and which would send the whole scheme out of control. But just what was it really — the talent of a genius or another consequence of my grandfather's experiment?

Understandably, thinking about this hardly filled me with the joys of life, and it was only because Lena and Arina were there that I couldn't just go and get drunk. It would've been a disgrace to let them see me in such a state. Which is not to say it didn't happen — they just didn't get to know about it.

Eventually, I'd read almost all the books. All that remained was the fourth floor, which, for the time being, I didn't have access to. Having nothing to do, I decided to sit in on Lena's classes, which, I could do, thanks to Khodkevich.

"Vetrov, come in, come in, quick, take a seat," the supervisor of Lena's group greeted me as soon as I walked into the auditorium. It felt like they were expecting me.

Mentally throwing out my hands, I did as he said in silence and sat down next to my student, who had until then been absorbed in making notes on the lecture.

"So, in this lesson, we went back over the basic techniques that the gifted use in battles at your level of knowledge," Khodkevich said, rounding off his speech. "But don't forget that, even though you're the strongest group in the year, there may be those among your comrades who studied with their relatives as well, which means that in some areas they might be at a higher level than you've been taught to so far. So, a magician's main virtue in battle is caution. You must never forget that underestimating your enemy leads to defeat, and in the real world — to death. Finding all this out in practice is what awaits you in what is the Academy tournament. Don't forget there's only a month left before it starts, so it's time to decide on the disciplines you'll be participating in and to assemble a team. That concludes today's lesson."

With these words, Khodkevich got up and left the room, leaving everyone to their own devices.

"Lena, do you want to take part in the tournament?" I asked her when her classmates had started to gather in small groups to discuss things. Remarkably, no one had approached us yet. "It'll be a good experience for you."

"But I don't really know how to use my powers yet," she said timidly.

"No worries. If the worst comes to the worst, you can always hit your opponent with brute force. And you don't have to win — the main thing is to gain experience fighting other magicians. Even if you lose the first battle, it's not critical. Except you need to be in a team to take part," I mused.

As if this was just what he was waiting for, the blond guy who I had to fight at the training ground appeared next to me.

"I'll join your team if you coach us," he said decisively.

"How many are there in each team?" I asked.

"Just four," said a beautiful brown-haired girl, coming up to us, who, according to my vague recollection, was one of the few who didn't try to ask me anything after the sparring match. "So, you can't do without me," she said, smiling cheekily.

"Okay," I said, as I didn't have anything against it. I didn't know the strengths and weaknesses of Lena's classmates, so this girl was no better or worse than the rest of them. "All we need now is one last person."

"Hah, no problem," said the blond guy. He went off for a few seconds and came back dragging his reluctant friend with him. He was all kind of disheveled and worked up.

"I'm not taking part in any tournament!" he muttered angrily, which only confirmed that he wasn't here by choice.

"Yes, you are," my sparring opponent said firmly, slapping his pal on the shoulder, which made him wince in pain. He responded by digging the blond guy under the ribs. It was his turn to wince. "That's all there is to it."

"Well, if everybody's happy..." I looked at the students carefully. The disheveled guy tried to say something, but the blond guy stepped on his foot, giving him something else to worry about. He managed to find some words, but they were a stream of obscenities, and him being an aristocrat, too. "So, introduce yourselves, please. I'm too lazy to come up with any names for you."

"Huh, you give a dog a name," the brown-haired girl said. "Call signs are more appropriate in our case."

"So, you'll be Vasilisa," I said, nodding at her.

"Why's that?" The girl looked at me with surprise.

"Did you not read any fairy tales?" I shot her an ironic look. "Vasilisa the Wise was exactly that, and since you like your wisecracks..." I said, shrugging.

"I'm not having that as a call sign," she said, beginning to backpedal. "I have a name."

"What is it, then?"

"Alisa Naryshkina," she replied, giving a slight curtsey.

"I might've known," I said with a smile, in response to which her shoulder twitched, and she kept quiet.

"Vladimir Orlov," the blond guy introduced himself and urged his friend to say something.

"Miroslav Bartenev," he mumbled reluctantly.

"Now answer my question." I paused and looked everyone in the eye. "Why do you want me to be your coach?"

"You might as well?" Alisa said, shrugging. "The others only want to train with each other, and since Lena has a strong mentor, then..." She gave a sly smile.

"Accepted." I nodded. "So, reserve a training field for us, and I'll be waiting for you there after classes."

I got up and left the auditorium. I had a training session to prepare.

* * *

"As you all already know, modern magic techniques are based on the willpower of the gifted." I began the training with a small introductory speech. "Unfortunately, I'm not able to channel any of the elements, which is why I'm not familiar with their features, but the magic energy that flows in us, whatever area your gift is in, is subject to change and control, and that's what we will be working on."

"That boring?" Alisa scoffed. "I thought we were going to do some sparring to hone our skills."

"There'll be no sparring until you pass my test. If you don't like that, you can go and look for another team. I'm not forcing anyone."

"We get it," Vladimir replied before Alisa could say anything. "What do we have to do?"

"It's all very simple." I kicked the bag next to me, and it fell over onto the ground with a gentle metallic rustling sound. "This bag contains empty aluminum soda cans."

"Do we have to destroy them?" Alisa said, grinning eagerly. "In a jiffy."

She was already getting ready to perform a technique, but I interrupted her with a gesture.

"No." I shook my head and pulled out one of the cans. "You just have to do this." I stretched out my arm so everyone could see and, directing my magic energy in two planes, like metal plates, I flattened the can into a thin sheet.

"Like that?" quietly gasped Miroslav, who'd looked unconvinced by the task prior to this.

"We're all able to manipulate magic energy, and it's only the area our gift is in that gives it its 'color', so any magician, even one not of the highest rank, can theoretically perform such a trick. The main thing is to get rid of the elemental component and use precisely this, let's call it, "colorless" magic that every gifted can use."

"But how do we do that?" Vladimir asked.

"That's for you to work out," I said. "And when you have, come and see me. Lena, I'll deal with you, now," I said, and I turned to my student.

"Why do we have to get on with this on our own? Alisa objected.

"Like I said, I'm not keeping anyone prisoner." I smiled slightly. "And Lena is my student, so... And if you suddenly run out of training materials, I'll bring you some more. Have fun."

I took Lena away, while her skeptical-looking classmates began to take the cans and discuss something between themselves.

"Do I really need to take part in this tournament?" Lena asked when we came to a stop.

"I need it too, so I can get into the closed part of the library," I replied. "There may still be books in there which will contain clues as to how to break our connection."

"Okay," Lena said, nodding her head resolutely. "I'll try."

"Well, don't try too hard," I said, laughing at her reaction. "As I said, you just need to put on a performance as, sadly, we can't talk about you having any serious control of your own magic yet."

"So, you're thinking of training this trio? But isn't this kind of technique a teacher's secret?" she asked anxiously.

"Hah, it's no secret at all. I read about the method in one of the books in the library, so they could easily have found it themselves. I had to brush up on it a little for the demonstration, but my control was already at a high level."

"Oh, I see..." Lena sighed with relief.

"Now show me what I taught you this month." I began with the important stuff.

It was only by seeing what Lena was now capable of that I'd be able to suggest where to go from there. Who knew that studying books on ritualism would allow me to better understand magic which I had no real flair for. Slightly annoying, even.

Lena stretched out her hand, and a small flame lit up in it.

"Not bad," I said, but at the same time on my student's face there appeared a triumphant smile, and more than a dozen similar flames ignited around her. "Really not bad," I drawled.

For someone who has only recently started learning magic, using a technique capable of summoning up so many elemental objects is a very good result, close to genius. Who were you before you became the victim of a demonic ritual, and how did the "Searchers" manage to miss you?

"How much does this spell consume?"

Each gifted is perfectly aware of their reserve and, knowing its limits, can roughly estimate how much their techniques have used in globally recognized conventional units.

"No more than ten units," Lena said proudly. "But unfortunately, I've not yet learned how to direct them at a target."

"Ah, don't worry," I said with a wave of the hand. "The main thing is to understand the principle and to feel your source and your element. Have you tried using your 'dark' fire like that?"

"I... don't dare, she replied after a short pause. "If I were to use that source for the technique, there'd be a risk of explosion due to the sharp rise in the resultant flow."

Only a month, and she was already using the scientific terms. If I hadn't spent so much time in the library, I'm afraid I would've embarrassed myself by having to ask her to explain what she meant. And I was still curious as hell about what Lena's other flame could do — it was so like what I'd seen from several dangerous demons.

"So, first of all, we'll work on your connection with your element so you can deploy your maneuver as quickly as possible while consuming less energy. For now, you're best only using black fire in case of emergency or as a last resort," I said. "Now let's start with this exercise..."

* * *

I honestly expected the three aristos, who wanted to be in Lena's group, to refuse to carry out the task I proposed, and try to force me to train them in some other way, but, maybe their pride kicked in, or something, and Alisa and Vladimir sat on the training ground until late in the evening, getting through the bags of metal waste I brought like a human combine harvester. Miroslav felt like giving up a few times, and he was quite animated in trying to get the others to do the same, but Vladimir kept sitting him back down, and they'd carry on with my task.

I deliberately didn't give them much to go on, keeping it to just one demonstration. I was honestly intrigued to see if they would throw in the towel or not, and if not, how long it'd take before they cracked it.

Well, I was, how can I put it, "less than correct" when I talked about using magic without elements. It's quite easy for me to use the power from the source without coloring it with an element, because that's something I can't do anyway. It was very difficult for those guys, who'd been trained since childhood to use the element they feel most at home with, to make do without it when using their magic.

I wonder how our ancestors, who used real magic spells that were spoken aloud, would've coped? Now most of these spells have been lost, and the ones that remain are the stuff of history books, but still.

So, the trio mastered the task, to one degree or another, in three days. Three days, and I reckoned it'd take them more than a week.

"Well, seeing as you say you've nailed it," I said, shooting them a quizzical look, "let's have it."

Vladimir stepped forward first, putting a can on his palm, gave it an intense look, and in a matter of seconds he'd turned it into a metal pancake. He did it almost cleanly, too, but my magic vision detected he couldn't manage without his wind element, which he used to compress the space above his hand like a vice.

He stepped back with a smile of satisfaction and let Alisa take her turn. She resorted to a little trick and, clamping the can between her palms, made them come together, crushing the can at the same time. Like a strongman in a circus. But there was still some magic to this. If Vladimir had created something like a press, then Alisa surreptitiously, or so it seemed to her, put a drop of water inside the can to make it more malleable, and therefore easier to crush, because of the water moving inside it.

Finally, after a shove from Vladimir, up stepped Miroslav, who, just like his comrade, showed us the can in his hand before squashing it as flat as a pancake in a matter of seconds. It might've looked like he completed the task better than the others, but this guy had an affinity with earth, which meant he could partially control the metal, so the task was easier for him. True, he channeled a minimal amount of his element for his technique, crushing the can almost purely using an emission of power. And this kid was even more work-shy than the others.

"Not bad…" I said afterward, "for commoners who only discovered magic a week ago." They didn't rise to it this time, but judging by the way Alisa clenched her fists, she was clearly finding it hard to restrain herself. "You're all so used to using your element in your techniques that you've forgotten that the other elements are also available to you, although to a lesser extent."

"But what do we need the other ones for?" Vladimir asked, which I was kind of expecting from him. "We're bound to lose using moves from the other elements."

"I agree with the last bit," I said, nodding. "An air element magician can create a fist out of air that will punch through a concrete wall, while a magician of the same level specializing in water can only scratch it, but that doesn't mean you shouldn't know at least a couple of techniques from all of them."

"What use is that?" Alisa said, frowning.

"What use, you say?" I looked her up and down, which caused her to flare up for a moment in righteous indignation, but she pulled herself together and adopted a steely gaze. "Vladimir, remind us what happened when we were sparring."

"I overestimated my strength and fell into a firetrap I couldn't escape from," he replied honestly, pausing slightly as he swallowed his pride.

"Correct," I said, pointing upwards. "But if you'd known at least something about fire magic, you could either have held out longer in the trap, or, with enough skills and smarts, get out of it altogether. You must realize you don't need to try jumping over a wall when there is a low yet uncomfortable gate next to it."

"So that's what this was all about!" Miroslav exclaimed suddenly.

"You should've been in touch with your own magic without using your favored element, just as you were putting your move together. That's the only way you can try to use the other elements. That's not to say they'll come easily to you, but in another instance, the power of your prevailing element would simply crush any such attempts," I replied. " I can't help you master your own element, but I can give you a better chance of winning if you can use non-standard moves. Yes, and knowledge of the enemy's techniques can be that straw that breaks the camel's back."

"But how are we going to study elemental techniques without a mentor?" Miroslav asked.

"What do you think the library's for?" I chuckled. "You're not going to be able to master anything really energy-intensive in the remaining time, but there are simple techniques described in some of the books, as well as how to practice them."

"Hmm, I didn't know there were such things in books," he muttered, somewhat perplexed.

"That's partly the problem with homeschooling, where everything is put on a plate for you. Try to get the information you need yourself. When you've learned at least one move, we'll be able to start training."

"But we're ready, now." Alisa, predictably enough, couldn't keep quiet. She was the ringleader of the group, and the voice of the others when they didn't dare speak out.

"Okay." I grinned in a way that made them all take a step back. "If you're ready, then deal with this." I stretched my left hand out to the side for greater effect, and a summoning seal was created on the ground under it. A second later, to my left, there was the fire hound Vladimir had encountered. It paid no attention to the students and began to rub itself against my hand. "This is the sweetie you need to beat," I said with a smile, patting the demon on the head, not worried at all that it was on fire. This creature knows how to make itself completely harmless when, of course, it wants to, and its contract doesn't allow it to harm the summoner. "Except there are two conditions," I said, looking at the trio who were momentarily distracted. "No magic techniques with a volume of more than fifty units and all without a fatal outcome. You're trying to immobilize the hound, not kill it, otherwise it'll respond with aggression, and I can't be responsible for the consequences."

It was this kind of demon that had evoked a deep and lasting association with normal dogs in me. Serby might have been to blame for a certain affection for these creatures, but they were also some of the smartest demons, they didn't demand much energy to be summoned, and you could use them for all sorts of things. The hound had now appeared in combat mode — its black skin and fur blazed with an internal fire, breaking out in red stripes, which ran in intricate patterns across its body like tattoos. Incidentally, you could distinguish one hound from another by these markings as they were unique enough for an observant person not to confuse them. In non-combat mode, and more so at night, these kinds of demons could disguise their fire completely, becoming like blurred shadows, and pursuing their prey to the bitter end. Very useful creatures, on the whole, if you ask me.

"But that's assault!" Alisa exclaimed.

"A training injury," I said, shaking my head. "No more. It's not my fault you decided to train without any preparation or a healer being present."

"That's where you're hiding." Arina's voice rang out, and then she appeared on the training ground. "And there was me thinking you got fed up with books already or weren't allowed into the Academy. But you're here, so you must be... training." She looked at everyone and, it seemed to me, her eyes rested briefly on Alisa, flashing with displeasure.

"That's how it turned out," I said. I wasn't in the mood for explanations.

"Oh, and this is something new." Arina had only just noticed the hound next to me and, stopping a couple of paces away, she looked at it with curiosity. "You summoned a much nicer creature that time... or created one," she said.

"Hah, and here's your medic, so stay safe, I'm gone." I gave a little laugh as I saw the puzzled faces of my audience, and I turned around, giving a command to the hound.

I didn't need the deaths of any students being pinned on me, so this time I summoned one of the smartest of the hounds, with which I managed to conclude a voluntary contract — not such a common occurrence in negotiations with an initially predatory creature. If the small spirits and demons gladly make concessions for the sake of energy they otherwise wouldn't get a sniff of, then these think they can get what they need just by killing their victim.

It's terrible to imagine what the world of spirits and demons must be like, with there being such a struggle for every scrap of magic. After all, someone has to be top of that food chain, and I suspect such an encounter wouldn't be to my liking at all.

While the three students were busy trying not to injure themselves, I went up to Lena, who was waiting patiently for me on another field. Overall, Lena made a wonderful student and, to be honest, she could've achieved more if I hadn't been her teacher, but our connection and her stubborn nature meant there wasn't any other option.

My entry onto the training filed was marked by the sound of a roaring flame, which my student had learned surprisingly quickly not only to create, but also to vary depending on the situation.

"Excellent 'Dragon's Breath', there," I said to her. "Try to squeeze it into a jet next time, and you'll see how the heat from it increases."

Yes, elemental techniques are still amazing. As a child, I dreamed I'd also be able to do something like that, but, as they say, my destiny lay elsewhere. Well, at least I can appreciate it when others do it.

"It's a shame I only have enough to do it about ten to twelve times," Lena said, sighing as

she completed the move by destroying a dummy, leaving only a handful of ashes.

"Your ambitions are too high considering that recently you couldn't even muster an ordinary flame," I said, putting the brakes on. "You've already made so much progress and later you'll be able to make this less energy consuming. All you need is time and practice."

"But what do I need all this for?" Lena asked, summoning up a fire in her hand. She looked absent-mindedly into its depths. "Why even study magic?"

"Why?" I asked as I too looked into the fire. "I studied magic to survive and to know myself. And once I'd reached a certain level, I just did what I wanted, without worrying about my power not being enough. Just set your goal and go for it. At this point in time, the Academy of Magic is probably the best place for finding the solution to this." I smiled at her tenderly. "Right, so let's continue. I remember last time you couldn't create a fire shield, and your reserve isn't depleted yet."

Lena demonstrated a dozen more different techniques she was told about in class and that were in the books, and we reproduced them as described. There are certain advantages to a new field of magic, when you don't need to memorize any multi-layered schemes to reproduce what you need. It's enough to imagine the result clearly — and there it is, right in front of you. It's better to understand each technique and visualize a simplified version of the way it works, and the better you can reproduce it in your mind, the more powerful it'll end up being. So, for two gifted people with the same chosen area of magic, the same technique can differ dramatically in terms of both quality and effect.

Lena's reserve had run out, so we headed back over to the other three students. I knew they hadn't destroyed the hound, as our contract hadn't come to an end, which meant it was still here in this world — something I could sense keenly through that, let's say, thread, between me and the summoned entity.

On the contrary, the hound was lying there on the ground with the rest of the group, its tongue hanging out. They all had burns, but Arina had used her magic to treat them, so, in fact, it was only their clothes that suffered, and, well, a little hair which would take a bit longer to restore.

"So, how are you?" I asked, and I patted the demon on the head, giving it some extra energy for a job well done.

"What kind of creature is this?!" Alisa asked, unable to restrain herself, looking at her singed lock of hair in horror.

"I have never seen techniques like that, or ones capable of sustaining themselves for so long without outside control," Vladimir said more calmly.

"Hah, there's a lot you've not seen in your life," I replied. "And this is just a demon I summoned."

"So, you're a summoner!" Arina broke off from treating Miroslav's hands and looked at me. "And all this time I thought they were complex illusions."

"Can illusions hurt you?" I did wonder, as I'd never heard of such a thing.

"There are experts," Arina replied vaguely. Judging by her expression, she'd blurted out something she didn't mean to and was now feverishly thinking how to get out of it. "So, you are a summoner, then?" she repeated the question rather than answering.

"I never really kept it a secret." I threw out my hands and bowed slightly to her. "I didn't come out and say it, either." Finished with the wound, Arina sighed wearily and looked at me attentively. "And how many other things haven't you told us?"

"Who knows," I said with a laugh. "I can see you've recovered already," I said, addressing the trio. "So, I give you permission not to hold back anymore and to try to destroy the hound." Hearing my words, the demon grinned widely. It struck the ground with its fiery tail a few times, leaving stripes burned into it, and then went and stood a short distance away from the students, who were still lying on the ground. "Come on, chop-chop!"

I waved my hand, and the hound, obeying the order given through our contract, rushed straight at the three of them.

Although the students were pretty tired from training and had exhausted their reserves, it seemed that wasn't enough for them to just not respond to the threat. Miroslav was lying down and stayed lying down, but he slapped his palm on the ground, and instantly in front of the hound there appeared stone pikes, which it had to jump out of the way of quickly to avoid impaling itself. This gave Vladimir and Alisa the time to get themselves together and get their own moves ready.

The demon rushed to the side, but at that moment Vladimir directed his technique not at the creature, but at the ground in front of him, creating a cloud of dust, which coated the demon's eyes and nose. Yelping with annoyance, the hound stopped and tried to shake the dust from its eyes. But as soon as it did, one of Alisa's water techniques caught up with it, knocking it down, and partially extinguishing its flames. Before their opponent could pick itself up, Miroslav touched the ground again, and where the demon lay turned into something like quicksand, preventing its escape. If they'd continued like this, the hound would still have broken free, but Vladimir was already forming a new air technique which looked like something classed as an air spear or a version of it.

"Enough." I stopped them. "So, you figured out how to combine each other's abilities."

"But Lena didn't take part, and she's a member of the team," Alisa objected, but it was clear she was very pleased that she'd been able to beat the hound, and that I'd acknowledged their success.

"Which is why, from tomorrow, you'll start training together," I said, nodding towards her. "And now you can tidy yourselves up and search the library for techniques from other elements."

Vladimir helped his pal get up, who, as it turned out, hadn't just decided to lie on the ground, but had twisted his ankle, which can't put right so quickly, unless, of course, you put a lot more energy into it. Arina didn't have to help them, so the students were grateful that she'd treated their burns and wounds at all. So, the three of them were battle-scarred but overall unharmed. The most important thing was that today they'd learned to work together, although I'd expected this to come a bit later. All in all, they were quite happy with their successes. Since I am, frankly, an average teacher, this could be put down to their skills and determination to grasp everything quickly.

"You said you were just Lena's teacher," Arina said as she approached me once the trio had left the training ground. "And then you suddenly start teaching others."

"Lena needs the experience of fighting with other magicians, and they asked to join the team themselves so they could take part in the tournament," I said, shrugging.

"Why don't you take part, then? After all, there's not just a team round, there's an individual one, too."

"Well, first of all, I'm not an Academy student," I began to explain. "And secondly, I don't have to."

"Why be the group's coach, then?" Arina wasn't going to let it drop.

"A whim."

"Gregor," she said very slowly, coming right up to me, and looking up into my eyes. "I'm dying of curiosity!"

"People don't die of curiosity, Arina," said Lena, who seemed very upset about something.

"I just need to get to the fourth floor of the library," I answered before the girls, who were looking at each other so malevolently, could clash. And it was hard to say who'd win, since at such a short distance Arina had the advantage — healing techniques can do more than treat people, something which many people forget. "Official coaches of the groups also go through a kind of tournament of their own, and if my team gets a decent result, then I'll be able to ask the Academy authorities for access to the restricted area."

"Couldn't you just ask through Lena's supervisor?" Arina looked at me with surprise. "Yes, not everyone is given access to the fourth floor, but it's the curators who petition the Academy council for this. And you, as far as I remember, are officially assigned to Khodkevich?"

"I honestly didn't know there was that option." I scratched the back of my head, bemused. I mean, Bukreev did say there was an easier way! True, it wasn't a done deal that Khodkevich would give me the go-ahead, but it was worth a try. "It's too late now, and, anyway, if my team wins it'll strengthen my case."

"Oh, it's a pity I can't join your group," Arina sighed.

"You can come to training," I suggested. "A healer would come in useful."

"Okay," she said, nodding, "but you'll have to show me that fairy again."

"What fairy?" Lena didn't understand.

"It's a long story." I waved away the need to explain and walked off the field, leaving the girls to themselves.

Looks like I'd done all this for nothing.

CHAPTER 14

WHEN LENA JOINED THE GROUP, the tournament was three weeks away. That might sound like a long time, but it wasn't enough to foster any real team spirit. So, I decided to concentrate on various battle scenarios instead, so their techniques didn't overlap and cancel each other out.

Raw material for their practice were my summoned creatures, which, despite their initial reluctance, allowed themselves to be wounded in exchange for the energy they got for fulfilling the contract. And they managed to negotiate better conditions, so that any damage would be repaired before they transited back.

I didn't feel sorry about one-time contracts as many of the summoned creatures weren't good at obeying commands, not having a brain or the ability to think as such. Many demons live solely by instinct, and submitting themselves to anyone doesn't come into it. Of course, in such cases, I always had the guys covered but, overall, they coped by themselves, and I didn't summon anything too serious.

The most interesting thing was no one in training asked me how summoned these beings. It seemed that was all taken for granted. While it didn't make sense for me to hide my abilities now, answering every single question was different matter.

All members of the group came to the training ground after classes without fail and practiced their skills in fights with the demons. Alisa stood out from the whole group. The fights put her into a berserker-like rage, and her comrades often had to protect her when she got too carried away.

It was also good that Alisa's reserve was quite large, and she used her water techniques, which in themselves were quite energy intensive, like a pro, almost perfectly, while also being economical. She learned the latter the hard way when, after one of the training sessions, she found herself one-on-one with a demon with a completely empty tank and couldn't muster anything. Only Vladimir's reaction and his drawing the blow saved her from a long time spent nursing her wounds.

Vladimir himself wasn't scared of getting injured, but it was clear he liked being thought of as a hero, and the looks Alisa gave him... I must say I was glad her attentions were now directed elsewhere. I had enough on my plate with Lena and Arina.

In public, both girls behaved almost like best friends, but they kept a noticeable distance from each other, as one was an aristocrat and the other a commoner. Yet, Arina only behaved like this with Lena — she spoke to me as an equal. Something was clearly going on between them, but in front of me both behaved in an almost exemplary manner, only allowing themselves the occasional bitchy comment.

With my gentle encouragement, after training, all four of them went to the library to baffle the Archivist (what a stupid nickname) with new books that could help them study the techniques for their element, as well as those elements that at least came to them to some extent. Lena had no techniques other than her fire ones, but this was most likely due to the other part of her gift, which could supersede the so-called affinity with the elements.

Despite studying all the available books to do with my search, I still had things to learn, and in this I was accompanied by Arina, who was keenly interested in anything that interested me.

I decided to take a break and look at a book that told you about other magic schools, the history of their origin and their most distinguished graduates. The one in my hands now was a volume in a series of books about the English Royal School of Magic. I did know something about it, but only the same sketchy information as everyone else, and I'd never had the chance to read about it in such a structured way.

Officially, the founder of the School of Magic was the famous Merlin, who set out to consolidate all the knowledge of druids and sorcerers somewhere it could be taught to the younger generation, which at that time was being persecuted by the common folk. Later, they were joined by witches and other magical people because Merlin was a guarantee of protection, and people wanted a quiet life, and not live in fear that their neighbors, ordinary peasants, would suddenly reach for their pitchforks because of some witchcraft performed by accident. The school then became the only safe place during the Inquisition, when magicians, who lost their powers in one fell swoop, began to be hunted. It's only about a hundred years ago they were able to recover, and then they gradually started gaining power and influence.

The School of Magic was different from our Academy in almost every way. We had alternative approaches to magic, and while the Russian Empire used a new method of applying techniques and willpower to the fabric of the world, the Great British Empire remained conservative in its views and continued to study magical sciences in the same way as their ancestors.

Noteworthy among English magicians was the inheritance of titles. All this led to each generation of magicians in England having their own Merlin, Morgana, Arthur and other figures of legend associated with the times of Camelot, where it all began.

Merlin and Morgana were chosen from the

strongest sorcerers and witches of their generation. They had to prove their skills and leadership qualities. And, needless to say, they were Britain's most adroit magicians. Historically, Merlin and Morgana opposed each other for many years, but those who now bore their titles weren't burdened by the kind of decisions they'd had to make, and most of the time they acted in concert, making a stand for the interests of their state and the magic community in England.

The situation with Arthur and his knights of the Round Table was much more interesting, though. Any who wanted to claim those titles renounced their magic abilities as such and completely devoted themselves to the art of being magic swordsmen — the first knights of Camelot. That's not to say they lost out making this choice. Yes, there were disadvantages, but there were also many advantages, too.

Magic swordsmen swept swiftly across the battlefield, leaving behind them the dismembered corpses of those who simply didn't have time to react. No kind of magic could stop such swordsmen as they used their own gifts to strengthen their body and protect themselves against hostile sorcery. But they still weren't immortal and, unfortunately, the healers couldn't help the swordsmen as they were directing their magic towards canceling out spells, so they had to recover themselves, which happened faster than with ordinary people, but still.

"I remember you mentioned studying at the

School of Magic?" I said, recalling a conversation I had with Arina at the Lazarevs' estate.

"Ah, they're not the most pleasant types who study there," she replied.

"Are magic swordsmen really as powerful as they're described in the books?" I asked, showing her the text I was reading.

"They are really powerful, but a bit creepy." Arina shuddered. "Did you know there was a project in Germany where they created their own version of magic swordsmen and turned them into magician killers?"

"Can't say I've heard of it." I said, shaking my head.

"A friend at the School of Magic told me that. They tried to hush it up as the knights of the round table dealt with the threat of the swordsmen but in doing so lost most of those aspiring to become new knights. Not the most illustrious chapter in their history. After that, they stepped up training of the knights, so they'd always be the best. Because of this, those who go into that field soon become very strange. They're shunned by all the gifted students there, so I never got the chance to talk to any of them."

"Did you want to?"

"It was interesting to see their battle techniques with my own eyes, but the swordsmen train separately from the rest." Arina sighed. "That's how all my studies in England went. Some snobs and druids, who were difficult to get a word out of." She fell silent for a few minutes, and then asked: "And what's it like to be a summoner?"

"What's it like to be a healer?" I batted away her question with another question." Each area has its own characteristics, and that's all there is to it. It doesn't make us special in ourselves. And I'm sure you know there are family secrets that aren't disclosed to outsiders."

"My uncle once said that you're actually an aristocrat." Arina seemed to have latched onto my mention of family. "But for some reason, you gave up everything and even changed your surname."

"What's the point in having that surname?" I replied without looking up from my book. "Out of my family, there was only me left, and all their property — an abandoned wasteland. There's no sense in me clinging to the past. That's why I gave up everything that reminded me of it."

"Sounds lonely," Arina said sorrowfully, giving me an inscrutable look.

"I'm from a family of dark magicians." I gave a joyless grin. "That's the norm for us."

"But even for dark magicians, family means a lot," she objected fervently, grabbing my hand.

"I don't have any family," I said, slamming the book shut. "I have to go," I said, practically ripping my hand out of hers, and, without looking round, I walked straight out of the library.

I flew at break-neck speed. A couple of seconds later, and I was on the ground floor. I slipped past the Archivist, who was frowning but didn't say anything. If he had, I'm afraid I wouldn't have been able to restrain myself.

I can't remember how I got there, but at some point, I found myself next to my bike and, without a second thought, I got on and started the engine. Maybe that's just what I needed. Out of respect for Bukreev, I didn't tear off at full speed, but quite calmly left the Academy grounds, so that, once on the highway, I could ride at full throttle. To an outside observer, it might have sounded like my engine was roaring wildly, but it was the whinnying of a demonic horse trapped in a motorbike, which had picked up on my mood, and the demon knew only one way to get rid of such feelings... breakneck speed.

*   *   *

I finally came to my senses somewhere on a wasteland on the outskirts of the city. From there, you could see the skyscrapers, but everything seemed to be derelict, like the place was abandoned. I wouldn't have been surprised if it turned out to be yet another ghost village, where the inhabitants moved to the city to earn more money. It would only be a matter of time before that wasteland became part of the city, and new high-rises were built there.

Breathing heavily, I looked at the corpses of the demons I'd killed and let out a mirthless laugh.

I didn't think Arina's words would bring back so many memories. After all, I really loved my family, whatever they were like, and their death hit me hard. So, I found it easier to forget who I was and become someone else. Strong and independent. But sometimes it all catches up with me and it makes me want to scream.

That's why I found myself there and, without giving it much thought, I just created a large summoning seal without any conditions or protection. At that moment, I didn't care who decided to answer my call. I summoned the demons not with any other aim but to kill or be killed. Everything was fair and straightforward, so the relevant beings responded.

It was also good that in the thick of it all, I didn't forget about my sword, which I preferred to keep near me after that visit from my aunt, in case I found myself in a tight spot. My magic, though, isn't suited to direct attack, and I'm weak in one-on-one confrontations. But an animated sword is not your usual sharpened piece of iron. And in this case, Miyamoto's cold reason balanced out all that cocktail of emotions that was seething inside me. Most likely, it was only thanks to him that I survived this time, because he didn't let me completely lose my head.

Meanwhile, another demon began to crawl out of the still active seal. It turned out to be too big for its whole body to appear, so it had to push its hand through first, and then, resting it on the ground, try to pull the rest of its body out. I was already too mentally and physically exhausted for another fight, so I just blocked the flow of energy to the seal, finally closing the corridor.

Before the seal imploded, there was a sound of

rage and pain from the unlucky demon, and its hand remained in this world, pouring blood onto the ground that was already pretty messy.

Looking around, I was surprised to see over a dozen different kinds of demons in various conditions, most of which I was seeing for the first time. Before that, I didn't care — there was only a goal, and me with a sword in my hand. Now the magician and researcher in me took over, and I regretted not being able to recall what they looked like before. There were only scraps of demons left, so putting the picture back together was rather tricky.

I once had the idea of compiling something along the lines of a bestiary, but somehow, I never got round to it.

Hmm, if my thoughts were going there, I must really have come to my senses.

Suddenly, I heard applause behind me and, swiftly turning around, I pointed my sword towards the potential threat.

"Awesome performance," said a vaguely familiar man in a brown raincoat as he carried on clapping. Except I couldn't remember where I'd seen him before. "I've never seen so many creatures in one place. Although, no... I'm lying... I have had occasion to see the corpses of demons."

"And who might you be?" I asked rudely. This was more out of habit than because I actually felt negative towards him. After the fight, I was mentally exhausted, and what I wanted most of all was to fall into bed and sleep.

"Gregor Vetrov." The man shook his head, lighting a white cigarette. "We met when you arrived in the capital. Konstantin Skuratov," he said, introducing himself with a slight bow of the head. "The Imperial Magic Security Service."

"And I'm supposed to believe you just happened to be here, eh?" Finally, I remembered where I'd seen this unshaven individual before. A lot had happened since then, and I'd plain forgotten about the man I found standing by my bike after the exhibition.

"I wouldn't say anything of the sort," Skuratov said with a shrug.

"So, are we going to keep playing guessing games?"

"Fine by me." He chuckled and puffed on his cigarette. "Actually, I'm in no hurry, but approaching a man with a sword in his hand..." He threw out his hands. "I think I'll pass."

On hearing this, I lowered the blade, without putting it back into its scabbard. It wasn't yet clear what his motives were.

"That's better," Skuratov said with a smile. "Now we can talk." He took another drag and continued: "I was assigned to you as soon as our service noted your appearance in the capital. Until now, you lived in Petrograd and were of no interest to us, but now you're in Moscow, that's a different story."

"Like you don't have your people in every city," I scoffed.

"Well, yes, but you were another department's

headache then, and now you're mine. So, that's the difference."

"Why the interest in me?" I asked warily.

"Are you joking?" Skuratov frowned comically. "A freewheeling summoner, not part of any family, and prepared to cooperate. Enough for you?"

"Hah, I must've missed that bit about cooperating."

"That was the task," the man answered honestly. "You took on jobs for money, and sometimes those jobs came from our Service. With your psychological profile, it wasn't hard to work out that you either wouldn't cooperate with an official request, or you'd try to inflate the price."

"Canny." I couldn't help expressing my admiration.

"We have specialists in their field." Skuratov threw out his hands as if to apologize. "The Petrograd branch was interested in working with you but couldn't see how to approach you directly without you refusing. They also worked to ensure you didn't attract any undue attention, by carefully manipulating the facts."

"The Voronovs," I said, hazarding a guess.

"Yes," said the employee of one of the most secretive and powerful organizations of the Russian Empire while still keeping his distance. "Your dear senior branch looked into all your affairs very thoroughly, but our specialists in such matters are much better than the servants of a not particularly influential family."

"Sounds like bragging to me, and I wouldn't

call them that." I was a little offended at the rather low opinion of my former relatives.

"Not bragging but a statement of fact. And about my attitude to that family... Try working with princely families and then you can compare," he said with a grunt. "As for you, a lot has changed since you showed up near Pushkino."

"But I didn't leave a trace!" I was indignant but didn't deny it.

Why? Because there was no point. People from that office wouldn't bluff let alone make contact if they didn't have all the evidence. And there was no point in not believing what Skuratov was saying, either. I suspected myself that some of my jobs were strange, but I put that down to the shady side of Petrograd or to some overly secretive employers.

"Magically speaking, yes," Skuratov said, lighting another cigarette. "It was very difficult to figure out what you did there, but you were unlucky an expert who loves solving such riddles arrived at the scene. The guy didn't come out of that apartment for almost three days until he was able to put together a general picture by connecting the fragments that were still there. So, in the end, we figured out that a summoning ritual was carried out in the place, one which someone stopped." He looked at me meaningfully. "It wasn't possible to find out exactly what happened and who conducted it, since the apartment was rented, and the owner didn't see his tenant in person, because all agreements were made through the internet. They also came to you thanks to a distinctive bike that a local hood remembered, and, well, the physical traces you left in the apartment." He paused for a few seconds, and then continued: "Your fingerprints clearly pointed to your involvement."

"Unfortunate," I growled, mentally kicking myself about the last point.

It was all logical, though. I'd erased every trace of any magic intervention, but I didn't suspect anyone would investigate the case so thoroughly. Usually, investigators only need to know a magician was at work for them to stop trying to find out the details. There's too high a risk of the investigation leading back to some influential family, who really wouldn't appreciate it.

"You're a talented self-taught magician. But no one taught you to cover your tracks, so no one suspects anything," he said, grunting again, and this time he took a step forward, but stopped cautiously when he saw me handling my sword.

"Since we're being so open with each other," I said, grinning, "why didn't you come after me as soon as you found out I was implicated in the ritual?"

"You were more use to us as a 'free mercenary' than behind bars. It didn't make sense to put you in jail. You destroyed all the evidence, and your presence at the crime scene is too circumstantial to open a case."

"So, what's changed?"

"Your being here. Entering the Academy of Magic, taking advantage of a loophole in the charter that few people ever read. The actions of the

Voronovs towards you. Too close acquaintance with the future heirs of influential families. Well, that just about covers it." He took out another cigarette and threw it at the body of the demon lying nearest to him. "At first, I thought something had happened to make you freak out, but, as I see, I didn't need to worry."

"Hah, no," I said, not taking my eyes off the man standing there so relaxed. "So, what next? Clap me in irons?"

"Why so black and white?" Skuratov raised an eyebrow in surprise. "On behalf of the Imperial Magic Security Service, I am authorized to invite you to become our freelance employee and consultant. The conditions, believe me, are quite good, and you'll be paid like you are for your usual jobs," he said, hinting again that their people had been here before.

"And if I say no?" I asked, still not lowering my sword.

"That would be a great pity," he said, sighing heavily. "But we'd be obliged to stop secretly covering for you, which means letting those dear relatives you 'love' so much come and have a word with you. Frankly, I'm being honest — we were only covering you because we planned to bring you into the organization. We wouldn't have used so many resources otherwise. There are plenty of other matters our personnel could turn their attention to, you know."

"An offer you can't refuse," I chuckled, relaxing slightly. "And what else haven't you told me?"

"A lot." Skuratov threw out his hands. "The snipers a couple of kilometers away in case you'd decided to act aggressively, for example."

"And there it is." I drawled and, removing the demons' blood from my blade with a violent shake, I put it back in its scabbard. Dramatic, I know, but I had to get my head together. "I assumed you were more likely to try to tie me up and make me work for you."

"Forcing a summoner to work brings its own problems," Skuratov said with a grimace. "Your kind don't tend to show their face if there's a big stick over them. It'd be easier for me to work with someone I can trust, rather than worrying about him at any moment summoning a creature that could bite my head off."

"You mean me?"

"Yes, if negotiations go to plan, I'll be your partner and liaison."

"Wait," I said, shaking my head. "Why are you being so open? I've heard too much now of what, in theory, should be a state secret."

"I already told you," he said. "We have professionals working for us, and your profile was created a long time ago. What it threw up was their best chance of you cooperating was by being extremely honest with you."

"So, the standard calculation?" I smiled a little, finally putting all my thoughts in order.

"Exactly," said Skuratov. "Can we finish this there? Isn't the working day already coming to an end?" He looked expressively at the sun approaching the horizon.

"Just like that?" I looked at him incredulously.

"I don't like all these conversations myself, so let's agree and we can go. Not a lot will change for you, on the whole, but some interesting jobs will come up, perfect given your profile. You don't really have any great options anyway. You can, of course, try to avoid the snipers' bullets and attack me," he suggested, narrowing his eyes. "Then try to escape, but still, you won't be allowed to leave the Empire. So..." He spread his hands.

"Okay, let's go."

I basically didn't have any choice. One person can't stand up to an entire state organization specializing in magic occurrences. At least not with my powers at their current level.

It's just a pity I wouldn't be able to get rid of any bodies now. Clearly, I was being monitored, but so I could demonstrate what I was capable of... No, better I leave that for now. I still didn't have much faith in what this old warhorse was saying, but I'd have to show compliance. As far as that was even possible for me, and then see what I could get away with.

* * *

Skuratov left his number on my mobile and got into a sports car parked at the edge of the abandoned village. It looked out of place against the backdrop of all the surrounding devastation. My bike also stuck out, but not quite as much.

"Hah, I see the office doesn't skimp on their employees, then," I said, eying the dark blue car.

"You won't find one of these in the service fleet," Skuratov replied with a shrug, as if there was nothing out of the ordinary for him. "For most operations, of course, low-key transport is required, but situations vary. Does your helmet have a headset?"

"Yes."

"Great. So, we can talk on our way back to the city."

Skuratov got into his car and, without waiting for me, sped off, gravel flying out from under his wheels, like live ammunition. It was a good thing the car was parked some distance away, otherwise I'd have had to jump out of the way to avoid it.

I had no choice but to catch up with the nimble servant. I was, of course, tempted to turn the other way, but I was sure I was being watched.

My engine roared contentedly, anticipating another trip, and I began to make up the sizeable distance from Skuratov.

"I didn't think that model could get up that kind of speed," came Skuratov's surprised voice over the phone when I caught up with him.

"Custom design," I said, not about to go into detail.

"Yeah, sure," he said incredulously. "Right, listen and remember. It's in my interest you give me as little trouble as possible, but I also can't refuse your appointment as my partner. So, please don't interfere with my work."

"Won't be a problem," I said, changing lanes after the car overtook me. "I actually have no intention of doing anything, anyway."

"Er, no, bro," Skuratov said with a laugh. "Now you're in our sights, you'll always be under surveillance."

"What, all the time?"

"No, not all the time, of course. But all major cases are being investigated, one way or another, and we already know your signature."

"Yeah, great, reeled me in." I shook my head even though Skuratov couldn't see me.

"Your conditions are still good, as the management is interested in voluntary collaboration with an independent summoner without any clan affiliations," Skuratov said, making his point again.

"So, the rumors that all summoners are carefully concealed by their family...?" I decided to test how open he'd be, seeing as he'd been instructed to answer everything honestly.

"A former aristocrat," — he emphasized with the word 'former' — "should understand perfectly well himself that 'the family has the right to use the resources of the family as it sees fit.'" Skuratov was quoting the 'Code of the Nobility' virtually word for word.

"What's someone from a princely family doing in service to the state, then?" I couldn't resist the question, as he hadn't answered my question properly.

"Unwillingness to participate in affairs of the family," Skuratov said with a chuckle. "I didn't want to become a pawn in my own relatives' games, so I asked to serve the emperor myself. I was younger than you at the time and may have acted stupidly, but I like my job."

"Sounds kind of strange." I didn't believe his story. "Well, okay. And what do you actually need me for?"

"Is it so hard to work out? Now our experts are carefully picking up all those pieces of demons' bodies to have a look at them. No one has ever summoned anything like them, so our investigators are falling over themselves to get their hands on it all." Skuratov laughed. "Well, up until now, we just didn't have an expert sufficiently well-versed in ritual magic, and you are just that. So, as you can see, the office is pursuing several objectives."

"All the same, that's not enough to first secretly watch me and shield me from too much attention, and then suddenly change your view," I said. I didn't believe him.

"They didn't give me all the details. But, as far as I know, there were several options for recruiting you, but your recent actions, especially today, meant they had to change their plans and act on the spur of the moment. The carrot and stick method, in my opinion, is quite effective in this case."

"But aren't you afraid that I might get angry because of the stick?"

"There's always that risk," Skuratov replied calmly. "Not a single magician so far has managed to outrun a bullet. I'm not even going to argue with the management's decision, although I don't like you being involved. After all, they answer only to the emperor. On the other hand, one person, no matter how strong, can so easily be overcome by a crowd. Yes, there'll be casualties, but the objective will be achieved. But these are just philosophical points."

Oh, yeah, an attempt to intimidate me, more like, but I decided not to pass comment.

"So, what now?" I asked after ten minutes of silence.

"So far, no orders," Skuratov replied straight away. "As I said, you threw a spanner in the works where your recruitment was concerned, so, put plainly, we don't have anything for you at the moment."

"So, I just sit by the phone, eh?"

"I'll come and get you up myself if anything turns up. You won't be registered as one of our employees, so you won't be able to go where I need to without an escort. Now, though, you may continue to go about your business," he replied. "By the way, how did you manage to recruit to your team three members of families in the top forty in terms of worldwide influence?"

"They came to me themselves after I beat Orlov in a sparring match," I said, not about to hide the fact.

"Man, you've got a death wish," Skuratov said, whistling.

"Explain." I didn't understand.

"If I remember correctly, Vladimir Orlov is second in line to Patriarch Orlov and tipped to become the clan's warrior. He's been groomed since childhood to head his family's military forces. The upshot is, Vladimir grew up to be a strong but arrogant young man, and just crossing his path isn't good for your health. How come you locked horns with him, and he didn't take revenge?"

"I just had to teach him not to put pressure on my student, otherwise he'd have me to answer to. And what you say about arrogance... Well, it seems one defeat was enough for the guy to think again. It looks like someone gave you wrong information, otherwise I really would be waiting for him to get his own back."

"Maybe, maybe," Skuratov said pensively, "still, try not to turn your back on him, you never know."

"Hah, concerned about your partner, now?"

"The top brass will be all over me if you die," he said with a sorrowful sigh. "And I'm quite attached to my hair — it has sentimental value for me. Bald wouldn't be a good look for me, but anyway. The main thing is to remember things aren't always straight forward where aristocrats are concerned."

"Says someone from a family of princes." I couldn't resist the barb.

"That's how I know," Skuratov said, agreeing with me unexpectedly. "Even if the students themselves don't have anything against you, their relatives may have a different opinion about their mentor."

"I'll deal with that myself."

"I don't doubt it, but I was duty-bound to warn you," and after about a minute of silence Skuratov suddenly said: "And try to make sure your team gets to at least the final of the tournament."

"Why?" I asked, surprised.

"I bet on you to win, and I don't want to lose my money." Skuratov gave a short laugh.

"Sorry to disappoint you, but I started all this to get into the restricted section of the Academy of Magic's library." I grinned to myself, glad that something of theirs wasn't going according to plan. It was too early to start fighting back yet but, a little victory — why not?

"So, it's true you've been all over the Academy library?" he asked before immediately continuing: "Well, if your group doesn't give a good account of itself, then there's no guarantee you'll get that access at all. Usually, it's granted to senior students and only then with a reference from the group supervisors. I can arrange access for you if you reach the final. How do you like that option?"

"I'll think about it, but I'm not promising anything."

Realizing there was no point in continuing the conversation, I ended the call and in a couple of seconds I overtook Skuratov's car and, after slightly adjusting the limiters on my motorcycle, I left it far behind me.

That round went to the Imperial Magic Security Service, but let's see how they try to control a black magician.

Ah, that really was the wrong time to lose it. It was all my aunt's fault, opening an old wound. Arina pushed me to behave like that with her questions, but she couldn't have known I'd react like that.

On the other hand, I now knew that for so many years my actions had escaped the attention of the Voronovs' servants. Somehow, I didn't believe they'd been unprofessional, but if there were experts of another level playing against them, then it wasn't surprising. And it was a pity it wasn't Christopher Lazarev — I could at least come to some sort of arrangement with him, since the patriarch of the Lazarev clan, for some reason, seemed to be kindly disposed towards me.

CHAPTER 15

ON THE DAY OF THE TOURNAMENT, it was if all those students at the Academy you never saw before suddenly came out of the woodwork. The building is quite large, of course, and the number of the gifted who get the chance to enroll here is relatively small, and they all spend most of their time in the classroom. So, if you don't go to class, you aren't going to meet many of them. And those you could see floating around tended to be loners who had something else to do.

These days, the annual tournament was open not only to students — who were exempted from classes after lunch — but the public, too. The Academy authorities had decided to make what had been an exclusive event much more inclusive. At the very least, having a separate category, which anyone, including commoners, could enter — it was in fact called the "The Commoners' Tournament" — seemed to put the Academy of Magic even more in the spotlight.

The event didn't even need the inclusion of commoners and other magicians without the numbers to study at the Academy to give it mass audience appeal. Having a prize of a hundred thousand imperial rubles up for grabs was too juicy an opportunity to turn down for many. Obviously, that would only go to the winner of the tournament, but there were some just as interesting prizes awaiting those who finished in the top ten. And there were contests in certain disciplines with smaller prizes, which anyone could enter. No one was going to stop anyone participating in several disciplines, but they did often clash, and any no-shows were automatically eliminated from that part of the tournament.

Until now, I'd seen the tournament as something of a show, but you only had to look beneath the surface to see how much there was to it all. And that was even without the betting, which, as it turns out, even the visiting dignitaries indulged in.

Unfortunately, I didn't know any of the people involved in that, so there was no point in betting on any of the supposed favorites. The risk of picking the wrong one was too high.

I didn't want to bet on my group either. We hadn't spent enough time training as I wanted to concentrate more on improving the control of source energy than on any real team cohesion. And as I told them more than once, I'm only a teacher... it would've taken a professional to whip the group into shape in such a short space of time.

Skuratov saying that he'd help me get access to the library was tempting, but I didn't have any faith in him. I still didn't know what to expect from his bureau, and there was no point in speculating either.

Ultimately, I was ready to try to achieve what I needed to under my own steam. Why rely on outside help only to be asked for something in return later? At least with my work I openly offer a payment option, and it's only then everything's left hanging a bit.

"I'm kind of worried," Alisa said, fidgeting with the cuff her dress, as she saw the people filling the stadium (the Academy had five of them). But, by the looks of it, she was more worried about the number of cameras and reporters.

"Hmm, don't worry, you look fine," I said, unable to resist getting a load of her rather open dress. "Everyone'll be wearing light training suits to avoid injury. And you're competing in the individual contests anyway."

"But that's..." Alisa threw her hands in the air. "We have to show what we're made of and not disgrace ourselves in front of everyone."

"Just go out there and perform. I don't expect you to win anything."

There was a separate zone at the stadium for the competitors, out of sight of the spectators. Probably so the youngsters didn't get too nervous, and to prevent any shenanigans. The good thing about the place was it was big enough for each group to have their own room, and there were screens showing the events inside the stadium. The room had a large sofa, several comfortable chairs, a table and a small kitchen where you could have a snack.

A kind of chill-out zone where you could relax before the next test and discuss tactics.

"That's not the point," Vladimir said, with a shake of the head. Until then he'd been standing next to Alisa, looking in silence at the crowd on the monitors that were broadcasting already. "It's also about our family reputations. Obviously all gifted vary in strength and preparation, but to lose to some junior branch..." He gave a sigh. "In the end, there's a lot at stake, and we can't let our families down. Failure means not just losing the prize but your good name, too."

"Well, if you're going to lose, do it with dignity," I scoffed. "Let them think it was an accident, and your opponent got lucky. You've got too many hangups on that score."

"Honor and dignity are what makes an aristocrat," Alisa said pompously.

"Great qualities to show in peacetime. In combat, everyone is guided by a much more basic survival instinct, and it makes no difference which stratum of society you belong to. But let's leave that for another day," I said, closing the subject. "Now you'd be better off focusing on your disciplines. As I understand it, everyone has chosen their own element?" All four of them nodded, and

I continued: "I know you want to show what you can do but try to restrain yourselves. Don't go all out."

"Why?" Alisa looked at me a little insulted.

"Huh, can't you guess?" I said, earning a disgruntled look from our water sorceress. Like I cared.

"You're afraid they might study us and be waiting for us in the team round?" Vladimir was the first to get it.

I'd noticed that Vladimir was the most intelligent of the group... Except for my student of course. Only when I got to know him better did I realize that on that first day he wasn't being a big-headed idiot — he was just employing the same tactics as me. Vladimir wanted to appear strong in front of the college group and become, if not the leader, then at least close to it. It's just he picked on the wrong person for that, and there wasn't much he could do about it.

"That's what I'd do if I was up against you," I said. "The best thing you can do is watch the other competitors later, so you get a rough idea what they're capable of."

"So, basically, keep your profile low and your eyes open," Miroslav said with a sarcastic smile.

"If you want to go as far as possible in the team round, then yes. Lena, the main thing with you is to give it your all," I said, turning to my student.

"I know, Gregor," she said, smiling sweetly at me. The others started looking at each other at this, but I pretended not to notice.

"So, what's the order of events?" I asked to break the awkward silence.

"First, there's the element stage," Alisa said. I'd asked her to prepare some information on the tournament beforehand. "Each stage proceeds according to rank, so senior and junior students are kept apart. They'll alternate between us to keep it interesting. After the elements, there are the healers and dark magicians of various kinds. There are, of course, those with very rare abilities, but they aren't separated into disciplines, so they participate in a mixed round of battles, with no restrictions on the type of gift. As for us, we're representing all the four main elements, and we come out in this order — water, earth, wind, fire. So, I'll be the first to show them just how strong our team is," she rounded off cheerfully.

"Love the attitude," I said. "Just be aware you tend to lose the plot in battle situations."

"As you like to remind me," Alisa muttered under her breath.

But it seems they'd decided to revise the tournament program and didn't start with the elements after all, as we were to find out.

Meanwhile, the tournament was about to start, and ten minutes later the third-year students were asked to show what they could do. With the element disciplines, it almost never came down to a fight, as it was more about mastering magic than combat skills. It could happen, though, in the event of a tie.

Arina Lazareva and Yura Volkonsky, who I met

at the race, easily distinguished themselves among the third-year students. I had thought about skipping that part of the tournament, but as I knew them, I wanted to see what they could do. Sure, it's interesting to see what the gifted are capable of overall, but it's the graduating students whose techniques are the most entertaining, even though they were up last.

The specific nature of their powers meant the healers didn't perform in the arena, but in special surgical rooms, where they were going to carry out a particular operation under professional supervision. As I found out later, the patients were all volunteers and didn't have to pay the healer in full for their work as it wasn't done by a specialist, even if everything was checked by a doctor afterwards. The more difficult the operation, the more points the student scored.

This was all displayed on the big screens, which would later focus more on the events in the arena. Thanks to the way it was broadcast, you could watch a dozen operations simultaneously. As they all ended at different times, as soon as one was over, the cameras moved onto the next.

Arina came up in the second pool. The students were confronted with patients with various ailments. Apparently, they were going with what they'd already proved they could do at school, otherwise, sadly, there'd have been quite a few failed attempts, and no one wanted to see that. Although, we did see this if a young healer was clearly very nervous or made a mistake somewhere, but it was quickly put right by the professionals.

Arina's task was to restore the left hand of a young man, which, judging by the slightly blood-stained bandages below the elbow, looked like it had been amputated recently. I knew a little about what healers do and understood that in such cases the body still "remembers" what it was like before the injury, which meant it would "help" Arina with what she was doing.

Unlike with element magicians, willpower only helped healers with simple things — treating wounds and scratches, cracked bones, skin conditions. What you could see, so to speak. But to grow someone a new arm, you needed to know its structure thoroughly and create a three-dimensional model of it in your head, then overlay it with techniques to make it real.

I went over to one of the screens and put Arina's test on full screen. She carefully removed the bandages from the stump and treated what hadn't yet healed with a solution. As I expected, the area around the incision was still inflamed, which meant it wasn't long ago that the young man had lost his arm. Arina carefully examined the limb and closed her eyes for a couple of seconds, asking the patient to hold his arm out to the side slightly.

The healer's hands lit up with a soft green glow, and she began to move them quickly over the arm, like she was weaving something. Gradually, you could see lines coming out of the stump, which started to interlace in a highly intricate pattern. To the observer, it was as if a green glowing tentacle had grown out of the guy's arm, pulsating and with a life of its own.

A hideous sight, but that's how this magic works.

Meanwhile, the assistants who were feeding the patient a nutrient solution through a drip hastily stepped aside to get out of Arina's way. Magic can do a lot, but it's always better to help the body with something extra rather than to try to compensate for it with source energy. The drip had to be refilled three times in all, as the effect of the magic regeneration made them run out incredibly quickly.

As far as I knew from the books, all healers perform in ways personal to themselves, but they do have some things in common. For example, in a case like this, any healer would start with creating the bones before grafting the other structures onto them. In fact, the tentacle Arina created was not only a frame that kept everything knitted together but was also itself the very basis for more subtle manipulations, which would be impossible without a highly developed understanding of one's own magic. Most likely, such a frame also allowed her to perform most of these procedures within a very small space.

I'm guessing all this, as only another healer can really tell you, and even then, sometimes the techniques in various families are drastically different, even if the result is the same.

Gradually, the tentacle stopped moving so

much and was already beginning to look more like an arm. A couple of minutes later and the patient's missing arm was recreated in minute detail by a green prosthesis. Arina held her hands over the limb. The green light went out, revealing the whole arm, but it was slightly paler in color below the incision. Arina corrected this flaw with another structure, making the skin tone the same.

Arina then asked the young man to try to move his restored limb, and he gently clenched his fist, unconvinced at first. Then he started to feel it with his other hand, as if he couldn't believe it was real.

That was the end of Arina's test, but I had no doubt that she'd finish in the top ten healers of the tournament at the very least as the others' operations were nowhere near as complicated.

There was another competitor who also stood out, though. He used structures so energy-intensive that they glowed as he was building them. His task was to almost completely restore the face of a girl about seven years old and treat her burns. It must've been that her parents couldn't afford such an expensive operation, so they decided to take a risk. The risk paid off, and the girl got her normal life back, as if nothing had ever happened.

This time, they didn't show everything the student was doing as he had to divide up his work and deal with restoring each element separately — not a spectacle for the fainthearted.

He ended up taking the most time and draining the storage devices he brought with him several times over, but he still managed it, and the final pictures showed the girl smiling and already trying, despite feeling very weak, to turn in front of the mirror and look at herself from different angles (they must have given her a shot of something for the cameras as such a patient would normally be extremely weak and drowsy and completely unable to walk).

Incredible and very painstaking work, so this guy certainly deserved his prize.

It was strange, though, that someone with his skills even decided to take part in the tournament. In my opinion, you shouldn't feel the need to prove your skills when you're at that level. Although... curing someone for free (it was the Academy of Magic that paid for it all), would've been a good way to promote himself.

Anyway, there were a lot more healers than I thought, and all their results were good, although not as outstanding as those two.

With Yura Volkonsky, however, it was his kit that made him stand out in his discipline. Instead of the standard light one, he'd put together something like a medium one, but without the helmet, weapons or other components that distinguish it. In fact, he'd taken a light set of armor and hung several straps on it which the military use for fixing extra magazines. In them, instead of magazines, were what appeared to be black metal plates.

Yura stood on the starting line of a small obstacle course made to look like a city street. They gave the signal, and he took off and ran inside. The event was covered by several cameras simultaneously, so we could watch the competitor from different angles. And find out what the straps were for. Yura used his magic to make some of the metal plates disintegrate. They then reassembled themselves as knife-like objects, which he directed at the targets that started to pop up everywhere. Now and then he'd jump to the side, hiding while he caught his breath, just like in real urban combat. In the end, it took him a little over two minutes to hit all the targets and make his way out the other side.

And Arina said he prefers organizing events. But this showed him to be a fine warrior who'd make a difficult opponent for anyone.

I wondered what sorcerers from the same element with a more developed source would be capable of. None of the other "metalists" did as well as him. The contender who finished closest to him completed the course in five minutes, so Yura was the winner by far.

It was a shame, though, for one freshman, who tried to imitate him. The metal frame he'd created for his knife wasn't strong enough, and it broke into pieces after three hits. And basically, Yura was the only one who thought to take enough metal with him for his technique, while the others were using ready-made weapons.

I forgot to mention — all their tests took place at the same time in different zones, so the audience could choose which one they wanted to watch.

After these warm-up performances, it was the turn of the masters of the four main elements to show what they could do.

First came the "waterists".

"Well, wish me luck," Alisa said, exhaling through gritted teeth.

"You don't need it," I said with a smirk. "Just show them what you can do and enjoy it."

"But that's..." She was about to boil over again.

All told, she was quick to flare up, but that wasn't my problem. Thankfully, once the tournament was over, so would be any need for me to ever train this group again.

"What?" I narrowed my eyes a little, asking her straight out, which stopped her in her tracks. "You're a freshman, and already rank as a Junior Master, when your most of your opponents are barely Apprentices. We didn't practice controlling our magic for nothing. So, you're bound to get a high score."

"Gregor's right," Vladimir suddenly agreed with me, and he put his hand on her shoulder. "You're one of the best in water, I know, and you'll finish in the top five for sure."

In true Alisa style, she snorted, turned on her heels, and almost ran out of our room, but I could see the tips of her ears had gone a crimson color. All because of Vladimir.

While no one could see, I gave the blond guy the thumbs up and winked, to which he just spread his hands slightly and smiled shyly, before quickly adopting a relaxed expression again.

Meanwhile, the screens started to show what awaited the waterists to see what level they were at. The gifted specializing in water had what seemed like a straightforward enough task — to carry a certain amount of water through from one end of a system of pipes to the other, and the less they lost along the way, the higher their score. Except the pipes were a real labyrinth, and weren't all at ground level, some of them twisted around in the air. They'd also done something to the liquid, so it wasn't as easy to control as ordinary water. And they'd also set a time limit of eight minutes, just for good measure.

So, the competitors had to rely on their powers to go through the whole labyrinth without looking, and, given how convoluted it was, do it quickly, otherwise they'd run out of time. It was a bit like those tasks that I'd given the guys so they could get in touch with their magic and control it better, only on a much larger scale. Transmitters inside the pipes allowed the viewers to watch everything the magicians did, and all the waterists could use was their magic, as they couldn't see through them.

A very interesting idea and, judging by the puzzled expressions, the first time any of them had ever attempted anything like it. I even wondered if Alisa would be up to it.

Five students had attempted it already, but none of them managed it within the allotted time — they in fact failed even to reach the end of the maze, getting lost in its twists and turns. The sixth competitor was to be our chestnut-haired smart aleck.

Alisa had seen all the previous failed attempts quite clearly and was looked nervous, but as soon as she approached the water bucket, she seemed to calm down. The countdown began as soon as the liquid entered the pipe, so everyone was patiently waiting to see what she'd do, but she was in no hurry, stretching her hands out over the water. A generous amount of energy went into the liquid, but it didn't seem to have any effect, other than it started to glow slightly.

Finally, Alisa came to life and waved her right hand making the water rush towards the pipes. She closed her eyes in concentration. Meanwhile, we could all see the maze from different angles and watch as she tried to find the way out.

It looked like Alisa deliberately saturated the liquid with her magic energy to control it better, and didn't try to do what the previous participants had done, which was to wrap the water in a kind of cocoon, so it didn't spill. No, she made the liquid able to move freely in the pipes, while keeping it all together so as not to lose a drop.

Then, Alisa moved further and further forward and stopped at about the same place where the other participants had got stuck. At this point, the labyrinth branched out in eight different directions, and it was simply unrealistic to try to work out which of them led to the exit, so it meant choosing the right one would be down to luck.

I turned to look at Alisa in time to see her lift

her hands up to her face and make several complex movements, drawing some kind of design using her magic energy. They don't teach this kind of thing at the Academy, so I looked at her design, which depicted a clot of liquid which she started to lead through the maze, with interest.

During our training sessions, Alisa had shown the best progress in improving her control skills, which was not so unusual for a hereditary water magician, because water requires the gifted to apply their powers to every particle, otherwise it they wouldn't even be able to transport a puddle. Now she was demonstrating her skills.

We could all see how the liquid split into eight roughly equal-sized water spheres, each of which took a different path through the labyrinth. Alisa had decided not to waste time searching for the right route, but to find it in her own way. She could only rely on her concentration and hope to able to put all the spheres back together again without losing any of the liquid.

"Crafty," I said when I saw she'd left small drops of liquid in the paths taken by her spheres.

It was easy to work out why she did this — the drops were to play the part of "breadcrumbs" to help her retrieve all the spheres when she finally found the way out. But keeping hold of eight small objects at once could still have proved to be something beyond a first-year student.

The cameras showed a droplet of sweat running down Alisa's face, and her tensely biting her lip as she gave the task her full concentration. And finally, her efforts were rewarded when she managed to find her way out of the maze two minutes later.

Alisa beamed and began to gather all the water spheres together. Unfortunately, her joy was premature, and towards the end she lost focus for a moment and two of the spheres were destroyed just seconds from the finishing line. Even so, it was the first time the task had been completed successfully, and within the time limit, too.

"Well done you," I said to her when she came back to our room. "I had no idea you could do that."

"Nor did I." Alisa smiled wearily, flicking aside a strand of hair soaked in sweat.

"So, you were improvising?" Vladimir asked, looking at her in surprise.

"I tried it with three spheres, but dealing with so many, and sending them in different directions..." She shook her head. "It was risky, but I was afraid of running out of time."

"So, did our training help?" I asked, grinning.

"Yes," Alisa said, nodding firmly. "Without honing the control of my power, I'd never have been able to pull this off. So, thank you." She bobbed ceremoniously, bowing her head slightly.

"Come on, now," I said, waving away such formal behavior. "Especially as it doesn't befit an aristocrat to bow before a commoner as if he were a prince."

"But I bow to the teacher." Alisa gave me a sly look, smiling as she rose.

"Which of us is next?" I paid no attention to Alisa's behavior, as she was obviously trying to get a reaction out of me. I wasn't going to play her game.

"I am," came the response from Miroslav, who'd been silent until now.

"I wonder what they'll think up for the 'earthists' given they came up with something like that for the 'waterists'?" Vladimir pointed towards the pipes and the next competitor.

"I don't care," he replied, yawning. "The sooner it's over, the sooner I can go."

"That's the spirit," I said. "You're always banging on about how impossible it is to win a prize."

"My family actually couldn't give a damn about my rank," Miroslav explained. "I only entered the Academy to annoy them, because now they have to pay for my studies," he said with a cheery grin.

"You're representing your family in this tournament," Vladimir said, shaking his head in disapproval.

"My older brothers are doing that just fine," he replied, smiling contemptuously. "Do I have to excel myself? I mean, I only got involved in all this because you dragged me here. That's all, I'm gone." And without giving Vladimir the chance to talk him round, Miroslav left the room.

The subject raised was something of a conversation-stopper, so we quietly watched the rest of the waterists finish their test. It turned out in the end that Alisa was the only one who managed to pass through the maze in such a short space of time. The others either failed, or they struck lucky and found the right pipe, pulling off the same maneuver as Alisa. Either way, their scores were a lot lower, so we congratulated the girl who was bursting with pride.

They quickly cleared the arena, and several gifted teachers came out into the middle of it. Arms aloft, they combined to create a structure in a matter of seconds. Being able to synchronize their magic energy like that without causing conflicts speaks of many years of practice and some serious skills.

Once all the preparations were completed, they gave the final supply of energy, and a four-meter-high golem started to rise out of the ground. One of the magicians took out a small gold amulet and even the cameras managed to pick up the luminous thread stretching from it to the stone figure. If I was right, it was a control thread, which meant this was a test to see how well the students could control such a large golem. Seeing as students from different years were to take part, the advantage was with the seniors, but it was quite possible that someone might cause an upset.

The subsequent performances from the students only confirmed my suspicions — the first two years couldn't do much with the stone dummy. They got into a muddle trying to control the golem almost straight away. It kept falling over, and the teachers had to go and take back the amulet and put the golem in place again. The seniors, however, showed themselves to be more adept. With them guiding it, the golem ran, jumped, and did push-ups. But it was the last competitor who stood out, making the golem perform a combination of moves a bit like shadow boxing, and it no longer looked so awkward and unwieldy. On the contrary, it danced around the arena, barely staying still for a second.

"Bad luck," Vladimir uttered quietly, but I still heard him.

"What do you mean?" I wanted to know.

"Next up is Miroslav, and that's his older brother, Yaroslav," he said, pointing at the monitor, where the guy who'd just competed was bowing to the audience and waving cheerfully into the camera with all the flamboyance of an actor. "They can't stand each other, and I'm afraid Miroslav will lose it. Then he'll be out of the tournament and might not be allowed to perform in our group."

"Hmm, but he seemed quite contained to me," I commented.

"Usually yes, but he's constantly having problems with his family," Vladimir said with a heavy sigh.

Vladimir's words were backed up when Yaroslav crossed paths with his brother. The cameras, unfortunately, couldn't pick up the sound, but they showed a verbal spat breaking out between them. It resulted in the elder brother taking it further and barging Miroslav with his shoulder as he went past, while he responded with an indecent gesture, before he approached the magician holding the control amulet with an impertinent grin.

From the outset it was clear Miroslav wasn't going to stick to the plan. First, he wouldn't take the control amulet and was talking about something with the teacher for quite a long time. The conversation ended with the man nodding to him and leaving the arena.

Miroslav then approached the golem and carefully examined it from all sides, even managing to get on top of its head. The usually apathetic guy was a whirr of activity and kept touching the golem's body with a dim green light. It wasn't yet clear why he was doing this, but I didn't think we'd have to wait long to find out.

Ten minutes later, Miroslav had finished his preparations and nodded to the magician, who still had the control amulet in his hands. Suddenly, rhythmic music began to play, and Miroslav made several intricate movements with his hands, culminating in a clap of the hands.

He slowly lowered his arms and for a few seconds stood in a pose imitating the golem. Stretching his arms out to the sides, Miroslav slowly moved his shoulder, and, after a slight delay, the stone idol did the same.

Unfortunately, the cameras couldn't show any magic if it didn't manifest itself visually, otherwise you'd have been able to see a lot of threads connecting him to the golem. It was one of the most difficult, and at the same time, easiest techniques in earth magic. Difficult to execute, as it required considerable skill from the gifted, and easy in terms of control, because at that moment all Miroslav's movements were echoed exactly by the go-lem, and with each passing second the delay be-tween their actions grew shorter, which meant he'd successfully adjusted to controlling the stone hulk. It was also good the golem had a humanoid shape — focusing on the body made it easier to control. It'd be more difficult, although quite pos-sible, to do this with, say, a spider made of granite, but it'd take some training.

By the time the music changed, Miroslav was completely at ease with operating the golem, and as soon as a Russian folk melody struck up, he broke into a dance, which the golem performed simultaneously. More than that — as one piece of music gave way to another, Miroslav changed his style of dancing to fit the new melody. Obviously, a golem can't have the mobility of a human, but as soon as it started to dance the lezginka, the sta-dium simply erupted.

Miroslav might not go on to win this contest, but there was no debating that the audience liked his performance the most. Although his brother, in my opinion, performed with more confidence and his golem moved more smoothly, the dances by the apparently cumbersome stone block, which for a short while resembled a human being, were very impressive. So, he was going to leave the arena a winner, whatever the result.

He managed to hold it together for the cam-eras, but as soon as Miroslav was back in our room, he immediately collapsed onto the sofa.

"God, I'm exhausted," he said, with a huge

sigh. By which point, Vladimir had gone over to him with a glass of water. Miroslav gave him a nod of gratitude but couldn't speak until he'd finished it. "There was so much to sort out before it'd work."

"And I thought you weren't going to bust a gut," I said with a grin.

"No," Miroslav said in agreement, "but my brother really got to me. What happened, happened," he said, waving his hand in a vague way. "Don't wake me."

And with that, he passed out.

"Shouldn't we get the healers?" Lena asked me, concerned, while Vladimir carefully rolled some towels up into a pillow and put it under his friend's head.

"They won't be any help," I said, not at all worried about Miroslav. "Everday magic exhaustion. He'll be fine in a couple of hours. Such ability, but it was all for nothing."

"You can't really use that in combat anyway," Vladimir retorted.

"Also true. But such a demonstration clearly reveals what our earthist can do — he's shown his hand, now." I looked at the screens again, which were broadcasting a less than successful performance from some girl, and I turned to my team. "At this rate, you all have a good chance of finishing in the top ten, if not the top five, for individual disciplines. I just don't know yet if that's a good thing or not."

"What's bad about it?" Alisa said, knitting her brows.

"If you'd performed truly badly, then no one would think much of our group, and your opponents would prepare accordingly. So, you," I said, turning to Vladimir and Lena, "there's no point holding back too much. The group's already given away that it's strong, so if you perform badly, that'll just raise even more questions. And that means they'll start gunning for us, and we don't need that."

Unfortunately, the contests for that day had to end early, as a couple of unlucky students made a complete mess of the arena, and the audience would've had to wait too long for it all to be put right. As someone explained to me later, this could well have happened during any of the contests, and we'd actually been lucky to get through so many of them as it was.

Okay, let's see what tomorrow brings.

END OF BOOK ONE

Want to be the first to know about our latest LitRPG, sci fi and fantasy titles from your favorite authors?

Subscribe to our **New Releases** newsletter:
http://eepurl.com/b7niIL

Thank you for reading *The Dark Summoner!*

If you like what you've read, check out other LitRPG novels published by Magic Dome Books:

NEW RELEASES!

The Hunter's Code
A Portal Progression Fantasy Series
by Oleg Sapphire & Yuri Vinokuroff

The One Who Changes the Future
A Dystopian Portal Progression Fantasy Series
by Boris Romanovsky

How I Built a Magic Empire
A Portal Progression Fantasy Series
by Konstantin Zubov

The Afflicted
A LitRPG Apocalypse Adventure Series
by Konstantin Zubov

An Ideal World for a Sociopath
A LitRPG Apocalypse Adventure Series
by Oleg Sapphire

The Healer's Way
A Portal Progression Fantasy Series
by Oleg Sapphire & Alexey Kovtunov

The Selected
A LitRPG Action Adventure Series
by Vasily Mahanenko & Yuri Vinokuroff

The Last Portal Jumper
A LitRPG Progression Fantasy Series
by Konstantin Zubov

The Dark Healer
A Historical Progression Fantasy Series
by Alex Toxic & Nadya Lee

The Strongest Student
A Portal Progression Action Fantasy Series
by Andrei Tkachev

A Shelter in Spacetime
A LitRPG Apocalypse Series
by Dmitry Dornichev

The Coming of God of Death
A Portal Progression Fantasy Series
by Dmitry Dornichev

The Village
A LitRPG Progression Fantasy Series
by Dmitry Dornichev & Alexey Kovtunov

Law of the Jungle
A Wuxia Progression Fantasy Adventure Series
by Vasily Mahanenko

Condemned (Lord Valevsky: Last of the Line)
A Progression Fantasy LitRPG Series
by Vasily Mahanenko

Living Ice
A Portal Progression Fantasy Series
by Dmitry Sheleg

Ghost in the System
An Apocalypse LitRPG Series
by Alexey Kovtunov

Crossroads of Oblivion
A Portal Progression Fantasy Adventure Series
by Dem Mikhailov

More books and series are coming out soon!

In order to have new books of the series translated faster, we need your help and support! Please consider leaving a review or spread the word by recommending *The Dark Summoner* to your friends and posting the link on social media. The more people buy the book, the sooner we'll be able to make new translations available.

Thank you!

Till next time!